I0728489

HOPE

NEVER

RESTS

HOPE NEVER RESTS

a novel

KATIE HART SMITH

Deeds Publishing | Atlanta

Published by Deeds Publishing in Athens, GA
www.deedspublishing.com

Printed in The United States of America

Cover by Mark Babcock
Text layout by Ashley Clarke

Library of Congress Cataloging-in-Publications data is available upon request.

ISBN 978-1-947309-10-4

Books are available in quantity for promotional or premium use. For information, email info@deedspublishing.com.

First Edition, 2017

10 9 8 7 6 5 4 3 2 1

Lovingly, for Jeff

Acknowledgements

I would like to thank the following individuals for sharing their expertise:

Captain Jon Spear, Gwinnett County Sherriff's Department: Captain Spear is the first registered bomb technician in the State of Georgia: a certified bomb technician with the Bureau of Alcohol Tobacco and Firearms and the Federal Bureau of Investigation.

Captain Ray Rawlins, Campus Police—Patrol Operations, Georgia Gwinnett College: Captain Rawlins is a former Forensic Examiner for Gwinnett County.

Captain Jeff Smith, Lawrenceville Police Department, Lawrenceville, Georgia: Captain Smith provides oversight for Investigative Services, to include: Criminal Investigations, Crime Scene Investigations, Evidence, and Forensics/Information Technology.

Mayor Jimmy Wilbanks, City of Dacula, Georgia: Mayor Wilbanks introduced me to the pellagra epidemic during his "Historical Overview of Dacula" lecture on November 2, 2016. He also mentioned that his father worked in Chattanooga making TNT. As a youth, Mayor Wilbanks asked his dad, "How did you make TNT without blowing up Tennessee?"

His father replied, "Very carefully!"

The Rich Beauty
of Helping a Child

He who helps a child helps humanity with a distinctness and with an immediateness with which no other help is given to human creatures in any other stage of their human life can possibly give again. He who puts his blessed influence into a river blesses the land through which that river is to flow; but he who puts his influence into the fountain where the river comes out puts his influence everywhere. No land it may not reach. No ocean it may not make sweeter. No bark it may not bear. No wheel it may not turn.

Sometimes we get at things best by their contraries. Learn the rich beauty of helping a child by the awfulness of hurting a child,—hurting a child even in his physical frame—hurting him still more in soul and mind. The thing that made the Divine Master indignant as He stood there in Jerusalem was that He dreamed of seeing before Him a man who had harmed some of these little ones, and He said of any such ruffian, 'It were better for him that he had never been born.'

If it is such an awful thing to hurt a child's life, to aid a child's life is beautiful.

— Bishop Phillips Brooks (1835–1893)
American Episcopal clergyman
Rector of Boston's Trinity Church, Bishop of Massachusetts
Author and lyricist of the Christmas hymn
"O Little Town of Bethlehem"

"The lotus flower blooms most beautifully
from the deepest mud."

Buddhist Proverb

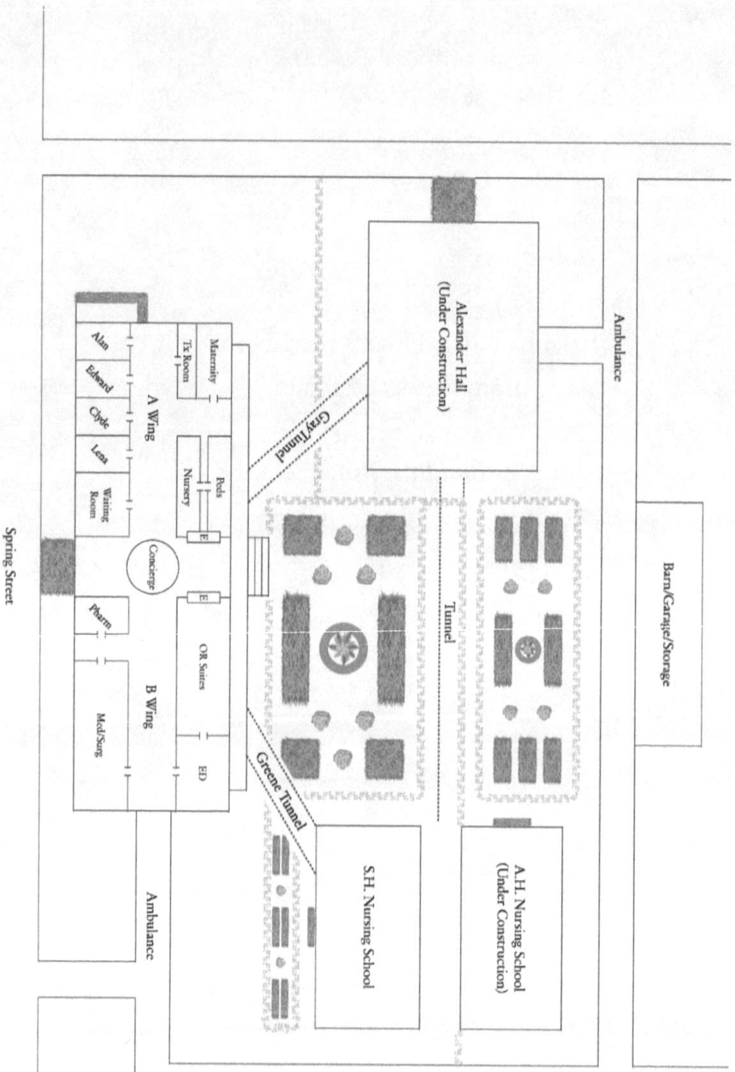

SACRED HEART HOSPITAL GROUNDS

1

Gang glanced over his shoulder as he gathered rocks by the fistful and shoved them deep into the front pants pockets of the lifeless body. He whispered, "Brother, we must be quick. Only matter of time before quarry workers come. Hope we've weighed him down enough."

Toot. Toot. Dinky's whistle sounded off in the distance from the city of Stone Mountain. The passenger train signaled it was on its way, bringing laborers and stone cutters to the quarries around the mountain. Dawn was breaking on the eastern horizon, erasing traces of the darkness and giving way to navy blue, dark purple, and violet. Chongan quickly flattened the rocks on the teen's chest before buttoning the dingy white shirt closed. The two picked up the limp body and tossed it into the wooden rowboat. Picking up their oars, the men directed the boat to the middle of the lake. A silhouette of an enormous granite outcropping emerged on the horizon—a mountain the indigenous Indians referred to as 'Lone Mountain' before the Georgia Legislature officially changed the name to Stone Mountain on Christmas Eve, 1847.

The brothers secured their oars and hoisted the lad. Pebbles and rocks slipped out from under the boy's clothes, striking the side of the boat as they slid the corpse into the water. Water rushed over the adolescent boy's freckled face, filling his mouth and nostrils. His blonde hair danced and waved around his face. Bubbles surfaced and popped as Gang and Chongan watched the body sink, disappearing into the murky depths below.

"That boy not follow Mr. Chang's rules," Chongan whispered as he pulled the oar handles towards his chest. "Mr. Chang lucky to have us, brother."

Gang nodded as he steered the boat towards the shoreline. He knew what they were called in Chinese: *xīnfù*. He had overheard Mr. Chang use the word in English once before. He whispered back, "Yes, brother, we are his henchmen."

WEDNESDAY, APRIL 1, 1914, SIXTH WARD, ATLANTA, GEORGIA

Addie paused and closed her eyes to reflect for a moment as the morning rays of sunshine kissed her cheeks. *What's behind me will not define me.* It was just a lesson. It's what's ahead that will. Mark Twain's quote came to mind: *"The two most important days in your life are the day you are born and the day you find out why." Maw, I'm on my way to find out why.* Addie opened her eyes and stepped over the marble threshold and through the front doors of Sacred Heart Hospital.

"Good morning to you, Miss Engel. Welcome to Sacred Heart Hospital and Nursing School. Nurse Hartman is expecting you."

Addie beamed, recognizing the face and voice.

"Come on. We don't have all day." Nurse Scott grabbed Addie's hand. "Duty calls, Red."

Addie stood in silence and disbelief.

Dressed in a heavily starched-white nursing uniform and cap, Nurse Scott stepped back, allowing Addie to enter the grand lobby of Sacred Heart Hospital. Paint fumes and the smell of plaster and wood filled the air. Hammering and sawing ensued while construction workers shouted instructions at each other and buzzed around like the carpenter bees on the front lawn. It was hard to make out the décor and layout, as tarps hung from the ceilings in the hallways to minimize the dust.

"What's wrong, Red? Cat got your tongue?" Nurse Scott chuckled.

Tears welled in Addie's eyes. She embraced Clair Scott. "What are you doing here? The last time I saw you, we were at Grady's Butler Hall, when Mrs. Gray passed away. You were a saint to me—to us." Addie stepped back to compose herself and wipe away a stray tear from the corner of her eye. "You taught me so much while I sat at her bedside and watched you care for those patients in that ward. What on heaven's earth are you doing here?"

"When you told me about the new nursing school opening at Sacred Heart, I made an inquiry with the Nursing Superintendent, Nurse Hartman, about open positions. I've been hired as the head nurse and will be assisting her with your training and education." Nurse Scott smiled and motioned for Addie to follow her through the main hallway, around a circular desk area that served as a hub for the converging four hallways, and out the grand back doors.

They stepped outside to another wide porch that ran the length of the building. Ramps flared off the sides while stairs in front of them led to a spacious walking garden below. A variety of flower gardens containing jonquils, irises, ferns, tulips, and rose bushes surrounded a round, gurgling marble fountain. Low profile, square-cut boxwoods bordered the beds and white pea gravel paths. In the distance, Addie made out three free-standing structures.

Nurse Scott pointed. "The two-story marble building closest to us is Sacred Heart's School for Nurses."

"It looks like a small replica of the hospital."

"Yes, it is. See that brick building beyond the brick wall they are constructing towards the back of the property?"

Addie nodded.

"That is the garage, barn, and storage area for any horses, wagons, ambulances, and extra hospital equipment." Nurse Scott waved at two men who were hand-painting the slogan adopted by the Sacred Heart leadership team last year on the sides of two ambulances—*Reliable. Reputable. Responsive.* "Mr. Alexander has even purchased fifteen bicycles for anyone to use on the property, even the patients! Can you believe that!"

"That's interesting. I've never ridden a bicycle before."

"Don't worry, Red. I can teach you."

"Really? That would be wonderful. But I don't want to become the first patient in our emergency room," Addie teased. "By the way, I heard from Nurse Hartman that there is a tunnel underneath us that connects the school to the hospital." Addie pointed towards the ground.

"Yes, there sure is." Clair stopped and looked back at the hospital. "And, there's another one between Sacred Heart and Alexander Hall, the hospital for colored patients slated to open in 1917. It runs under the front lawn and under the brick wall to the other hospital. To complete the underground triangle, the third tunnel is being finished over there. It will connect with the first tunnel under the Colored and the White nursing schools. Nurse Hartman will explain what they will be used for during your tour with her." She pulled out a piece of paper from her skirt pocket and unfolded it. "According to my notes, you will get a tour of the property from our founder, Mr. Edward Alexander II, after lunch. He's a great man. You will really like him."

"Great!" *Thank goodness I didn't formally meet him at his Christmas party last year when I was with Mrs. Gray's nephew, Lester Schwinn. Lester was a good for nothing snake oil salesman! I hope his soul is burning in hell! This time, I look forward to meeting Mr. Alexander under a new set of circumstances.* Addie felt her cheeks flush and hives welled on her chest. She loosened the yellow silk scarf around her neck.

With fifteen minutes to spare, Addie walked into the nursing school and dorm. Nurse Scott escorted her to Nurse Hartman, who was sitting behind a small maple drop-leaf table in a long hallway lined with windows that overlooked the Sacred Heart gardens.

"This is Miss Addie Engel, Nurse Hartman. However, I prefer to call her *Red.*" Clair excused herself as she tugged on one of Addie's auburn tendrils.

"Good morning, Miss Engel. Or, is it Red?" Lena put a mark by Addie's name and noted her arrival time in her notebook entry. "It's good to see you this morning. In a manner befitting a professional, I must insist that we refer to each other using last names." She winked at Addie and smiled as she referred back to her clipboard. "Your trunk has arrived and has already been put in the dorm for you."

"Yes, Nurse Hartman. I understand." Addie spotted another familiar face, Mr. Alexander's daughter, Opal. She was mingling with a group of girls gathered in the hallway. They had already met on two previous occasions: the Alexanders' Christmas party and at a luncheon at Nurse Hartman's apartment last month.

"Feel free to join the others. We'll begin promptly at zero nine hundred hours."

"That sounds wonderful!" Addie was so excited that she started walking away, pivoted on her heels, and returned to the table. "Uh, what did you mean exactly by zero nine hundred hours?" she whispered.

"That is military time for nine o'clock in the morning. That's good, Addie. You came back immediately to clarify something you didn't understand. That's the mark of a great nurse. When in doubt, always question and clarify. You've already managed to master the first lesson."

"Gee! Good to know I passed my first oral pop quiz on the first day of class!"

Nurse Hartman's eyes gave her away as she restrained herself from laughing out loud and turned her attention to register the next student, who now stood behind Addie. Addie joined Opal and the other girls, who introduced each other and made small talk as they watched the remaining nurses check in. Addie counted heads in the room as an ornate grandfather clock at the end of the hallway tolled nine bells. Lena got up with her roster in hand and approached them. Addie had counted only nine heads when the last bell chimed. Someone was missing.

Lena rapped her pencil on the edge of her wooden clipboard. "Ladies! May I have your attention please? My name is Miss Lena Hartman. I am the Nursing Superintendent for Sacred Heart Hospital and Nursing School." Nurse Scott returned to the room and took her place next to Nurse Hartman. "I'm going to call roll in alphabetical order. When I call your name, please line up here against the wall." Using her pencil, Lena pointed to the white wall in front of her.

The gaggle of girls fell silent, anxious for their name to be called. Addie fidgeted and began to bite her thumbnail, then heard Mrs. Gray's voice in her head. *Please keep your hands out of your mouth. Doc Gray use to say that was one of the most important ways to prevent infection and stop the spread of diseases, in addition to good hand washing.* Addie complied and clasped her hands behind her back. She squared her shoulders and stood tall.

Lena looked over at Opal. "Opal Alexander. Alexis Carmichael."

"Please call me Lexie," a fair-haired girl said as she passed Nurse Hartman.

"Actually, I will call you Miss Carmichael. Your friends can call you Lexie when you are outside the classroom or when you're chatting in your beds late into the night. While we are together, we will refer to each other by our last names. When you are working your shifts in the hospital, you will be summoned as Nurse Carmichael. The physicians will be acknowledged as Doctor, not Doc, mister, or 'hey you.'"

The girls stirred and giggled. Lexie blushed, unsure if she had just been reprimanded. She nodded and stood next to Opal.

Lena continued. "Addie Engel. Isabelle Esposito. Alice Fein. Charity Johnson."

No one acknowledged the last name.

"Charity Johnson? Well, she is either late or absent. She just earned ten demerits." Lena made a note by Charity's name.

"Roberta Jones."

A short, stout girl stepped forward. She had the face of a cherub. Her freckled, rosy cheeks glowed.

"I go by Bertie." She bubbled over with enthusiasm as she walked passed Nurse Hartman. "That is, when I'm not being called Miss Jones or Nurse Jones."

Addie knew right then and there that she wanted to get to know her.

"Thank you for letting us know, *Miss* Jones." Lena continued to read the remaining names. "Susan Kessler. Mary Margaret O'Malley." One girl, void of any effervescence in her spirit, stood alone in front of Lena. "And you must be Deborah Owens."

Addie looked her over. Dark, cold eyes met hers. *Yikes! That isn't someone I want to get to know. I bet she has ice water running through her veins. Where have I seen that look before? Oh, God, in Paw's eyes...and Lester's eyes!*

Deborah took her place against the wall with the rest of the students.

"Now, I'm going to take you on a tour of this facility and the dorms. Please follow me."

"Nurse Hartman! Nurse Hartman!" Joshua Goode ran past the fountain and up the garden path, passing the long line of windows. Lena met him on the front steps. Joshua removed his straw hat. "This telegram was just delivered for you, ma'am. It's marked *urgent*."

"Thank you, Joshua. Come in for a moment." Lena took the envelope as they stepped through the front doors. "Ladies, this is Mr. Goode. He is in charge of housekeeping and maintenance on the hospital grounds." Joshua bowed and acknowledged the nursing students while Lena opened the telegram and read it. She wadded it up, stuffed it into the envelope, and drew a line on her roster. "Well, it seems that Miss Johnson will not be joining us. According to her telegram, she eloped with her boyfriend last night." Lena shoved the envelope into her uniform pocket.

The young ladies gasped and murmured while Deborah, disinterested in the whereabouts of the newlywed, glared at Joshua. Addie observed Lena, noting the girl's reactions and Deborah's disapproving mannerisms. Addie could tell Lena was miffed, not only at Deborah's initial reaction to the black man standing in the room with them, but to the vacant nursing position, knowing that spot could have gone to a deserving candidate.

Nurse Hartman patted her pocket. "Well, better to know now than to have to manage a student whose heart was elsewhere. Is there anyone else who feels that they will not be up for the task these next three years? Speak now or forever hold your tongue."

The girls glanced down the line at each other. No one spoke.

"Good. Let's proceed with the tour. Follow me." The students walked behind Nurse Hartman single file, like baby ducklings following their mother.

Joshua departed.

They had walked about six steps when the line came to a halt in front of the main arched doorway.

"This is the main entrance to the nursing school. Mr. Alexander and I designed this building so that you have maximum exposure to the beautiful outdoor gardens. White rockers and wicker porch furnishings are expected to be delivered later this afternoon. In case of inclement weather, the furniture can be brought inside and placed here in the hallway so that you can still have a peaceful place to retreat to." Lena pointed toward the end of the hall to her left. "The grandfather clock was a donated to this school by my parents. They taught my brother and me that, all day, from the first time you hear the bell chime in the morning to the last time it rings before you fall asleep at night, you should ask yourself, 'What did I do today that helped another human being?'"

"Why?" Deborah shrugged her shoulders, absent of any emotion.

"Why, you ask, Miss Owens? For starters, I believe, in this great big world of ours, that we all have a purpose. We are all meant to help guide one other along our journey through life. It is through compassion that we find connection." Lena sensed Deborah's cold and unfeeling manner was a mask. Time would reveal what was underneath, but not today.

Pointing to the other end of the hallway, Lena continued with the tour. "That is the coat closet and hat rack for you and our guests to use." Lena turned around and proceeded down the main hall. "The room on your right is called Classroom A, and to my immediate left is our library and parlor." The group crossed through an intersection with the back hallway, which also ran the length of the building. Lena walked toward the back doors, stopped, and turned around. "To your right, you will find a fully stocked kitchen. It is always open for your use. We have no maids on the premises. Therefore, it is your duty to keep it clean and to clean up after yourselves. Failure to do so will result in demerits that you will have to work off." Lena pointed to the room on the students' left. "Beyond these French doors is Classroom B. Now, follow me down this hallway, and we'll take the stairs up to the second floor."

Once at the end of the hall, Lena directed the girl's attention to a silver-handled, square door in the wall. "This is our laundry chute. You will find another door just like this one upstairs. You can use this one for dirty kitchen towels, napkins, table clothes, and dish rags. In the pantry, you will find laundry bags marked, *SHNS Kitchen*. Discard your soiled linens in there, cinch it up, and send it down the chute. A canvass cart catches the laundry bags in the basement tunnel below us."

A hand shot up. "Excuse me? I have a question," Lexie said. "What happens to our dirty clothes and unmentionables?"

"Good question. Mr. and Mrs. Wu will be operating our laundry department for the hospital and the nursing school. Because we don't have the funds for maid service, I will create a weekly work chart that outlines your chores for that week. One of which will be to roll the dirty laundry cart through the tunnel to the laundry room every day. Mr. and Mrs. Wu will wash, dry, press, and fold everything to include the laundry bags. It will be your job to retrieve your clean clothes. For those assigned to kitchen or bathroom duties that week, you will return those items to their rightful places."

"Did I sign up for nursing school or labor camp?" Bertie mumbled, causing those closest to her to burst out laughing, to include Addie and Opal.

As Nurse Hartman ascended the stairs, she said, "I heard that, Miss Jones."

Bertie wrinkled up her face as she mouthed, "Oh, crap!"

Addie called up to her, "Nurse Hartman? Will you explain the tunnels to us?"

"Yes, I'll tell you all about them when we get upstairs."

The entire group assembled in the large dorm situated in the front of the school that overlooked the garden and walking paths below.

Thoughts whirled through Addie's mind as she processed her new surroundings. *This room looks so institutional and lacks the charm of my bedroom at Mrs. Gray's house.*

The only hope of color was from the rays of sunshine cascading through the window panes that cast rainbows on the white bed linens. The polished pine floor appeared bleached out by the white walls and metal frame beds. Brass electric lights lined the walls above the wooden bed tables that separated the rows of beds. Addie found a bit of warmth in the fireplace at the end of the room. The bookshelves on either side of it were stocked with a variety of reading materials. Porcelain white angels, glass vases in a variety of pastel colors, and a few brass bowls containing silk flowers and greenery were carefully staged between the books in an effort to soften the stiff spines of the literary collection.

"Mr. Alexander had tunnels built so the physicians, staff, and nurses could come and go between the buildings freely without having to mix with the general population. They will be extremely helpful especially on rainy or blustery days. There will be a total of three tunnels configured in the shape of a triangle. They are well marked and provide underground access to all of the buildings for the housekeeping, culinary, laundry, and maintenance staff, too."

"What about to the garage?" Deborah asked.

"That building is the exception. There isn't a tunnel to that structure. However, private driveways off Spring and Alexander Streets will provide the ambulances access to the emergency departments at both facilities and ultimately circle around to the back property and connect in front of the garage."

Lena walked toward the fireplace and stopped. Nurse Scott and the group followed.

"Your trunks have been placed at the foot of your assigned beds. You will also notice that your uniforms are ready for you."

Since everything was white, Addie missed seeing the folded pile of white clothes on top of each bedspread.

"Please follow me into the dressing room and your bathroom area."

The young ladies crossed the hall and entered another large room at the back of the building. The mirrors above the white porcelain sinks reflected their images. Addie caught Opal and Bertie making faces; she nudged them with her elbows and stuck out her tongue.

"Your shower stalls are to your left, the bathrooms are here, and your lockers and dressing room are to your right."

The group followed Nurse Hartman. The black and white mosaic tile floor gave way to a navy carpeted dressing room where pecan lockers and chests of drawers lined the periphery while two brass chandeliers divided the room. Gold, brocade-up-holstered benches sat in front of the cabinetry. Addie noticed the windows along the back of the school were frosted behind the parted curtains.

"Hey! Me name is written on this locker," Mary Margaret sang out in an Irish brogue, pointing to a locker directly in front of her.

"Yes, Miss O'Malley, they're already assigned to each of you. Now, go and stand in front of your locker."

The girls separated, searched out their names, and complied with Lena's instructions.

"You will see there are no locks here. Look to the person on your right, look to the person on your left, and look at the person behind you. You are all sisters. You will not borrow without asking and you definitely will not steal. If you do, you will be immediately removed from this institution, placed under arrest for theft, and thrown into the pokey."

A few of the students stood straighter.

"Open your lockers."

Addie, like the others, unlatched her door to find a navy blue, wool cape with a deep gold lining hanging in the wardrobe on a wooden hanger. Embroidered in gold colored thread on the left side was the name *Sacred Heart Hospital*. The caduceus was underneath. "Oh, this is so beautiful! Thank you so much!" Addie tried hers on and was the first to thank Nurse Hartman. The others followed suit. Upon further inspection, Addie couldn't believe her eyes. "Oh, my heavens! My initials have been embroidered inside."

The young ladies flipped open their capes to see their initials hand-stitched in dark navy on the inside left panel.

Lena glanced at the watch pendant pinned to her nursing uniform. "I have one more thing to show you before I meet back up with you in Classroom B for lunch. On the board hanging on the wall outside of this room in the stairwell, you will see a posting of notices, hospital shift assignments, and your weekly chores. That is where I will also post notices about your class schedules." Struck by another thought, she added, "Oh, and before I forget, this building does have central air conditioning, an ice machine in the basement, and two phones. One is located in the main hallway upstairs and the other is downstairs. Please note that it is a private number. You will be allowed to use it once a week for fifteen minutes to call home. And, of course, you can use it to call me for late night emergencies."

"You don't stay here in the dorms with us?" Deborah's eyes darted to Lena then back to her locker.

Lena could tell Miss Owen's was plotting late night escapes and rendezvous.

"No, I reside at the Ponce Apartments a few blocks away and will bicycle to work every day. My number is posted by the phones should you need to reach me in the night for any reason. Believe me when I say when it's lights out at twenty-one hundred hours, it's lights out. Mr. Alexander has hired night watchmen, or should I say off-duty policemen, to patrol the hospital grounds and tunnels, especially since much of the property is still under construction. They will also see to your safety at night." Anticipating they were about to inquire about Nurse Scott's residence, she continued. "Nurse Scott resides in an apartment not far from here in the Fifth Ward. She, too, will bike to work."

"Great." Disappointment washed over Deborah's face.

"Regarding the phone calls to your families, I will have a sign-up sheet on the board before the end of the day. You can call them every Sunday afternoon and evening. If I find you gabbing on the phone in the middle of the night to some beau you have left behind, what will you receive?" Lena cupped her hand to her ear.

Gosh, who would I call? I don't have a family of my own anymore. Mrs. Gray is gone. Garrett is the only person I have ever loved. Garrett and Mr. Darling don't own a phone and have to travel into Hope to the local mercantile store to place a call. Addie reached deep inside her dress pocket. She pulled out the pebble her childhood friend gave to her before she left her rural roots in north Georgia. Rolling it around in the palm of her hand, the flecks of iron pyrite, Fool's Gold, caught the light and sparkled. She recalled telling Garrett, *'I plan to keep your stone with me everywhere I go. It's a constant reminder of you, my past, my Hope, and my tomorrows.'* Addie had hated saying good-bye to Garrett on Mrs. Gray's front porch. I know life has so much in store for me. I'm ready to let go to see where it takes me. She remembered Garrett saying, *'While a part of me wants to snatch you up and carry you back to Hope, I know that you long for more. I can't deny you that life. Before I go, promise me that you will write to me from school. I want to know that you are happy and doing well. That's my wish for you.'* She imagined his breath on her skin and his whisper in her ear. *'I love you, my dear Addie. Come back to me someday.'* Addie's heart sank like the stone she dropped into the depths of her dress pocket. She hung her cape on its hanger and returned it to the closet.

"Demerits?" Both Bell and Alice answered.

"Good, Miss Esposito and Miss Fein. You are right. I expect

to see you downstairs for lunch with our founder, Mr. Alexander; Dr. Williams, our medical director; and our Chief Operating Officer, Clyde Posey, at eleven thirty." She glanced at her watch. "According to my watch, you have exactly one hour to change into your new uniforms and unpack your belongings. Please leave your empty trunks at the foot of your beds. This afternoon, Joshua and a few of his men will carry them to the basement, where they will be stored. Nurse Scott will remain with you to lend a hand."

Lena walked out of the dressing room. As she descended the back stairs, she heard the sound of feet running between the dorm and the dressing room. Returning to the kitchen, she found Joshua standing close to Maybelle Reed.

Joshua looked up and winked. "I'm just lending a hand to Sacred Heart's prettiest new cook." He continued to help her unpack two wicker baskets of prepared dishes.

"Ha!" Maybelle fired back. "I'm Sacred Heart's only cook!"

Lena laughed right along with them. "Joshua, I must say, you did a great job helping me this morning. Maybelle, thank you for getting this kitchen stocked. You both have been invaluable in helping us get this school ready."

"I'm happy to be of assistance, Nurse Hartman." Joshua turned to Maybelle. "If you don't need me for anything else, I've got to rally a few men to help me carry the students' trunks to the basement this afternoon. Ladies, if you'll excuse me."

Joshua smiled at Maybelle. It was a loving smile, Lena observed.

Maybelle's mocha cheeks blushed as Joshua exited, whistling the hymn "Love Lifted Me." She slipped into her starched, white iolite apron, and addressed Lena as she cinched her bow. "Yes, ma'am, the pleasure is mine. I've prepared lunch for y'all today. I hope you like turkey and cheese, pimento cheese, and cucumber finger sandwiches, cheddar cheese straws, potato salad, fresh apple sauce, and pickles. I even brought some homemade lemonade and sweet tea."

"That sounds delicious! I'm sure the girls are ravenous."

Maybelle took out two large Mason jars and uncapped them. Finding glass pitchers in the cabinets, she poured the beverages into them and stored them in the refrigerator. Maybelle grabbed an empty ice bucket. "I'm going downstairs to fetch some ice. You need anything while I'm down there, ma'am?"

"No. Thank you."

Maybelle exited the kitchen.

Lena looked up at the ceiling as the students continued to run back and forth between the rooms. She beamed. "This place finally has a heartbeat!"

Addie donned her uniform and ran into the bathroom to find an available mirror. She twisted her hair into a bun and pinned her cap in place. She was taken aback. Her uniform transformed her into a vision she'd long thought could only be a dream. Gone were all traces of the beaten-down farm girl from Hope. The young city lady had also been erased, as she no longer wore a hair transformation or any traces of lipstick, blush, brow pencil, or powder. Her faint perfume was also washed away. Addie radiated as she embraced her new appearance, making last minute adjustments to her uniform and adjusting her stockings. *I look so smart. I can't believe I actually look like a nurse! I hoped and prayed for this day to come. Gosh! If only Maw could see me now.* Addie stared at her image in the mirror and her blue eyes connected to her inner soul. She felt her spirit becoming overwhelmed with a sense of peace.

Opal ran up to her. "I see Nurse Hartman assigned our beds and lockers together. Isn't that just grand? Oh, look at you, Addie! Here, let me fix the bow on the back of your apron."

Addie's bow was crooked. She turned around so that Opal could retie it. "Let me check your bow-tying skills, too," Addie said. Opal spun around and popped her backside out. There were no adjustments to be made. Opal had tied the perfect bow. *I bet her bandaging skills are going to be sheer perfection, too!* "Your bow's perfect, Opal."

Nurse Scott ushered the girls downstairs and into Classroom B. They found Mr. Alexander, Dr. Williams, Clyde, Lena, and Maybelle already in the room making introductions with the other students.

Edward saw Opal enter. "Oh, look at my little girl. You are so grown up." Opal spun around in front of her father and then pecked him on the cheek.

Opal grabbed Addie's hand. "Daddy, this is Addie. She's the girl I've been telling you about that Nurse Hartman introduced me to last month."

Addie shook Mr. Alexander's hand. "It's a pleasure to meet you, sir."

"You look mighty familiar. Where have I seen you before?" Edward rubbed his chin as he pondered for a moment. "Oh! Yes, now I remember."

Addie flushed and held her breath. *Oh heavens, if he remembers me passing out at their Christmas party, I will die from embarrassment! Doc Gray's tonic combined with champagne did me in.*

"I saw you at Mrs. Gray's funeral."

Oh, thank the dear Lord above! Relieved, Addie relaxed and exhaled. "Yes, sir. I was her nursemaid after her husband passed away."

"She was a fine woman. Her late husband was an admirable man and respected physician. In fact, I plan on dedicating the tunnel that connects Sacred Heart Hospital to Alexander Hall in Doc Gray's honor at the grand opening. I'm sure she told you that he was going to be our medical director until he suffered a fatal heart attack."

"Yes, sir, that will be quite an honor to bestow upon him. I only wish Mrs. Gray was alive to be a part of the celebration. She always talked so highly of you and Nurse Hartman."

"It's a pleasure to meet you, Addie. Please take care of my Opal." Edward patted Addie on the back as he excused himself to address the group. "Well, as my daddy use to say, 'let's get to it and just do it.' Welcome to Sacred Heart's School for Nurses. Everyone fill your plates, find a seat, and we'll get started."

Clyde turned his back on Edward and rolled his eyes. Catching him in the act, Deborah made eye contact with him. She nodded as he winked at her and turned his scowl into a hint of a grin. He licked his lips.

Lena witnessed their exchange, making a mental note to keep a close eye on Miss Owens.

"Miss Owens, please come sit over here by me, will you?" Lena motioned her over, pulling out the empty chair beside her.

Deborah's eyes turned frosty as she joined Nurse Hartman at the table.

Edward turned to watch Addie and Opal scamper off and

rejoin the group at the buffet table. His heart burst with pride. He wiped a tear from his cheek, knowing his dream to make a difference in this world was finally coming true.

2

The Holy Cross Orphans' Asylum, a white shiplap home located on Chapel Street, was nestled in Atlanta's west end amongst the city's working class. Pressures of poverty forced the labor class to abandon their children in search for work. This orphanage was among approximately two dozen others sprinkled between Atlanta, Augusta, Macon, and Savannah. While some homes were designated for boys or girls—Christian, Jewish, Catholic, white, or colored children only—Holy Cross accepted only white boys ranging in age from newborns to thirteen years of age.

Since Georgia's economic development revolved around cheap child labor, the law permitted children as young as ten years of age to work up to eleven hours a day. As a result, numerous mill and factory owners set up their businesses in the southern city and shanty towns cropped up. Times were tough and thousands of laborers and their families lived without the luxuries of indoor plumbing, gas, or electricity.

Boys, ten years of age and older, housed at Holy Cross, were hired out to work for the railroad companies, cotton or textile mills, or to other businesses. Their wages were deposited into the orphanage's coffers to help offset the costs of room, board, food, and clothing. A few dollars were always skimmed off the top for "operating and living expenses" by the founders, Father Joe and his real-life sister, Ida Preti. While adoption fees also helped to assuage costs, desperation and greed fueled the fire for the Preti's desire to seek out additional sources of revenue.

Sow seeds of hope so you can reap your future potential was cross-stitched on yellowing fabric that was framed and mounted in the hallway of the orphanage. Ida stopped in front of it, taking time to relish in the countless hours it took her to sew her masterpiece. Embroidered corn stalks, cornucopias filled with fruit and vegetables, and scrolling borders filled the hand-made oak frame. She adjusted the picture to hang perfectly straight, aligning the top of the frame with the line of one of the boards on the white-washed shiplap wall. She ran her fingers over the bumpy knots and various colored threads. "Perfect!"

Ring. Ring. Ida waddled—her short, plump frame shifted from side to side down the hall—as she raced to answer the black candlestick phone. Pushing her tightly-curled salt and pepper hair away from her ear, she picked up the phone and placed the earpiece against her ear. "Hello? Hello?" breathless, she sang into the mouthpiece.

A man with a staccato Chinese accent chimed back. "Is this Holy Cross Orphans' Asylum?"

"Yes, yes, it is. May I help you?"

"Yes, this Mr. Chang. Please let Father Preti know that I want to meet with him tonight to finalize our arrangement. Tell him not at my emporium, but rather in the parking lot of the National Pencil Company Factory on Decatur Street."

Ida mulled. "Isn't that the place where that poor young girl was murdered in the basement almost a year ago?"

"Yes. I will be in the area on business. Tell Father Preti I will see him at eight o'clock sharp." The phone line went dead.

"Hello? Hello?" Ida clicked the switch hook a few times with her index finger. "Hello? Hello?"

Ida heard the sound of heavy footsteps behind her. She spun around.

"Who was that on the phone?" Father Preti inquired.

She hung up the phone and returned it to its place, making a few minor adjustments. "Perfect!"

Joe smacked Ida's hands. "Quit trying to make everything so perfect. We aren't and life isn't. I'll ask again. Who was on the phone?"

Irritated, Ida shoved her hands in her dress pockets. "It was Mr. Chang. He wants you to meet him in the parking lot of The Pencil Factory on Decatur Street tonight at eight."

"Did he say anything else?"

"No. Do you plan to finalize our new business arrangement with him?"

"Yes."

SATURDAY NIGHT, FOURTH WARD

Father Preti steered the Galloway motor wagon into the parking lot of The Pencil Factory parking lot. He spotted Mr. Chang's black Model T. Pulling up to the passenger's side window, the driver pointed toward the back of the car. Mr. Chang popped up, emerging from underneath a worn wool blanket. He tossed his long, black, tightly-braided ponytail off his shoulder.

"I'm not popular in this town. I make this quick." Without moving his head, his dark eyes shifted left and right.

Father Preti turned the key and shut off the engine. "So, what's gonna be our arrangement?"

"You send me boys ages six to eight. Tell them they are going to loving home. Before you bring them to me, give them this." Mr. Chang tossed a large tonic bottle into Father Preti's empty passenger seat.

"What's this?" Picking it up, he read *Mr. Chang's Hypno-Sedative. Ingredients: Indian hemp. Potassium bromide. Chloral. Indications. Use for hysteria, sleepiness, dysmenorrhea, Epilepsy, spasms, neuralgia, and other nervous disorders.*

"Give them one to two teaspoons depending on size. Mix in drink."

"What do my sister and I get in return?"

"Twenty-five dollars per boy. Not negotiable."

"What if we start running low on inventory?"

"Not my problem." He fanned his hands in the air. "You find children roaming in streets or abandoned at hospitals. Set up meetings. Let them know you are willing to take the wayward bastards and orphans off their hands. After all, you are doing them a favor. Oh, there's a new hospital opening next month in Sixth Ward called Sacred Heart. Contact a man by the name of Clyde Posey. Schedule meeting with him. He'll be expecting your call…Father."

"What are your plans for the boys?"

Mr. Chang shook his crooked, bony fingers in the air. His long fingernails caught Father Preti's attention. They were filed to mimic claws. "Not your concern. Should you ever get caught by police, you not know me. If you don't listen, you and your sister will be torn apart by the dragon," Mr. Chang snarled, revealing his lower row of teeth, chiseled to sharp points. He disappeared under the blanket and tapped on the floorboard. The chauffer started the car, driving off into the darkness without turning the headlights on.

3

The passing seconds on Addie's wrist watch turned into minutes. Minutes turned into days and the days into weeks. Addie discovered she had an insatiable thirst for knowledge. New thoughts and ideas spurred with every medical topic introduced by Nurse Hartman.

During the first week, the students learned about the origins of medicine, hospitals, and nursing from a textbook called *A Short History of Nursing*. In the second week, the textbook dedicated to Lilian Wald, a pioneer in public health nursing, called *Hygiene and Sanitation for Nurses*, was introduced. Subject matter ranged from the origins of water supply, hazards around water closets, pipes and fixtures in the home, the care, storage and preservation of food, and the duties of public and school nurses. The book also reviewed infectious diseases and their prevention. Obstetrics and pharmaceuticals were presented in the third week, continuing through the end of the month.

The grandfather clock signaled the end of a lesson every time it chimed on the hour. Today, as it chimed on the half hour,

Addie watched the rain pelt the window panes in the hallway outside of Classroom A. Wind gusts scattered the water from the fountain. Addie tried to follow along in her textbook, *Obstetrics for Nurses*, as Nurse Hartman reviewed the anatomy and physiology of the reproductive system on the blackboard. Addie's thoughts kept wandering back to that unforgettable night with Garrett in her bedroom at his Aunt Olive's house.

Addie rested her chin in her hand. *Chapter Two doesn't mention anything about the steamy romance, passion, sweaty kisses, and the explosive exhilaration of an orgasm like the one I experienced when Garrett and I made love. Gosh, the medical dissection of the act of sex is stripped down to our basic human instinct to reproduce and pass on our genes. The author fails to mention how sex is so much fun.* A goofy grin appeared on her face. She reached deep into her apron pocket and fumbled with a few extra bobby pins and the rock Garrett gave her. She decided to keep it with her at all times for fear of losing it.

Lena scanned the attentive faces of her students and saw Addie gazing outside with a silly smirk. She chose to awaken Addie from her daydream. "Miss Engel. Can you tell me what connects the placenta with the child in utero?"

A hush fell over the room. Addie sensed people looking at her. Her vision of her passionate night with Garrett quickly vanished. She mentally emerged back into Classroom A, where she found Nurse Hartman staring at her. "I'm sorry, Nurse Hartman, did you ask me a question?"

"Yes, Miss Engel, I did." She tapped the piece of white chalk in the palm of her hand.

Addie squirmed. She felt her cheeks get hot and her chest flushed with hives. "Can you please repeat it?"

"For the second time, can you tell me what connects the placenta with the child in utero?"

Having assisted with numerous livestock deliveries on the family farm in Hope, Addie was relieved to know the answer. She had cut a few for the cows and helped one of their old mares unwrap it from around her foal's neck. Addie answered, "It's the umbilical cord."

"Correct, Miss Engel." Pointing the stick of chalk at Addie, she added, "May I ask that you remain present in mind, body, and spirit for the duration of the class?"

"Yes, ma'am."

Some of her classmates snickered. Opal, who sat beside Addie, kicked her leg under the table. Addie kicked her back.

At the stroke of twelve, the class recessed and enjoyed their lunch break together in Classroom B. Maybelle had prepared fried chicken, green beans, corn, and fresh corn bread, complete with an array of jams, butter, and honey. Addie avoided sitting with Opal during lunch for fear of having to field probing questions about her behavior earlier today.

As Addie spread butter on her hot corn bread, she reprimanded herself. *Addie, don't get into trouble. Stop day dreaming.* Then, another voice popped into her head, answering and rationalizing. *Addie, dear, you are in nursing school. How much trouble could you possibly get into here? Relax and quit obsessing.* Opting to shut off the internal conversation, she shoved a piece of corn-bread in her mouth and jumped in the conversation with Alice and Bertie about the best way to treat diaper rash.

The rain showers continued as the latter half of the afternoon was dedicated to reviewing the *Materia Medica for Nurs-*

es. Weights and measures, solutions, antiseptics, and astringents were reviewed. Addie continued to fumble with the pebble in her pocket to prevent Nurse Hartman from calling her out again for daydreaming. As the clock struck five bells, Nurse Hartman wrote their homework assignment on the board.

Obstetrics for Nurses, Chapter 3 — The Stages of Labor

Principles and Practice of Nursing, Chapters 5, 6, 7

"Holy moly! We have a lot of reading to do tonight. My head is so full. I think I'm on the brink of being overloaded." Opal closed her book, stood, and stretched. "Hey, where did you go today during sex ed?"

Addie gathered her books and notebooks, shoving her pencils in her uniform pockets. "What? I'm not sure I know what you mean."

"Sure you do. Who was or is he?" Opal waited to hear something juicy. She searched Addie's blue eyes for a hint. There wasn't one.

Dismissive, Addie flipped her hand. "Oh, it's nothing worth mentioning. I'm just tired. It's like you said. We're being taught so much. I was just taking a mental break to watch it rain outside."

They made their way up the stairs to change out of their uniforms and study and relax before dinner. Addie threw herself on her bed, agitated by being called out by Nurse Hartman and the fact that she still hadn't made any effort to contact Garrett yet. She listened to the rain pelt the tile roof. Memories returned to the night she ran to Garrett's house and hid in their barn. She rolled over, turning her back to Opal, who sat on her bed reading one of her textbooks. Thoughts about Garrett continued to stir her soul. *Mrs. Gray's Will and Testament left the house and money to me. Garrett's aunt and uncle must be so embarrassed about Lester's Doc Gray and Doc Otto tonic scandal. How ironic that he was poisoned to death! He was pure evil. He finally got what he deserved.* Addie's flurry of thoughts continued. She stewed, thinking back to the moments when Lester had been so cruel to her and Mrs. Gray. *I can't even imagine what he would have done to me. He would have surely set Mrs. Gray's house ablaze with me in it rather than rather see me happy and living in it. Bastard!*

The rain continued, lulling Addie to sleep. Opal closed her book and hopped off her bed. She considered rousing Addie for dinner, but decided to let her remain undisturbed. She pulled a blanket over Addie's shoulders and joined the others girls downstairs for the evening.

Hours later, a great white flash of light illuminated the garden outside and a crack of thunder shook the window panes, startling Addie awake. She rubbed her eyes and scanned the room to see eight bodies in their beds under the covers. *What time is it?* The grandfather clock downstairs chimed one bell in reply. Addie got out of bed, put on her pink silk kimono, and tied the sash in a bow. Opal rolled over and saw her silhouette.

"Are you okay?" Opal whispered.

"Yeah, I'm fine. I can't believe I missed dinner." Addie was still a bit foggy-headed.

"You were sound asleep. I thought it best to not wake you. Where are you going?"

Restless, hungry, and anxious to tackle some of her homework, Addie whispered back, "I'm heading downstairs to grab a snack and do a bit of reading. Since it's so quiet, I think I'll be able to get a lot accomplished in a few hours."

"Have fun," Opal mumbled and rolled over, pulling the covers over her head.

Addie grabbed *Obstetrics for Nurses and Principles* and *Practice of Nursing*, making her way through the darkness. The storm raged on as thunder rumbled and lightning flashed. The wind drove sheets of rain against the windows. Addie could tell the storm system was strong, and it was almost on top of them.

Addie turned on the kitchen light and set her books down on the table. Grabbing the cold, silver handle on the refrigerator door, she opened it to find a plate of leftover fried chicken. She heard grumbling, unsure if it was from her stomach or thunder from the storm.

As she reached for the plate, there was heavy pounding on the front door. Startled, she slammed the refrigerator door closed. She peered around the kitchen door, affixing her gaze down the long hallway. Through one of the sidelights, a night watchman peered through the window and spotted her. Sensing something was horribly wrong, she ran to open the door for him.

Officer Evans, according to his brass nameplate, was dripping wet. As he removed his navy-blue hat, water ran off the top and splashed Addie's bare feet. She didn't feel it. Addie was fixated on the worry in his green eyes as he spoke frantically. *What would cause a policeman to need help at this time of night in the middle of a terrible storm?* In an attempt to remain calm, Addie rapidly searched for a rational explanation. *Tornado? Fire? Prowlers? The Atlanta Ripper?*

"Baby? Did you say baby?"

"Yes, Miss. A woman and her husband were driving by and thought that Sacred Heart Hospital was open. My partner is escorting them here so they can get out of the storm. Her water has already broken and she said her contractions were about two minutes apart."

"Here? As in here?" Addie pointed towards the floor.

"You all are nurses? Right? You do this kind of thing all the time."

"Um, we're just nursing *students*. We're in training."

Lightning crackled across the sky. Addie made out three images scurrying through the garden. Two men, one in uniform, supported a very pregnant woman. She stopped and howled as thunder rumbled. Her knees buckled as she clutched her belly. If it weren't for her husband and the other night watchman holding her up under her arms, Addie knew for sure the woman would have collapsed to the ground. Addie could tell she was having a contraction. They had to let it pass before she could make her way up the stairs and into the school.

Officer Evans looked scared. Addie reached out, touched his shoulder, and felt his body tremble.

He started to cry. "I don't want her baby to die like ours did last year when my wife gave birth to our son alone at home. Please help her."

Addie immediately focused on what logical steps needed to be taken next. *Think.* She recalled the country doctor's instructions when she helped him out with neighbors' deliveries in Hope. *Secure the patient in a safe place, prep the room and the patient, and let nature take its course. Prepare for any one of the three common childbirth complications: asphyxiation of the child, postpartum hemorrhage, and shock.* "We will. We all will. Please take her into the back classroom, across from the kitchen. I'm going to call my nursing supervisor and wake my classmates. I'll be right back."

Addie ran to the telephone in the hallway and rang Nurse Hartman, who in turn said she would call Dr. Williams. Lena assured Addie that help was on the way. In the meantime, she was told to refer to her *Obstetrics for Nurses, Chapter V, Obstetric Operations* and follow the textbook's instructions.

Addie ran into the kitchen and grabbed her book as she called up the back stairs. "OPAL! GIRLS! I NEED YOUR HELP! WE HAVE A MEDICAL EMERGENCY. OPAL?" She flipped to *Chapter V.*

"Coming. We're coming," sleepy voices randomly called back.

Addie heard bare feet hitting the wood floor overhead, stampeding towards the stairs. She stood at the bottom and directed the sleepy students above her. "We've got a woman in active labor. Her water has already broken."

Deborah yawned and rubbed her eyes. "How'd they end up here?"

"Is that really an important question to be asking now?" Addie snapped. "Here's what we are being presented with. We have a patient that needs our immediate attention. I called Nurse Hartman and she is summoning Dr. Williams. They will be here as quick as they can."

"How do ye know this isn't a wee test? You know, like a pop quiz?" Mary Margaret adjusted her nightgown.

A woman screamed out from Classroom B.

"Miss? Where are you? We need you NOW!" Officer Evans called out.

Addie shot a look back at them. "Does that sound like a pop

quiz to you?" Addie ran into the kitchen. The girls followed. "We're coming," she called out to Officer Evans.

Addie pulled out a white apron from one of the drawers. Setting the book on the counter, she scanned the text and then began reading *Preparation for operation* out loud. She directed the girls gathered around her. "Deborah and Susan, you two boil pans of water, find a hot water bottle, soap, a pillow, and a large basket. Mary Margaret and Alice, fetch blankets, sheets, towels, string, safety pins, a razor, and newspapers. Meet us in Classroom B." She turned to the next pair of girls. "Lexie and Bell, I need you to prepare one bowl of one percent Lysol and one bowl of 1:1000 bichlorid, a pitcher of hot Lysol solution, and a saucer containing scissors and tape soaking in one percent Lysol for the cord cutting."

"Okay. We're on it." Lexie and Bell scurried off.

Addie showed Bertie and Opal *Fig. 113* and *Fig. 114* in the textbook. Addie thrust the open textbook into Opal's hands. "You keep reading aloud and follow me. Bertie, get the officers to help you and prepare Classroom B. Arrange the tables, chair, blankets, linens, and newspapers just like you saw in the photograph and the illustration."

"Got it." Bertie, bright eyed and wide awake, was eager to tackle the task.

Addie, Bertie, and Opal ran out of the kitchen across the hall into Classroom B, propping the French doors open.

"Ohhh! I feel another contraction coming on." The pregnant woman's husband held her as she breathed through the agonizing pain. Sweat beads popped up on her forehead and upper lip.

"Ma'am, my name is Addie. We are all nursing students and

we're going to help you until our medical director and nursing supervisor arrive."

"We thought you were already open. We didn't know what to do. We're the Millers. This is my wife, Amy," Mr. Miller explained.

Amy attempted a smile as she breathed heavily through pursed lips. "This is our fifth child."

Fifth child! That baby could come at any moment! Addie remembered that ladies typically had a longer labor with their first born, but with each sequential birth, labor could progress rather rapidly. *Time isn't on our side. We must move quickly.*

"Officers, please help me arrange three tables and a chair in this fashion," Bertie said as Opal showed the picture in the book to them.

"Opal, start reading." Addie instructed. "What do we do next?"

"For births at home, soap out the windows or tape newspaper across the windows to prevent nosey neighbors from peeking inside."

"No, no, after that."

"Obstetric operating is bloodier than any other, sometimes urine, bowel movements, blood...." Opal looked up. "Give me a moment." She glanced back down, hastily scanning the pages with her fingers. "Ah, here we go. The nurse should call some courageous women to hold the limbs of the patient while on the table. The husband usually cannot be relied on; he is likely to faint."

Opal looked at the husband and the officers, who finished arranging the furniture. "Gentleman, I need to ask you to leave this room. Please have a seat across the hall in our parlor. Close the door behind you, if you please."

Opal ushered them out as Bertie, Mary Margaret, and Alice covered the three tables with sheets. On the center table, they made a Kelly pad by rolling old copies of *The Atlanta Dispatch* into a tube with string inside. They configured it into the shape of an "n", tying the string ends in a bow so the roll kept its shape. Over the top of the pad, they laid unfolded March issues of *The Atlanta Constitution*, letting half of the paper overhang. They secured the corners with a safety pin to make a funnel that led to a roasting pan below. A clean towel was placed on top. They placed a rolled-up blanket at the head of the table to serve as a pillow. A classroom chair sat on the spread-out copies of the newspaper on the floor in front of the basin and funnel.

Between contractions, whimpers, and moans, Addie helped Mrs. Miller undress and assisted her onto the table. Addie covered her with a blanket while Mary Margaret and Alice wrapped her legs and feet in a sheet, leaving only the perineal area exposed. Lexie and Bell placed their basins filled with instruments and solution on the right table. Deborah and Susan set the pitchers of hot water and a basket containing the hot water bottle covered with a pillow on the left.

Opal continued reading. "Preparation of the patient. Hold the patient's legs in modified lithotomy position or place them in the modified Walcher position." Opal rushed over to Addie and pointed to *Fig. 118* in the book. The woman's legs were spread apart and draped over the backs of two wooden, kitchen chairs. Looking up at each other, they both shook their heads and pointed to *Fig. 117*. The picture illustrated two women holding and supporting the legs of the patient.

"Deborah and Susan, I need you to hold Mrs. Miller's legs like so." Opal showed them the picture. They complied.

Addie sat in the chair and watched blood-tinged secretions stream through the funnel and drip into the metal roasting pan. *Ting. Ting. Ting.*

Opal turned the page. "If the labor is very rapid, part of the proper surgical preparations may have to be omitted — the bath, the enema, the shaving, but not the antiseptic washing. Wash your hands and fingernails thoroughly."

Addie washed her hands.

"Now drench the vulva and neighborhood with one percent Lysol solution. Remove as much hair with the razor as possible and avoid getting hair and soap into the introitus."

Bertie prepared Mrs. Miller by relaying the steps Addie was taking. Addie lathered the area in soap. She retrieved the razor soaking in the basin and shaved in a downward direction.

"Ooo–owwwww. The baby's coming," Mrs. Miller hollered.

"Disinfect the rest of the area like so using the bichlorid solution." Opal showed Addie the diagram.

As Addie leaned in to proceed with the next steps, she caught a glimpse of *The Atlanta Constitution* headline dated March 19, 1914: "New 'Jack the Ripper' Now Held on Charge of Robbing High School." Blood dripped down the article about the Atlanta Ripper cases and a potential suspect in custody. Three years ago, Addie began hearing gruesome stories and rumors circulate about the serial murders in downtown Atlanta. Ripper victims tended to be young, colored or mulatto women in their twenties, who were found with severe, crushing blows to the head and their throats slashed from ear to ear. News about the Atlanta Ripper sent shivers up Addie's spine.

"Ohhhh! I want to push! The baby's coming. I want to push NOW!" Mrs. Miller screamed.

Bertie patted her reassuringly as she wiped her brow with a cool wash cloth. Mary Margaret and Susan scurried to the head of the table to support Mrs. Miller's shoulders as she grabbed the backs of her legs and pushed.

Addie watched a dark-haired head crown as the vagina opened wider with each push. Various secretions cascaded into the funnel and the pan below. The baby's head popped out. Its face turned to the right side as the baby untwisted its neck and the shoulders rotated inside the pelvis.

"Oooo." Opal and the other students stared in amazement.

Addie remembered the country physician referred to the baby's actions as external restitution. She heard his voice in her head. *There will be a short pause before the shoulders are immediately followed by the rest of the trunk.*

Belle elbowed Deborah. "Have you ever seen anything like this? This is a miracle. Why am I crying?" She wiped the tears from her cheeks.

Addie supported the head and assisted with the shoulders as the rest of the slippery baby entered the world into her awaiting hands. She cradled the wet infant and cleared mucous from its mouth using her little finger, which was covered with a linen cloth.

Opal continued to read as Bertie ran to the foot of the table, taking the bluish-colored baby from Addie. "Tie off the cord and cut it."

Addie complied. She handed the newborn to Bertie, who held the baby upside down and gently smacked its bottom. The baby immediately inhaled, turned pink, and wailed at the top of its lungs.

Mrs. Miller propped herself up on the back of her elbows as Mary Margaret dabbed a cool, damp cloth over her face. "Is it a boy or a girl?"

Bertie cradled the baby in her arms and turned to Deborah, who held out a blanket. An arc of urine splashed Deborah in the face. She gagged, tossed the blanket at Bertie, covered her mouth, and ran out of the room.

"It's a boy!" Bertie yelled out so the men in the parlor could hear her. Both rooms erupted with shouts of "Congratulations!" Tears and hugs followed.

Addie turned back to the patient, knowing the third part of labor was eminent. She needed to deliver the placenta. Bertie showed Mrs. Miller her infant son before attending to him and placing him on the warmed pillow in the basket.

Opal turned a page. "Bertie, tie the umbilical cord one half inch from the skin margin using the surgeon's knot like so." She directed Bertie to the photograph in *Fig. 120*. "The cord is severed one fourth inch from the ligature." Bertie used sterilized scissors and followed the instructions.

"Addie? Girls? Dr. Williams and I are here!" The familiar voice of Nurse Hartman called out, followed by the sound of footsteps running up the hallway.

Help has finally arrived! Addie sighed with relief.

Dr. Williams appeared in the doorway carrying his black, leather doctor's bag. Nurse Hartman stood behind him and assisted him in removing his black rain coat and hat. He scanned Classroom B to find the various students in their nightgowns and robes as they attended to the mother and child.

Addie jumped up from the chair. "Dr. Williams. This is Mrs. Amy Miller. She just gave birth to a baby boy. We don't have any silver nitrate for his eyes and the placenta still needs to be delivered."

Opal clutched *Obstetrics for Nurses* to her chest and ran over to Lena to debrief her.

Dr. Williams pulled out his stethoscope to assess the newborn. "Addie, come here, my brave girl. I need you to hear this." He placed the earpieces in Addie's ears and placed the bell-shaped chest piece over the baby's heart. *Ba-dum. Ba-dum. Ba-dum.* The heart beat was strong and rapid. Addie's eyes widened as she gazed upon the tiny infant, Dr. Williams, and her classmates. Dr. Williams removed the stethoscope from Addie's ears. He retrieved medications from his bag and administered them to the baby. Then, he instructed Bertie to attend to the newborn while he turned his attentions to Mrs. Miller.

"Mrs. Miller, you have a beautiful, healthy baby boy. What are you going to name him?"

"Judson Davis Miller." Mrs. Miller looked over at the basket where she heard him cooing.

Dr. Williams summoned Nurse Hartman into the room as he rolled up his sleeves. She helped him to cleanse and disinfect his hands. "Will you please bring me my bag and we'll finalize this last stage of delivery. Ladies you are doing a fine job attending to Mrs. Miller. We're almost done now."

Addie stepped backwards as she watched Dr. Williams deliver and examine the placenta to make sure it came out complete. She knew any torn fragments left inside the uterus could lead to infection and possibly death.

Addie looked down at her hands. They began to tremble. She tried wiping them on the front of her apron. Blood and secretions saturated her apron, her kimono, and gown. Her hands shook uncontrollably. The smell of iron permeated the air. Memories resurfaced. *Oh, the blood!* Addie recalled pricking her finger on the rosebush in her yard while Maw and Paw fought and the droplet of blood that fell onto her apron. Replacing that memory was the image of Maw lying in the tub with blood seeping from her slit wrists onto her white, cotton apron. Addie turned ghostly white. She darted out of the room, ran through the kitchen, and headed upstairs to the bathroom. Addie ran her fingers though her hair. "I've got to get it off me now!" she yelled out.

"What's gotten into her?" Nurse Hartman excused herself and ran after Addie.

As Addie ran through the dressing room, she tore off the apron and bathrobe. Still wearing her stained nightgown, ran into a shower stall, and turned on the water. Taking the bar of soap, she scrubbed at her hands and her skin. She watched the bar turned reddish-pink. She dropped it, crying out, "No, Maw! No! Why did you do it? Why did you leave me?" She sank to her knees.

Lena found Addie huddled in the corner of the stall. Water cascaded over her. Lena repositioned the spigot away from Addie and sat down next to her. "What's wrong, Addie?"

Addie began sobbing and rocking, staring off into a distant past. "I don't think I can be a nurse. There's so much blood!"

"Yes, that's true. There is a lot of blood sometimes. But, based on what I've heard and have seen tonight, you are going to make one incredible nurse, Addie."

"I don't think I can do this." She continued rocking. "I didn't tell you how my Maw really died. She didn't die in the fire with Paw like the paper said. Paw was mean to us. He turned to liquor and cards after my little sister and brother died from Scarlet Fever. Paw never recovered. He used to yell and beat on my Maw and me. One day, my Maw just had enough. She grew too tired… and she cut her wrists."

Lena's tears mixed with the water splashing on her face. She let them flow as she listened.

"I watched her leave this earth. In her dying breath, she said, 'I love you very much. I will always be your guardian angel, Addie.'" Addie looked at Lena. "My Paw came home and found her. He wanted to *kill* me. He thought I made it happen. So, I ran away, seeking refuge at the only place where I knew I'd be safe, with Garrett at the Darling's house. The next day, Mr. Darling and Garrett found our family farm house and barn ablaze, discovering the remains of Paw cradling Maw on what was left of the front porch swing."

Lena wanted to say something, anything of comfort. Instead, she remained silent.

"Tonight, when I looked down at my hands and my apron covered in blood and I could smell the blood in the room, those memories came raging back. I'm just no good to you. I'll never be good enough, just like Paw always said."

Lena took Addie's hands in hers. "Addie, my dear girl, I am so sorry for your loss. However, I need for you to look at your hands now."

Addie looked down.

"Do you still see the blood?"

"No." Addie flipped her hands over to examine them. "It's gone."

"Let the water wash it all away, the painful memories, the hurt, and try to forgive your parents. Your mother knew the woman you could be if given the chance. Do you know that you managed to accomplish the most amazing feat tonight by bringing life into this world? Addie, Judson is here right now because of you. You even heard his little heart beating. Can you feel the warmth and love in your heart?"

Addie searched her heart. *Addie, I love you. I will always be your guardian angel.* "Mrs. Gray use to say that, too. She said she could always feel the warmth of Doc Gray's love in her heart."

Addie clutched her chest. "I do. I do feel it. I feel Maws, Sissy's, Ben's, Paw's, Mrs. Gray's, and now Judson's."

"Addie, you will always have a connection to that child. He will always be a special memory for you. Move past the pain and forge forward. Tonight was a life-changing experience for you, for all of us. I need you to lean on your inner strength and faith. The more faith you have in God, the less fear controls you. Find that peace in your heart."

Addie nodded. "I let my fears take hold of me, didn't I?"

"It's perfectly alright, Addie. You're so young and still have much to learn about yourself and life. Everyone carries some kind of tragedy or painful experience inside them. It's how we choose to deal with it and learn from it that's most important. What you learned tonight is that you weren't alone. You took charge of a very scary situation. Your instincts and inner spirit took over. You followed your heart to a place that helped another human being. A nurse is exactly who you were born to be."

Addie looked up at Lena. "What did you just say?"

"A nurse is exactly who you were born to be."

"Oh, thank you, Nurse Hartman. I really needed to hear that, those exact words." Addie hugged Lena.

Lena whispered back, "It's alright to call me Lena right now. My mother had a saying when I became upset or distraught over something." Lena imitated a very old Southern woman's voice. "'Lena, you need to bounce right back like a red rubber ball and not break like a bone china plate.'"

Addie pulled away, managing a slight smile as she dried her tears and wiped her nose.

"Oh, and one more thing. I noticed you haven't signed up on the roster to call anyone on Sundays." Lena hushed Addie before she could speak. "You can call me." Lena rose to her feet, turned off the water, and extended a hand to Addie. "Now, come on and get dressed. We've got to help the Millers and Dr. Williams right now. I need you on your feet and reporting back to your duties, Miss Engel." Addie obliged and stood up.

Addie glowed with renewed spirit as she changed into dry clothes and returned to assist her classmates in Classroom B.

Dr. Williams accompanied Mrs. Miller and Judson Davis in the ambulance to Grady Hospital for her postpartum care. The night watchmen escorted a very proud Mr. Miller to his car as they toked on cigars through the rain and passed a pewter-curved hip flask back and forth between them.

An hour later, Lena debriefed her students on what they learned from Chapter V and rewarded their accomplishment by cancelling classes the next day. "Yes, I am granting you a free day. You are free to leave the campus and enjoy the day," Lena said before departing.

Adrenalin rushed through some of the young ladies who chose to remain downstairs in the parlor to recap the birth of the fifth Miller baby. Exhausted, Addie opted to return to the dorm. Opal followed.

"We make an amazing pair, don't we?" Opal removed her bathrobe and crawled in bed.

"Yes, we do. Thank you for everything you did tonight to keep us on task. We couldn't have done it without you either." Addie slipped under the covers. "What a night!"

The storm moved on and only faint flashes of light flickered in the clouds in the night sky. *Ba-dum. Ba-dum. Ba-dum. I actually heard little Judson's heartbeat!* Addie smiled with a heart filled with warmth and love as she covered her heart with her hand. *Maw, I feel the warmth of your love in my heart. Like Garrett's pebble, I hope to carry it with me everywhere I go. I hope that feeling and sense of purpose never leaves me.* Addie looked out of her window at the stars breaking through the clouds. *Hope never rests, does it, Maw?*

4

It had been two days since mock operations at Sacred Heart Hospital began. With the final stages of construction complete, new staff busied themselves setting up their respective departments and areas. Addie and Bertie watched the new blue-eyed pharmacist, Shelby Lee Maddox, dressed in a tan suit and a vest that matched his eyes, walk past them as they stood by the concierge desk.

Bertie nudged Addie. "Couldn't you just imagine running your hands through those dreamy, blonde locks?"

Addie chuckled. In a low tone, she replied, "Bertie, you have such spirited aspirations."

A woman with dark, curly hair popped up from behind the desk like a Jack-in-the-box. The girls jumped back. "I definitely could. Isn't he a peach?" Moira threw her arms on top of the desk and folded them. "Hey! My name is Moira." Addie began to introduce herself. Moira waved her off. "Don't worry, I can read your name tags. It's a pleasure to meet you." Whispering, she continued, "I heard that he is single and comes from a very wealthy family from Chattanooga. I believe his daddy has something to do with the railroads. His daddy is a close friend of Mr. Alexander."

Bertie wrapped herself in Moira's every word as they watched Shelby walk down the hallway to the apothecary. He turned to catch the three women stealing a glimpse as he opened the department door and closed it behind him.

Embarrassed, Moira disappeared behind her high-profile desk. Addie grabbed Bertie's arm. They rushed off in the opposite hallway towards the wing referred to as 1-A, which contained the leadership team's offices, patient waiting area, maternity and pediatric rooms, and nursery. Wing 1-B housed the medical-surgical unit, the emergency room, surgery suits, and the new, peachy pharmacist's department. The medical library, boardroom, doctor's offices, and storage closet were on the second floor, 2-A, while the TB ward was on 2-B. The nurses had fun saying that the TB patients were going to be on 2B, turning the popular Shakespearean phrase into 'TB, or not TB, that is the question!' Nurse Hartman informed Edward and the rest of the leadership team at their meeting last week about the nurse-coined phrase. Appreciating the nurses' humor, they embraced it—for internal use only.

Addie glanced down at her watch. She converted the time on the face of the clock into military time in her head. *0950.* Nurse Hartman had scheduled an anatomy class with Dr. Morgan Paine in the morgue today at ten o'clock. *We've got only ten minutes until class begins.* They turned right down a small hallway that led them to the maternity unit on their right. There was another small corridor on their left that separated the pediatric unit from the nursery. Turning the corner, they stumbled into Sacred Heart's pediatrician, Dr. Randall Springer, carrying a stack of textbooks. A few slipped from the top of the pile and fell to the floor.

"Oh, my goodness! We're so sorry, Dr. Springer," Addie apologized as she and Bertie scooped up the books. "Where are you going?"

"I was heading up to the second floor to put these in my new office. Will you help me?"

"Yes, of course." Addie glanced at her watch again as they walked down the hallway, past the concierge desk, and waited for an elevator to arrive. She nervously tapped the floor with her right foot. *Fiddle sticks! Nurse Hartman is going to give us our first demerits for being late.*

Sensing Addie's anxiety, Dr. Springer asked, "Do you need to be somewhere?"

Addie, feeling rushed, flushed as the three entered the car and rode it up to the second floor. She spilled out, "Nurse Hartman scheduled an anatomy class at one thousand hours with Dr. Morgue today."

Confused, he contorted his face. "Huh?" Stepping out of the car, Dr. Springer turned left and walked down 2-A towards his office. Realizing Addie was on edge, he detangled what she said. Laughing, he translated it back to her, clarifying, "Oh, you have anatomy class with Dr. Paine in the morgue at ten."

"Right, that's what I said...isn't it? If we're late, we'll get demerits." Addie looked at her watch again—*1003*—and then back to Bertie, who shook her head and shrugged her shoulders.

Bertie was lost in Dr. Springer's baby blues. She blurted, "Has anyone ever told you that you and Mr. Maddox look alike?"

"He's the new pharmacist from Chattanooga, right? Uh, no. You're the first, Nurse Jones." He winked.

"Are you single? Married?" Bertie needed to know.

"Bertie, what's gotten into you? No, he's not married." Addie, realizing she was sounding like the gossipy Moira, who so often popped up from behind her desk downstairs, fell silent. "Here."

Addie shoved the books into Dr. Springer's hands and stepped out into the hall, looked at her watch again, and began pacing. She resisted the urge to bite her thumbnail, remembering Mrs. Gray's instructions.

Taking the remaining books from Bertie, Randall set them on his new cherry desk. "Don't worry, you two. I'll escort you back to the basement and explain to Nurse Hartman that you have been helping me. In fact, I'd like to stand in and watch. It never hurts to have a refresher course every now and again."

They returned to the elevators and Dr. Springer punched the "B" button. During their descent, he turned the conversation towards Addie. "I want to thank you for letting me rent your house, Addie, while you are here in school. Please know that you are more than welcome to come home anytime if Nurse Hartman grants you leave one weekend. It's still your place. I'm just a guest."

Feeling invisible, Bertie shrank into the corner to give them privacy.

Addie's cheeks cooled. "I really miss that house, the warmth, the cozy fire, and Mrs. Gray." Realizing Bertie was still in the car with them, she made it plain. "Just let me know the next time you go out of town. I may consider the offer of taking a respite at the house. Thank you, Dr. Springer. You are too thoughtful."

The elevator doors parted. They could barely make out the top of Mr. Wu's head as he stood behind a laundry cart piled high with clean linens, towels, and washcloths. "Good morning." He bowed to each of them as they passed. Bertie bowed repeatedly. "Laundry going 2-B."

"That's great, thanks, Mr. Wu." Addie tugged Bertie's arm as they turned the corner and proceeded down the basement tunnel under the A wing.

"You understood him? What's the laundry going *to be?*" Randal asked.

"No, silly. He's taking it to 2-B, the TB ward." Addie punched him in the upper arm. "See, we have this saying…." Realizing this was a medical doctor and *not* Garrett, she panicked, stopped in front of the closed laundry room doors, and threw her hands up. "Oh! I'm so sorry, Dr. Springer. I didn't mean to hit you. It's something I use to do with a best friend of mine when we joked around."

"Addie, would you relax? You're wound tighter than a watch on your wrist. You know, my father had a saying: 'Worrying gives small things big shadows.'"

At that moment, the double wooden doors flew open as Mrs. Wu pushed a laundry cart into the hallway, striking Dr. Springer and Addie. Addie fell into Dr. Springer's arms as they were thrown against the wall. They fell in a heap on the floor. Linens exploded into the air like confetti from a rocket. A falling towel knocked Addie's cap over her eyes.

"Dr. Springer! Addie! Are you alright?" Bertie rushed over to help Dr. Springer to his feet.

"So sorry! So sorry! So sorry!" Mrs. Wu ran over to them,

clasped her palms together, and bowed repeatedly as she apologized. "So sorry!"

Dr. Springer said reassuringly, "There's no need to apologize, Mrs. Wu. We're just fine."

Addie flipped her cap back as she took Randall's extended hand and was assisted back onto her feet. He looked up to find a washcloth draped over his head. The three doubled over in hysterics. Addie removed the washcloth and ran her ringers through his tossed, blonde locks.

Bertie interjected with outstretched hands, "Oh, here, let me help you."

Randall laughed and stepped back. "I'm fine, ladies, thank you. Come on. Let's help Mrs. Wu with this mess."

Addie glanced at the time as she hurriedly picked up towels and sheets, throwing them into the cart. *1015. Oh, Lordy. Nurse Hartman is going to have Bertie and me scrubbing the toilets for a month! We have got to go now!* Grabbing Bertie, she said, "Nurse Hartman is going to have our heads for being so late!"

Addie, Dr. Springer, and Bertie ran to the closed, windowless doors marked Morgue, Room B-A.

"Come on, it's time to go into the *room-bah*." Erasing his jovial, childish smile, Dr. Springer combed his hair with his fingers.

Bewitched, Bertie watched his every move.

Randall straightened his tie and white coat and, with complete authority, opened the doors. "Sorry, Dr. Paine and Nurse Hartman, for our tardiness." Addie and Bertie shuffled in behind him. "Nurse Hartman, Nurse Engel and Nurse Jones were helping me. I completely lost track of time. I'm to blame."

The nursing students gawked as Addie and Bertie squeezed

next to Opal, who stood around the examination table with the other students. A ghastly looking Dr. Paine, cloaked in a black, rubber apron, raised his grey, wiry eyebrows. Addie noticed that each hair darted off in its own direction. He held up a scalpel with black, rubber-gloved hands. Then there was the smell. A pungent, putrid, and astringent odor filled her nostrils.

"Breath through your mouth or try putting this eucalyptus balm under your nose." Opal leaned over and handed her a tiny white jar. "It helps…kind of."

Addie caught Deborah's dark eyes. They seared through her skin.

Deborah's tone was cold. "Nurse Hartman, aren't you going to give Addie and Bertie demerits for being late?"

"Ah, about that. Nurse Hartman may I have a word with you in private?" Dr. Springer ushered Lena out of the room.

Addie rubbed the balm under her nose and handed the jar to Bertie. *Oh, fiddle sticks! He's going to tell Lena that I ran into him, knocked his books out of his hand, gossiped that he was single, and punched him in the arm. I'm going to be on bedpan duty for a year!*

"As I was saying, when I make the initial incision…" Dr. Paine threw back the sheet, revealing a very wrinkled, blue-ish-white, elderly female cadaver. "I begin here just above the clavicular area, like so." Being right handed, he reached across her body and skillfully pierced the scalpel through the skin over her left shoulder and sliced towards the midline of the chest, stopping just above the nipples. He did the same on the other side and then made a "Y" as he cut down the center of the abdominal area, stopping just above the pubic region.

There's no blood! Addie watched him intently, making mental notes and studying his every move.

Dr. Paine retraced his incisions at the top of the chest, making them deeper, excising the skin from the bone. He retracted the v-shaped flap of skin and folded it under the chin, exposing the muscles and bone underneath.

Addie looked up and noticed sweat beads on Susan's forehead and upper lip. She was pale and swaying. Dr. Springer and Lena returned to the room. Susan stepped back, her eyes rolled up, and she fell backwards. Randal sprang into action, catching her before she slammed the back of her head on the floor. He scooped her up and carried her out; Lena followed him.

Without skipping a beat, Dr. Paine said, "I'm sure glad to have another physician around to help me today. If any of you other girls plan to fall out on me, please do so away from the body.

If you feel light-headed, go and take a seat over there." He pointed to eight heavy, wooden chairs in the corner of the room. "Put your head between your legs and let the blood rush back into your brain."

He raised his scalpel and plunged deep into the abdominal cavity. He retracted the skin, revealing the liver, stomach, intestines, and other various internal tissues and organs. He set his scalpel down on the instrument tray and reached for what Addie thought looked like pruning shears.

How interesting! They look like the ones I used to prune Maw's rose bushes, Addie thought.

"It's just like cutting up a chicken." Deborah snickered under her breath.

He clipped the ribs, separating them from the sternum. Mary Margaret and Alice grabbed hands, looked at each other, and ran to the chairs in the corner. They bent over at the waist and threw their heads between their feet.

"I don't think I'll ever be able to eat chicken again." Alice gagged.

Snip. Crack. Snip. Crack.

He ripped apart the chest cavity and continued to dissect the area, revealing the lungs, heart, and diaphragm. Bell and Lexie stepped away from the others, joining the girls on the chair in the corner.

"Come back and rejoin us when your strength and resolve return, ladies," Dr. Paine called after them as he moved to the abdominal area, plunging his hands deep inside. Squishy noises ensued.

"This is absolutely remarkable." Addie leaned in closer to examine the internal organs. "They look just like the organs in a deer, a cow, or any other animal."

"It is, isn't it? Miss..." Dr. Paine peered over his spectacles at her name badge and looked at

Addie's face. "Miss Engel."

He removed his hands. "If you would like, don an apron and some gloves. You can help me as I remove the organs."

"Oh, I'd love to!" Addie slipped into the protective coverings and returned to his side.

Lena reentered the room and scanned it like the general on a battlefield. She found the wounded. Four students were bent over in chairs in the corner. Alice had removed her cap and was retching in it. Then, Lena identified her fighting soldiers. The ones who remained standing tableside, shoulder to shoulder with Dr. Paine, included Opal, Bertie, Deborah, and Addie, who was clad in a matching rubber apron and holding the woman's liver in her hands. Before turning her attention to the impaired, she smiled at Sacred Heart's future medical-surgical nurses.

WEDNESDAY EVENING, FOURTH WARD

As Dr. Springer readied himself for bed in the master suite at Mrs. Gray's house, he found himself without a clean washcloth to rinse off with. The housekeeper he had hired wasn't due for her scheduled visit until the morning. He lifted up the lid on the white, wicker clothes hamper and sifted through the dirty towels, clothes, and underpants. The sour aroma of something formerly wet stopped him from rummaging further. He decided to borrow a washrag from Addie's room down the hall. Dressed in his silk, navy blue bathrobe and tan leather slippers, he walked down the hallway, turned the glass knob to Addie's closed bedroom door, and stepped inside.

Although Addie had not resided in the house for over two months, the faint smell of lilacs still lingered in the air. He recalled smelling that sweet, floral fragrance a few hours earlier when she fell into him in the basement tunnel. He knew in his heart that there was something special about Addie. Nurse Hartman said that she was one of only four left standing next to Dr. Payne when she returned into the room—holding the woman's liver of all things! Randall's stomach flipped. A sworn bachelor dedicated to the art of medicine and pediatrics, he couldn't believe he found himself thinking about her. But she piqued his interest. He wanted to get to know her better.

Even though he was the only one in the house, he didn't like the awkward feeling he was getting from being in her bedroom and didn't want to linger. He retrieved a washcloth from her bathroom. As he made his way out of the room, a swooshing sound and swaying movement from something hanging on the back of her bedroom door caught his attention. He closed the door for a closer inspection. He steadied the object, stopping it from moving.

He held it in his hands as he studied it. Glued on a piece of cardboard and hanging from a corn silk blue ribbon tacked to the back of her door hung a heart-shaped collage. Magazine pictures of cosmopolitan women and newspaper photos from faraway places in the United States and Europe were surrounded by dried flowers. Inscribed on top was *Dreams are an aspiration of your heart, so dream big!*

He believed he had found the key to unlocking Addie's heart.

5

Edward's foot tapped to the beat of the brass band as they played "I'm Going Back to Dixie", a ragtime classic written by Irving Berlin. He scanned the crowd as he, the Sacred Heart leadership team, the priest from the Shrine of the Immaculate Conception, Governor Slanton, and Mayor Woodward sat on the wooden stage erected on the side lawn. Borrowed American flag banners that had been displayed on the Atlanta National Bank to celebrate the International Shriners Convention last week hung from the platform.

Governor Slanton had just completed his speech and Edward was seconds away from being introduced by Mayor Woodward. Gentle breezes blew the banners and rustled the trees. Edward removed his pocket watch; it read ten thirty. The program was right on schedule. Following his speech was the blessing by Father Kennedy and the ribbon cutting ceremony. Edward's heart leapt out of his chest. It was a proud and momentous day for him and his family. He continued to inventory the attendees. He found some familiar faces in the press, among the alderman from various wards, and his Rotary Club and Masonic Lodge. Movement from a group dressed in white caps and dresses wearing navy capes huddled together on his far left caught his attention. Opal and Addie eagerly waved at him. His eyes locked with his precious daughter—his favorite daughter, but he would never say it out loud. He beamed and nodded in return.

"May I introduce to you the founder and director, Mr. Edward Alexander II." The mayor shook Edward's hand as he returned to his seat next to the Governor. Edward adjusted the microphone and cleared his throat.

"I want to thank y'all for coming out here today for the grand opening of Sacred Heart Hospital. It has been a life-long dream of mine to build a facility that provides quality medical care to all Georgians as one Sacred Heart."

The crowd cheered and applauded.

Edward waited for the noise to subside; he continued. He pointed to Dr. Williams and Nurse Hartman, who sat directly behind him. "I'd like to thank my wonderful leadership team who worked tirelessly to make sure the Sacred Heart Nursing School opened in April." Edward directed the crowd's attention to the group of student nurses on his left. "Here, in front of you, is our first class of nursing students. Please give them a round of applause."

Hoots, hollers, and whistles ensued. Edward continued to recognize the rest of the hospital staff, including the employed physicians and nurses. He proceeded with a dedication of the Greene tunnel and presented Mrs. Greene with a commemorative plaque honoring her late husband, Tom. He had hated losing his friend to a collapsing tunnel wall five months earlier.

Luckily, Tom's brother stepped in to take sole ownership of the Greene's Construction Company, thereby keeping the hospital building projects on track.

"Without further ado, we will conclude with a blessing from Father Robert Kennedy from the Shrine of the Immaculate Conception followed by the cutting of the ribbon." Edward stepped back as Father Kennedy stood. "Father, if you please."

Edward stepped behind him, removed his bowler, and bowed his head in silence. The crowd followed suit. Following the prayer and the blessing of the hospital and the staff, Edward replaced his hat and stepped down from the grand stand, walking hastily towards the hospital porch. Reporters chased after him.

"Mr. Alexander. I have a question for you," a young man called out. The white card in his hat band read *Press* in bold, black print.

Edward thought he said he was a reporter from *The Atlanta Dispatch*. He didn't catch his name, and it didn't matter who he was reporting for. Any news coverage was good coverage for Sacred Heart.

The reporter asked, "What inspired you to build this building out of marble versus bricks like Grady or other hospitals in town?"

Edward stopped for a moment to answer. Reporters encircled him, scribbling notes in pencil in their spiral-bound flip pads. "Fellas, I was inspired as a teen by my European travels to Italy and France. I fell in love with the historical landmarks like the Roman cities, amphitheaters, and the Coliseum. Centuries later, they still stood and the stone remained white. I found out they were all built using travertine, which weathers the elements over time. That's what I wanted for this hospital facility. I wanted Sacred Heart to be a landmark in Atlanta and to stand the test of time." He continued speaking to bowed heads. "Travertine is even being used in Paris's latest construction project, called La Basilique du Sacré-Coeur de Montmartre." Edward backed away from the group. "Now, if you'll excuse me, fellas, I've got to cut the ribbon." He called back to them with a hand in the air, "As my daddy use to say, 'let's get to it and just do it.'"

Clyde overheard Edward. He rolled his eyes.

The crowd shifted to the right and congregated in front of the hospital for the ribbon cutting ceremony. The police closed off part of the street, which allowed people to file off the lawn, onto the sidewalks, and overflow into Spring Street. Opal took Addie's and Bertie's hands as they made their way over for the ceremony.

"What time does your shift begin today?" Addie asked Opal and Bertie.

"I have to work on the pediatric unit tonight. I wonder if Dr. Springer will still be around." Bertie squealed.

Opal chimed in, "I'm scheduled to work in maternity right after this ceremony is over. Where did Nurse Hartman assign you to work today?"

"I'm working on the medical-surgical unit right after they cut the ribbon." Addie glanced around at the faces around and behind her. A familiar looking copper-haired man caught her attention. He wasn't wearing his usual denim overalls, white cotton shirt, and straw hat. Rather, he was clad in a dashing, rich brown, felt bowler. Addie recalled seeing it in a "Hats for Spring" advertisement in the paper a few weeks earlier. The style was referred to as "Marquis" and made by the Stetson Company. He was dressed in a white collared shirt, light brown pinstriped suit, and matching vest. Her gaze fell to his shoes. *Boots.* He wore brown, leather boots the color of his hat. He turned and caught her gaze. *Garrett.*

Her stomach flipped; her heart raced. She released Opal's hand and began walking towards him. She searched his eyes. They narrowed as he smiled. He rushed through the crowd towards her.

She ran into his outreached arms. Her heart overflowed with joy and tears welled up in her eyes. As the ribbon was cut, the brass band began playing another lively tune and the exuberant crowd clapped along. Garrett scooped her up in his arms, twirling her high in the air. Addie clutched her cap as tears streamed down her face.

Bertie's mouth fell open. "Holy cow, Addie's sure getting swept off her feet in the occasion. Who is that gentleman?"

Opal leaned close and, in a hushed tone, said, "Oh my!" She watched the exchange between Addie and the dapper young man. "I think it's Mr. Sex Ed."

"Who?"

"Never mind. I'll explain it to you later...in private. I've got to run along for my shift. Keep track of the time. Make sure Addie doesn't dilly dally. If she's late, Nurse Hartman will issue demerits for sure. Dr. Springer won't be able to bail her out this time."

"Will do." Bertie kept an eye on Addie, whose hands flew excitedly in the air as she spoke. Bertie temporarily resisted the urge and then inched closer to overhear the conversation.

Addie reached deep inside her apron pocket. She pulled out the pebble Garrett had given her before she left Hope.

"I can't believe you still are hanging on to it." Garrett stared at it in disbelief.

"What are you doing here? I'm sorry I haven't written to you yet. We've just been so busy."

"It's okay. I know you've got your hands full. Look, I've got a bit of news for you. Remember when I worked alongside my father and our neighbors to put out the fire on your family's farm?" Garrett watched Addie nod her head. "I felt a keen and clear sense of purpose that night. It awakened something inside of me. I knew then exactly what you meant and how you felt about nursing school. I discovered I felt the exact same way about firefighting. It was difficult to tell my father that I didn't want to be a farmer anymore. Can you believe that I'm no longer going to be a country mouse?"

"What? I'm confused. You're leaving Hope?"

"I am. I can't actually believe I am saying this. I'm becoming a town mouse and moving to the city. I've been hired by the City of Atlanta's firehouse number six. I start my training next week."

The boy Addie fished, swam, and caught frogs with on the muddy banks of the pond had vanished. A spirited, young man with a sense of self and purpose reestablished stood in front of her. "That's wonderful news. I'm so proud of you." She ached for him, recalling their passionate night together.

"I'm looking for a place to stay. Aunt Mary told me at Lester's funeral that you have rented Aunt Olive's house to a pediatrician." Garrett hesitated and then asked, "I don't suppose that I could stay there in the other guest room while I am in training?"

Addie didn't respond. She pictured Dr. Springer in his bathrobe standing outside of Mrs. Gray's bedroom door. A few feet away, Addie, clad in her robe, stood outside her room, staring across the hall at Garrett in his night clothes.

At that very moment, Dr. Springer burst forth. "Are you going to introduce me to your friend?" His right hand stretched out toward Garrett. "Hey! I'm Dr. Randall Springer."

"Greetings to you this fine morning, I'm Garrett Darling." The fact that Dr. Springer was wearing a white lab coat—and based on the description his aunt Mary had provided—led him to believe that this was the fair-haired, blue-eyed pediatrician renting his late aunt's house.

Garrett added, "I'm Dr. and Mrs. Gray's nephew."

Addie watched their exchange.

"I've heard plenty of fine things about your uncle. He was a legend in this town. In fact, I understand they are dedicating a tunnel in Dr. Gray's honor when they open Alexander Hall in a few years."

"Yes, that's true."

"So, what line of work are you in? Are you in the medical profession, too?"

"Oh, heavens no!" Garrett pulled on his suit collar. "I'm not cut out for that line of work. Actually, I'm going to be a fireman. I've been hired by firehouse number six. I'm looking for a room to rent in town close to the station."

Addie noticed Garrett had purposefully omitted that he was a farmer from Hope.

"You know that I am renting your aunt's house, right?" Randall looked at Addie as Garrett nodded. "Isn't that fire station just down the street on the corner of Wheat Street and Boulevard?"

"Yes. It's definitely within walking or biking distance," Garrett clarified.

"Why don't we work out a deal so that you can use the guest room? Lord knows that with the hours I'll be keeping at Sacred Heart, I won't be there often. When I am home, I'll be catching up on my sleep. With your new line of work, Garrett, it sounds like you'll be doing the same." Randall turned from Garrett to Addie. "Let me clear this with my landlord."

"I'm fine with whatever you both work out amongst yourselves."

Bertie grabbed Addie's hand and interjected, "If you will excuse us, we must be off. Addie's shift begins in just a few minutes." She batted her eyes at Dr. Springer. "I start my shift tonight in the pediatric unit. I look forward to seeing you then, Dr. Springer."

Addie left Garrett and Randall standing side by side as they watched Bertie lead Addie through the throngs of people before they disappeared through the front doors of Sacred Heart Hospital. Bertie pulled Addie around the concierge desk. *Ring. Ring.*

Moira responded to the incoming call. "Is it sunny out?" she howled. "Of course not, it's very cloudy right now." She hung up the receiver.

Alan Waxman, Sacred Heart's Chief Financial Officer, stood on the opposite side of the desk, listening to Moira. He adjusted his spectacles, noticing rainbow prisms of sunshine beaming through the circular window over the main doors in front of him. Thinking it odd, he made an entry in his notebook. Excusing himself to the strangers standing around him, he escaped the hordes of people and exited out the back door.

Bertie left Addie standing outside the medical-surgical unit on the B wing. Addie strained to hear the winding siren of an ambulance in the distance. She adjusted her cap and readied herself to enter the unit. As she opened the door, a steel tray filled with hemostats, gloves, and gauze pads was shoved into her hands.

"We've got a bleeder in bed number two." Nurse Scott pointed to a bed across the room. "A worker from the Georgia Soap Company was brought in during the ribbon cutting ceremony. He got his left arm caught in one of the machines. We need to stabilize him before the doctors take him to surgery." Nurse Scott grabbed Addie by the arm and commanded, "Come on. We don't have all day. Duty calls, Red."

6

"To Sacred Heart Hospital on Spring Street," Ida commanded the taxi cab driver. She had convinced Father Preti to ride uptown in a taxi versus taking the wood-bodied truck. "Appearances matter," she had told him as she called for the service. Ida waved her hand fan vigorously to cool the perspiration from her brow. Coarse curls shot out like sprung springs from under her yellow hat.

Father Preti scooted into the backseat alongside his sister. He closed the door. "Help me with this, would you?"

Ida reached over and adjusted the priest's collar; it had folded over on itself. "There, that should do it." She patted the priest's shoulder. "Ready to secure another account?" Ida counted on her fingers. "We already have three others, including Detective McGee from the Atlanta Police Department."

"We must be careful who we trust, Sister. We're starting to play with fire."

"By working with the police, we will never be suspected of any wrongdoing. We're doing God's work." She tapped her fan against the palm of her white-gloved hand.

"After our stint in Boston, I'm rather enjoying this warm southern climate." He cleared his deep, low voice. Catching his reflection in the car window, Father Preti smoothed down the sides of his short-cropped hair.

A twenty-three-minute cab ride landed them in front of Sacred Heart Hospital. Ida retrieved a few bills from her handbag and handed them to the driver. He pocketed the money and got out to open her car door. Tipping his black cap, he watched Ida scoot her large frame out of the vehicle. "Thank you, ma'am. Father."

"Have a blessed day," the priest said in a reverent tone. He followed behind Ida as she teetered up the walkway through the front doors.

Moira popped up from her chair from behind the concierge desk. "May I help you?"

The priest remained silent. Ida stepped up to the desk. Breathless, she managed to eke out, "We have an eleven o'clock meeting with Mr. Clyde Posey. He should be expecting us."

Knowing Clyde was not religious, Moira sized them up as she stepped out into the hallway. "Please follow me." She motioned the visitors to follow her. Moira was dying to know why a priest and a middle-aged woman, whose high forehead, prominent nose, and broad chin favored her religious companion's facial features, had a meeting with Clyde. "What brings you to Sacred Heart?"

Ida and the priest exchanged glances. Ida took her cue and spoke. "Father Preti and I represent Holy Cross Orphans' Asylum. We're here to meet with Mr. Posey to discuss helping orphan boys who may be brought in for medical care or abandoned while at Sacred Heart." Ida looked at the priest, then back at Moira. She refrained from imparting any further details.

Moira pointed her finger at the two of them. "Are the two of you related? You both really favor each other."

The priest answered. "Miss Preti is my sister. She and I work together for the service of God and those less fortunate."

The three came to a stop in front of a heavy walnut door with a large frosted glass pane. Moira gently knocked on the glass.

"Come in." Clyde's voice echoed from inside the office.

Moira opened the door, made introductions, and closed the door behind her. Dejected, she returned to her post after realizing that there wasn't anything tantalizing to learn from a meeting with a priest, his sister, or their orphanage.

Clyde's visitors sat in two chairs that faced him. Appearing unsettled and confused, Clyde took his seat behind his expansive executive desk. A moment of silence passed before he uttered, "It was my understanding from Mr. Chang that I would be meeting with the Preti sisters this morning." Directing his comment to Father Preti, he asked, "Who the hell are you?"

Unfazed by the profanity, the priest put his hands on his thighs and leaded forward. "My name is Josephine Preti. But, you can call me Jo, or if I'm dressed like this…" Jo sat back and pulled on her black suit lapels, then leaned forward again. "Please refer to me as Father Preti, Father Joseph, or Father Joe. Got it?"

Clyde connected the dots. Josephine dressed like a priest to give the appearance of validity to the Holy Cross Orphanage. He chuckled to himself, thinking they were far from pretty sisters. Intrigued, Clyde inquired, "So, tell me how you operate your orphanage and what's in it for me?"

Ida crossed her arms and rested them on her ample bosom. "Jo and I run the orphanage. All we need from you is referrals in the way of orphan boys, from newborn to thirteen years old. On the front end, we run a legitimate placement agency. One the backend, we cherry pick those kids we think will be a good fit for Mr. Chang's brothel. What he does with them is none of our concern."

As Ida spoke, Clyde sized Jo up. She aroused him—Jo definitely was in keeping with his motto, 'The bawdier, the better.'

Sensing that Clyde's mind was wandering, Ida stopped speaking. She rapped her fingers on his desk, interrupting his promiscuous thoughts. "Look here, Mr. Posey, my sister and I don't make a habit of mixing business with pleasure."

Clyde pounced. "I'm not interested in you." He pointed at Jo. "I'd be interested in you."

Jo sat back in the chair and crossed her legs in the manner befitting a man. "Like my sister said, we don't mix business with pleasure."

Clyde shifted the conversation back to Ida. "So, what's my cut?"

"Five dollars a kid." Ida reached inside her handbag and pulled out a business card, sliding it in front of him. "Call the number on the card when you know of a child that need placement. When they are ready to be discharged, I'll pick them up and take them to the orphanage."

Clyde picked up the card and waved it in the air. "Make it ten dollars and you have a deal."

Ida uncrossed her arms, clasped her fingers, and rested her hands on her grey skirt. "Ten dollars. Not one penny more."

Clyde stood up, reached across the desk, and extended his right hand. "You have a deal." He shook Ida's hand. "It will be a pleasure doing business with you." He reached out and shook Jo's large hand. As she released her grip, she raked her middle fingernail across his palm, sending a chill of excitement through Clyde. Goose bumps erupted on his forearms and he jumped in his skin.

TUESDAY NIGHT, FOURTH WARD

Lost in thought, Clyde rolled off of Moira and propped himself up in his four-poster, canopy bed.

Charlie Finch, senior reporter at *The Atlanta Dispatch*, had been pressuring Moira since the grand opening of the hospital for some newsworthy nuggets. Eager to learn anything of interest from Clyde's numerous business meetings today, she probed, "Darling, you've had quite the busy day today. What's weighing heavy on your mind?"

He scratched at his coal-colored strands with both hands. "I've got a new business arrangement. I'm just trying to iron out the details in my head." Clyde pulled up the purple silk blanket over his legs. He leaned over and looked at her.

"What?"

"Actually, I could use your help."

"How?"

"As part of your job duties, you maintain the status of all patient's admissions and discharges in your ledger books, right?"

"Yes." Moira pushed her unruly brown curls away from her face and inched closer.

"How do you document the orphans—the ones that come in on their own or the abandoned kids—when they are discharged?"

Moira rolled over onto her stomach and flipped a few contrary ringlets away from her eyes. She rested on her elbows. "The nurses in the nursery or on the pediatric unit tell me if a child has been discharged into the care of a local parsonage or home. The child may even leave on their own accord, meaning they are simply discharged back onto the streets of Atlanta."

"I need your help to refer newborn boys up to thirteen years old to Holy Cross Orphans' Asylum."

"Why?" Moira's heart skipped a beat, knowing there was more to learn about this meeting with the priest and his sister.

Clyde chose his next words carefully. "Keep me informed of any parentless child that gets admitted to the hospital." He grazed his pale, thin fingers over the curve of her back. "I'll take care of the rest."

"That's it?"

"That's all."

Moira frowned.

Clyde lifted her chin so his eyes could meet her faraway gaze. "What? You don't seem too excited about helping these troubled youth."

"I just thought there would be more to the story."

He shrugged his shoulders. "There's no story to tell." He hoped he sounded reassuring, refraining from a full confession about Father Preti's true identity. He looked forward to getting to know his new irreverent friend.

7

SATURDAY, JUNE 27, 1914, FOURTH WARD

The telegraph came in from a call box at 7:56 p.m. to firehouse number six, a two story, neo-Romanesque, red brick building located at 39 Boulevard Northeast. The recently mechanized station served the affluent colored community, dubbed "Sweet" Auburn. Within minutes of the notification, the firemen slid down brass poles, piled into the red firetruck, and set out towards a section of the Georgia Railroad's tracks south of the freight depot in downtown Atlanta. Sirens wailed.

"How does this kind of thing happen?" Garrett hung on to anything he could as the truck darted and swerved through the streets and intersections.

"Actually, it happens all the time. Kids get bored and come down to the tracks to play. The brave ones dare each other to jump aboard the moving train. The one's who make it start climbing all over it, and even try to walk on top of the moving cars," a fellow firefighter shouted back.

Once on the scene, Garrett hopped off the truck and pursued his colleagues.

"Prepare yourself, just like I trained you, Garrett." Lieutenant Randy Jones ran past him.

Garrett observed that the train wasn't moving. A small crowd of railroad workers and the conductor were gathered around an area between two cars. Garrett made out the face of an adolescent boy sandwiched between the boxcars. He estimated his age to be around fifteen or sixteen. He appeared to be alert and was talking. Everyone was unusually calm, including the boy. However, upon closer inspection, Garrett saw that the youth was pinned between two freight cars.

"What's your name, son?" Lieutenant Jones inquired.

"My name is Timothy. My friends call me Tim." He looked down. "I can't see my feet. I can't feel my legs, sir."

"Don't look down, Tim. Just keep your eyes on me. Do you hurt anywhere?"

"No sir. I'm not in any pain."

Turning to Garrett, the lieutenant said, "I need for you to be this boy's source of strength in his final moments. Go to the other side of the cars, hold his hand, and start talking to him."

"About what?"

"About anything." The lieutenant's tone was grave. Turning back to the boy, he said, "Tim, do you have any family close by?"

Tim shook his head. He started to cry. "Am I going to be okay?" He started to fidget.

Lieutenant Jones reached out to Tim. "Son, don't move. Do you have any relatives in the city?"

"No. I don't have a home. I just take odd jobs and lay my head where ever I can."

The conductor whispered in the lieutenant's ear before running toward the train's engine.

"Tim, is there anything you want to say before...." Lieutenant Jones choked back tears. "Are you the praying sort, son? Would you like us to pray with you now?"

"Why?" Tim grew anxious. "Whatever do you mean? I'm okay, right? I don't hurt anywhere."

Garrett took Tim's hands in his as the lieutenant spoke. "Tim, the conductor is going to restart the train's engine. When he does, the cars are going to pull apart."

"Then you will pull me free, right?" Tim was frantic, looking at the faces all around him.

Some of the men looked away, avoiding eye contact at all costs, while Garrett began reciting the Lord's Prayer. Tim, the lieutenant, and the others joined in.

"Amen."

The train cars lurched forward, separating the freight cars. Blood gushed and spattered onto the tracks as the lower half of Tim's severed torso and legs fell to the ground. The smell of gastric contents and bodily fluids was overwhelming. Tim lost consciousness. Garrett grabbed Tim underneath his arms and pulled him away from the train. He lay Tim's lifeless upper torso to rest on the ground and hastily covered him with a blanket.

Garrett knelt by the body and wept.

Lieutenant Jones came over and gently placed his hand on Garrett's shoulder. "You did well today."

Garrett took a moment before asking, "Why did you ask if Tim had family close by?"

"He's what we call, in these instances, 'a living dead man'. He couldn't feel anything below his waist because his spinal cord had been severed. We give the trapped individual a chance to say good-bye to their loved ones before we separate the cars. As long as the cars stay together, the victim won't exsanguinate, bleed out."

"This isn't the first time for you, is it?" Garrett regained his composure and stood up.

"Regretfully, no. It won't be our last, either. Come on, son, we've done all we can here." He changed the tone of the conversation and said cheerfully, "Perhaps the next call into the station will be from Mrs. Sawyer down the street to rescue her cat from her Dogwood tree." The lieutenant refused to discuss suppressed memories and dredge up gruesome visions from the past. It was these moments, he'd tell his men, 'you can't un-see.'

SATURDAY EVENING, FOURTH WARD

Randall heard the front door open and close as he cleaned his supper dishes. Garrett's heavy boots clomped immediately upstairs, indicating that it was one of those tough days he couldn't discuss. *Squeak.* The second to last stair always gave away one's location when one was ascending or descending the stairs. "I've got to fix that loose floorboard," Randall muttered under his breath.

He opened the basement door and switched on the stairwell light. He walked down the wooden stairs, immediately greeted by the smell of must, dust, and damp cool air. He rummaged through the shelves, moving old canning supplies, in search of a hammer and nails. He spotted a wooden-handled hammer and a cardboard box of nails on the second to bottom shelf. As he reached for the brown box marked *Nails* in bold white letters, a tiny brown field mouse scurried into view.

"Ahhh!" Randall cried out, quickly retrieving his hand. His startled response was followed by nervous laughter. Not much scared him, but critters jumping out from dark spaces did.

He watched the unaffected brown rodent scurry down the shelving unit, disappearing through a crack in the wall. Intrigued by his furry friend's quick get-away, Randall inspected the area closer. Scooting the wooden shelf away from the wall, he discovered a small door. He unlatched it, ducked his head and walked inside. Immediately, he swatted at the air; he had walked into cobwebs. Making a hasty retreat into the main basement, Randall found an oil lamp and a set of matches sitting on a makeshift pine table that was pushed against the far wall. He lit the match and the wick and returned to the hidden behind the wall. Holding up the lamp, he made out a stack of dusty, gray wool blankets in the corner. Next to that lay a pile of papers and three oil lamps. Randall reached down to pick up the papers and then stood up. He decided to kick at them first with his boot in hopes of scaring anything away that might cause his heart to skip a beat. A cloud of dust rose from the sandy floor. Relieved that nothing else skittered away, he picked up the papers and left the room, closing the door behind him. He laid the dusty papers on the table and blew on them. A white cloud shot up in the air and lingered for a moment before vanishing.

The yellowed, brittle papers appeared to be hand-drawn maps, void of any street or city names. The only directional marking was a tiny arrow in the top right corner; *North* was written in black ink above the point. The route appeared to go through squiggly lines, which he assumed were streams or rivers. Upside down Us and Vs looked like they referenced hills and mountains.

A shadow appeared on the wall. Either it was the same mouse that greeted him earlier or one of his friends. Randall chose to not find out and scooped up the maps, hammer, and nails. He blew out the lamp and hastily retreated upstairs.

8

MONDAY, JUNE 29, 1914, FIRST WARD

Scout knocked on the oak office door. Charlie Finch, Senior Reporter was painted in black on the frosted glass.

"Come in." Charlie's head materialized from behind a tall pile of old copies of *The Atlanta Dispatch*. The two chairs in front of his desk were occupied, filled with stacks of clippings and files.

Scout removed his tweed cap and blurted out, "Hey, Mr. Finch. I checked out the story down at the Georgia Railroad tracks. It appears that a group of teenage boys were playing Chicken, daring each other to run between freight cars as they were being coupled. Unfortunately, one kid wasn't so lucky, got squished between them, and died." Scout wrinkled his nose.

"Did you find out anything else?"

"The kid's name was Tim. He was an orphan. No family. No home."

His response was met with silence. Charlie made notes on his spiral pad. "Sorry, Scout. I'm a bit preoccupied. We just got news over the wire that the Archduke Ferdinand and his wife were assassinated yesterday morning by a nineteen-year-old

Serb. Diplomatic tensions are running high between Austria and Serbia today. My gut tells me this is going to turn out to become a much bigger story." He stopped writing. "Time will tell."

"Is there anything else you want to know about the railyard accident?"

"No, kid." Charlie pulled out a side drawer in his desk, reached inside a box, and pulled out a fifty-cent coin. He tossed it across his desk at Scout. "Here. Thanks for the checking into it. I wanted to see if there was anything more to the story. I've been hearing rumors about young boys being murdered. Between the Atlanta Ripper going after young colored women, there's some other deranged lunatic in town targeting white boys. I have a source at the APD that's giving me some leads. Perhaps I need to check in with my sources at Grady, St. Joes, and Sacred Heart Hospitals." Charlie sifted through the pile of papers on his right and then shifted his attention to the pile on his left. "Now, some misguided young man on the other side of the world is targeting royalty. What's this world coming to?"

"I don't know, sir."

"Is anybody safe anymore?" Charlie huffed.

"I just don't know."

MONDAY AFTERNOON, SIXTH WARD

Ring. Ring. Moira answered the phone as she watched various visitors, doctors, and nurses walk by her desk. "Good afternoon, thank you for calling Sacred Heart Hospital. How may I help you?"

"Yes, this is Father Preti at the Holy Cross Orphans' Asylum. My sister received a message from Mr. Posey this morning. I understand there is a young boy who broke his arm that is ready to be discharged into our care today?"

Moira flipped though the patient ledger book. It was large, dark green, and bound in leather, and it tracked admissions and discharges. She ran her right index finger down the rows to find *Pediatrics*. "Yes, I have a Billy Swanson, eleven years of age, ready to be picked up."

"Excellent. Let Mr. Posey know I will be there within the hour."

"Yes, Father. I will." Moira spotted Clyde leaving his office. "Cly…" She quickly stopped herself, making an immediate correction. "Mr. Posey. Excuse me, sir?"

Clyde pivoted on his heels and walked towards the concierge desk. "Yes, Miss Goldberg?"

"Father Preti from the orphanage just called. He'll be here within the hour to pick up the homeless boy, Billy Swanson."

"Great! Thanks for letting me know."

"My pleasure, sir." She made sure no one was looking and winked.

Clyde looked forward to seeing Jo. He hoped he could convince her to drop by his home one evening. He wasn't sure exactly how to broach the subject with her, concluding it might be best for her to come to him. He walked around the desk towards the surgical theater and suite on the B wing. He approached the closed doors marked *Medical-Surgical Unit, 1-B*, overhearing Nurse Scott giving direction as he passed.

"No, Addie. See how his dressing gapes here and here." Nurse

Scott pointed out the gaps in white gauze bandaging wrapped around the hairless calf of a fifty-year old man.

Addie undressed the bandage for the third time, exposing the catgut-stitched, six-inch laceration sustained from an ax accident while chopping down a pine tree in the patient's front yard. Addie thought the name 'catgut' was funny, especially after learning that that type of suture was really made out of sheep or goat intestines, not actual cats. Dr. David Leventhal, one of Sacred Heart's surgeons, informed her class that he prefers to use catgut stitches on those patients who lived in the rural areas of Georgia. This type of suture was dissolvable. In his experience, this clientele was less than compliant about returning to the hospital to get their stiches removed by a medical doctor. However, they would return if the wound reopened or got infected.

"You can't leave gaps. The flies will lay their eggs in his wound and they will hatch. The next time you undress that wound, his leg will be filled with maggots. I would say that he might be a tad bit upset to see something like that, don't you think, Nurse Engel?"

Exhausted and embarrassed, Addie took a deep breath and redressed the wound for the fourth time, this time without gaps.

"Excellent job. Practice makes perfect, Nurse Engel." From across the room, a commotion stirred. Nurse Scott spotted Nurse Fein and Nurse Esposito trying to administer an enema to a very resistant patient. "No! Stop! That's not the correct patient!" Nurse Scott ran over to intercept them. "The enema is to be given to Mr. Chadwick in bed number three, not to Mr. Danbury in bed number four." She grabbed the red rubber enema bag and tubbing out of their hands and moved the white cotton screen.

"Must I have to do everything for you girls?" Claire apologized to Mr. Chadwick and turned her attention to the patient in the other bed. She lowered her voice to a whisper as she spoke to Alice and Belle, her tone stern. "I swear to all that is Holy, if you ladies don't pay attention to the details, you are going to kill someone, or worse yet, you're going to kill yourselves. You must be mindful of what you are doing. Wisdom is knowing and doing. Knowing without doing is useless; doing without knowing is useless. It's my job to teach you to know what you are doing, to whom, and why you are doing it." She pounded her right fist in her left palm as she made her points. "Discipline and wisdom, ladies! And, as Nurse Hartman preaches, 'question and clarify' always!"

Deborah overheard the last part of Nurse Scott's conversation as she administered a morphine injection to a sixty-four-year-old male, who was in his final stages of life after battling pellagra in bed number five. She snickered under her breath.

Nurse Scott shot her a look. "What's so funny, Nurse Owens?"

"Nothing, ma'am. Nothing at all." Deborah gathered her supplies, placed them on the silver tray, and left the room. Stepping into the hallway, she spotted Clyde leaving the surgical theater. She caught his eye. Disinterested, he kept walking.

Clyde walked around Moira's desk and proceeded down the A wing. He took a right turn halfway down the corridor, another right, and then an immediate left, stepping into the pediatric ward. There, he found Father Preti speaking to Dr. Springer at the bedside of Billy Swanson. He remained in the doorway.

"Please be sure to bring him back in six weeks. I will x-ray his arm again and if everything looks okay, I'll remove his cast." Dr. Springer handed Father Preti a small brown corked bottle. "This is for pain. Give him one tablet by mouth every six to eight hours, as needed."

"I will. Thank you, Doctor." Father Preti shook Dr. Springer's hand.

"Nurse Jones, would you mind escorting them out?" Dr. Springer summoned Bertie, who was sitting at the nurse's desk, writing a note in a patient's chart.

Clyde interjected and stepped into the room. "I'll be happy to do that. Come, Father Preti." Clyde motioned the priest and the boy over.

"Billy, go on ahead of me. I'll meet you by the front door. Mr. Posey and I have some business to discuss." Jo stepped out of the ward and over to the far corner of the hall. Reaching into her pants pocket under the robe, she pulled out an envelope and discretely handed it to Clyde. "This should take care of it. And, as for other matters…"

"Yes, what did you have in mind?" Clyde fidgeted, turned away, and quick-stepped down the corridor. Jo pursued. Taking a left into the main hallway, they came to a stop again. Clyde reached inside his suit jacket and pulled out a white card.

"This has my home address on it. Tonight? Let's say after midnight? I have a few things to attend to."

Jo shook Clyde's hand. "I look forward to it." She raked her middle fingernail against Clyde's palm as she unclasped her hand.

Clyde quivered and bit his lower lip to keep from smiling. The thought of his new conquest excited him.

MONDAY EVENING, FIRST WARD

"It's time to take your medicine," Ida sang. She whirled two glasses of water through the air as she tottered towards fair-haired twin boys, Landon and Logan, who sat next to each other on the side of a twin bed.

"But, I'm not sick!" Logan protested.

"Isn't that a good thing? This medicine prevents you from getting a cold. Must be working like a charm." Ida shoved the glasses into their hands. "Come now, boys. Don't dawdle."

The boys obliged, emptied their glasses, and returned them to Ida.

"It's lights out for you, boys." Ida cackled as she left the room, closing the bedroom door behind her.

Jo and Ida let a few hours pass before loading the boys into their truck. Remaining in the First Ward, they drove through the darkness to Mr. Chang's opium and massage emporium.

Following Mr. Chang's explicit instructions to the letter, Jo pulled the vehicle into an ally behind the establishment. "Stay here."

"Will do." Ida turned to check on the unconscious boys in the back seat.

Jo slid out of the driver's seat and adjusted her sage colored dress before walking over to the door. She knocked on the solid wood frame. Jo heard the sound of chains followed by the clanking metal noises of bolts and locks. *Creak.* The heavy black door opened a crack. Jo leaned in and said in a hushed voice, "Mr. Chang is expecting us. I have a delivery." The door opened wider; two men walked into the ally and approached the truck.

"They're here," said Ida in a sing-song manner as she pointed to the backseat.

Gang spoke to his brother, Chongan, in Chinese. Chongan threw an envelope into the front seat. Ida snatched it up, lifted the bottom of her brown dress, and shoved the envelope up the left leg of her bloomers as they each grabbed a boy and disappeared back into the building. The door closed. *Creak. Clang. Clang. Click. Click. Click.*

Jo hiked up her dress and hopped back into the truck. "I'm going to drop you off at home. I've got somewhere to be." She hit the gas pedal.

Ida knew not to press Jo for details.

"Man?" Chongan inquired as they carried the boys over their shoulders down a long hallway. "Man wearing dress?"

"No. Woman."

9

American flags waved in the gentle humid breeze on the lawn of Sacred Heart Hospital. The construction noises next door had ceased so the men could celebrate America's Independence Day with families and friends. Mr. Alexander had made arrangements for the staff's family to join them in the back lawn for a picnic that afternoon.

Sparing no expense, he even hired a band and a fiddler named John Carson. He first saw him play last April at the inaugural Georgia Old-Time Fiddler's Convention in Atlanta's Municipal Auditorium. While Carson came in fourth place then, this year, he won first. Edward thought the Fannin County farmer was dynamite. Carson was winding his fiddle to the tune "Listen to the Mockingbird," a favorite of President Abraham Lincoln's. Edward agreed with the President's assessment of the ditty: "It is as sincere as the laughter of a little girl at play." Edward walked around a large maple tree, acknowledging the McDaniel brothers with a tip of the hat and salutations as he walked past them.

"I hope an' pray the emergency room will be q-u-i-e-t today,"

Brice McDaniel boomed. "I know never to say the 'q' word for fear of bad luck." His ruddy Irish skin glowed red under the shade of the maple tree. "Jesus, Mary, and Joseph, I believe me pipe and me plums are glued to me leg. It's so bloody hot out 'ere!"

Rob and his twin brothers, Tim and Jim, who were also ambulance attendants for Sacred Heart, howled.

"Perhaps, ye need to get your pipe blown. It'll cool you down a wee bit, 'ey?" Tim interjected.

"Bugger me balls. I'd say it do quite the opposite, lil brother." Brice smacked the back of Tim's head so hard, he stumbled forward and almost fell into Clyde as he walked by.

Not amused, Clyde rolled his eyes, strolling past the men in silence.

"I believe he has a stick up his arse," Tim mumbled under his breath.

The McDaniel brothers broke up in hysterics as they mimicked Clyde's aristocratic gait behind his back, mindful no one was watching their antics.

On the other side of the maple, Addie sat at a long picnic table covered with a red and white checkered table cloth. Fresh cut flowers from Sacred Heart's garden were placed in Mason jars and served as center pieces. A variety of hospital staff and nursing students were engaged in lively conversation. Dr. Springer noticed an empty space next to Addie. He observed that she wasn't participating in any group discussions, but rather appeared to be lost in thought, watching various people crossing the hospital grounds.

"Is this seat taken?" Dr. Springer removed a Skimmer straw hat with a red and blue band.

Addie looked up to find Randall without his white coat on. Instead, he wore a blue and white striped suit, white shirt, and red, white, and blue bow tie. She thought he looked so handsome. Aware she was getting flushed, she looked away and said, "Why no, please have a seat." She tapped the space next to her with her fingers. "I must say, Dr. Springer, you look very dapper today. I'm seeing more and more men wearing this type of suit lately. It's becoming very popular." Addie looked out over the hospital yard and raised her hand to point out a few gentlemen in the distance playing croquet with their wives and girlfriends on the side lawn.

"Seersucker suits are all the rage now. A New Orleans merchant developed this blend of fabric a few years ago in his search for a lighter-weight suit that could withstand the summer heat and humidity."

"I had no idea."

"Do you know where the name 'seersucker' comes from?"

"I have no idea." Addie shrugged her shoulders, thinking she was beginning to sound like a parrot. *I had no idea. I have no idea. Pull it together, Addie, and say something intelligent in response next time.*

"'Seersucker' comes from the Persian word for 'milk and sugar'. The rough blue stripe represents sugar and the white stripe symbolizes milk. This new crinkled textile is so comfortable. It really stands up to perspiration."

Before she had a chance to think, the words spilled out. "I had no idea." *Oh, fiddle sticks!*

"Pardon my manners. I must be boring you to death."

Addie reached out and touched him reassuringly on his

shoulder. "Oh, heavens no. Please pardon me. My brain is mush. Nurse Hartman and Nurse Scott have been teaching us about so many topics, my senses are numb. I even had a complete meltdown the other day after receiving my first monthly report card."

"I heard that Nurse Hartman doled those out. If you mind me asking, how'd you do in June?"

Addie had memorized her grades in each category. *Cleanliness, Work—C; Cleanliness, Person—B; Reliability, Patients—C; Reliability, Records—C; Economy—C; Adaptability—B; Observation—B; Industry—B; Disposition—B; Executive Ability—B.* "My marks were average." Addie refrained from divulging the details; it was against Nurse Hartman's rules to discuss their grades. She accidently overheard Alice and Belle talking in the dorm bathroom. They had been put on probation for their carelessness and poor marks. "I still have a lot of work ahead of me."

"Don't get discouraged. One of my medical professors used to tell me, 'Only God is perfect, so don't let your ego get in the way of practicing good medicine.' After all, we're only human and the art of medicine isn't an exact science. Our patients are going to teach us life lessons about ourselves—our resolve and our character. Not everyone is going to recover, heal, or respond positively to the medications and treatment we provide them. Everyone is unique and no two people have the exact same reaction to surgery, pain, and illness. We manage their care to the best of our trained abilities. Throw in a few prayers, and the rest is out of our hands."

Addie chuckled, amused by Randall's efforts to cheer her up. "I appreciate the pep talk, Dr. Springer."

"Please call me Randal, since it is just the two of us talking." He looked around the picnic table to make sure no one was eavesdropping. "I'm quite aware of the rules around here," he whispered in her ear. The faint scent of lilacs reminded him of when they'd fallen on top of each other—after Mrs. Wu knocked them over with her laundry cart—and of Addie's bedroom and the secret aspirations and dreams poster hanging behind her door. He refrained from mentioning it. "Sometimes the rules need to be bent a little."

Addie laughed. "Yes, they do." It felt like the burdens of her studies, report card grades, and patient care had lifted. *Garrett. I've neglected to ask about him.* "So, how's your arrangement with your new tenant working out?"

"Since you are our landlord, I promised Garrett that I wouldn't divulge too many of our gentlemen's secrets with you," he chided. "Actually, he is doing great. He said to tell you hey when I saw you. He would have loved to come to the picnic as my guest, but he had to work today."

Fiddle sticks! I was hoping to see him.

"He comes home exhausted and likes to share the stories of his latest life-saving heroics. And, then there are days when we don't talk about his work. I know those untold tales are tragic and heart-breaking, ones that just can't be put into words. They are so horrific that they are pushed into the deep, dark recesses of his mind to be forgotten. Addie, he's truly making a difference in this world and in the community he serves. You'd be proud of him. I can tell he loves his new line of work. It's dangerous, but he loves it."

"How marvelous! I've always hoped for the best for him. It seems that Garrett has found his calling."

"He really has. I've even been teaching him what I know about the medical management of shock and hemorrhage, and pressure bandaging in the field. As a result, he spoke to his lieutenant and they've invited me to give them instructional courses on first aid. If the firefighters are trained to stabilize the patients, it is my hope that those patients will have a better chance at survival when they reach us at the hospital."

Addie hung on his every word. Randall intrigued her. His ability to see the bigger picture unexpectedly ingratiated him to her.

"By the way, I happened to be down in the basement of Mrs. Gray's, er... I mean, your house looking for some carpentry tools to fix a loose floorboard on the stairs."

"Oh, I know the one, the second to last stair?"

"Exactly! That's the one. Were you aware that there was a secret room in the basement?"

"Gosh, no. Wherever did you find it?"

"It was behind the wooden shelves against the wall."

"What was in there?" *Cases of Doc Gray's tonic?*

"Not much. I found some old, dusty, wool blankets and oil lamps." Then Randall recalled running across something else. He rubbed his forehead, trying to remember. "Ah! Maps. There were hand-drawn maps indicating some kind of route, but there weren't any street or city markings on them."

"Did you ask Garrett about the room? Perhaps he knows what his uncle and aunt used it for."

"I haven't had the chance to yet. Lately, we've been passing like ships in the night."

"Red! Red!" Nurse Scott called out as she ran up to Addie.

"Come with me, Red. I promised that I'd teach you how to ride a bike. I finally found two bikes that weren't in use. Joshua is reserving them for us." She turned back and waved at Joshua in the distance. He only nodded his head, unable to wave because he was holding the handles of two bikes, one painted red, the other bright green.

Addie leaned over to Randall. "Please excuse me, Dr. Springer. It appears that Nurse Scott is going to teach me another invaluable lesson today." Addie popped up off the wooden picnic bench and ran off hand in hand with Claire.

"I hope you don't end up in our emergency room, Nurse Engel," Randall called out.

Addie glanced at him over her shoulder. The sun's rays illuminated her face. "I promise!" she called back. "I hope I'm a quick learner."

Randall felt his heart skip a beat.

SATURDAY EVENING, FIRST WARD

"Nighty, night, Billy. Don't let the bedbugs bite!" Ida tucked in the boy picked up from Sacred Heart Hospital almost a week ago.

"Good night and God bless you, Miss Preti." Billy waved at her with his left hand. His right arm was in a plaster cast that immobilized his wrist and his elbow and was secured to his chest in a cloth sling to minimize movement and pain. A defensive wound had left him with a broken ulna according to Dr. Springer's x-ray findings. Billy sustained the injury from an Irish textile owner who liked to beat his workers with a shillelagh, a thick, knotty-wooded walking stick made of oak or blackthorn and commonly used as a weapon in his homeland.

"Good night, Miss Preti," said the other four boys in the room. The sixth boy, named David, was already under his covers, snoring.

Ida closed the bedroom door behind her and walked to the living room.

Jo adjusted her reading glasses as she read yesterday's copy of *The Atlanta Dispatch*. She scanned the pages for any news about orphaned or abandoned children in the Atlanta area. Flipping the newspaper closed, she folded it and handed it to her sister, who took a seat next to her on the pale blue couch. "I think you'll find the news about the assassination of Archduke Ferdinand and his wife while they visited Sarajevo interesting. They escaped a bomb thrown at their car, only to be shot and killed a few hours later by a lone assassin. The Austrian-Hungarian government is up in arms with Serbia." Jo stood up and stretched. "That's one way to start a war."

"It sure is." Ida picked up the paper and unfolded it.

"I'm gonna take a short cat nap. Wake me when it's time to go."

"I will."

"Did you give the boy his medicine tonight?"

"I did. I mixed it in his milk at supper. I didn't want the others to get too suspicious by trying to give him medicine at bedtime. We've got to be so careful, especially around the older ones. By the way, what are we going to do with Billy? We can't hire him out to work."

"No, but until his cast comes off in about a month, he'll be useful to us here in the house and around the property doing light work. Not to fret, dear sister, I've got it all under control."

Ida fell asleep while reading the paper. When the clock on the fireplace mantle in the living room chimed twelve times, she awoke. She got up off the couch and retrieved her sister from her bedroom in the back of the house. Jo had slipped into a dark blue dress and hoped none of the boys were awake to notice she wasn't wearing her priest garb. She carefully opened the boys' bedroom door and tiptoed over to the snoring boy. She pulled back the sheets and picked him up. Billy stirred in his bed. She froze in place and waited a few seconds before exiting the room. Ida closed the door behind her, turned the key in the lock, and removed it.

Billy opened his eyes and let them adjust to the darkness in the room. He scanned the beds; one was empty. He heard a truck engine turn over, the sound of rocks crunching under the rubber tires, and then there was silence. He slipped out of bed and walked over to the door. Billy twisted the glass knob to the right and pulled. Nothing. He twisted it to the left and pulled. Nothing. He crossed the room and carefully parted the curtains. He inspected the windows and noticed they were nailed shut. But why? Why would orphaned and homeless boys want to leave this place unless they were adopted? Three square meals, a roof over his head, clothes, a job, and a bed to sleep in was more than he had ever had. Yet, they were locked in the bedroom and there was no escape. He wondered if the other boy's bedroom, which housed four younger boys and two empty cribs, across the hall was also locked.

Billy returned to sit on the edge of his bed. He wedged his fingers between his cast and his skin, scratching at the itchy, hot skin under the heavy plaster. Where had Father Preti and Miss Ida gone with one of the boys in the middle of the night? Billy knew it could be dangerous to ask too many questions. He had learned his lesson from Mr. McCray after he tried to rescue a thirteen-year-old girl from his mill office before he could violate her. He opted to be less vocal and more observant this time.

Headlights flashed through the curtains, casting shadows on the wall. Billy's feet quickly disappeared under the covers. He closed his eyes. He heard the rocks crunch. The truck engine shut off. He heard footsteps on the back porch followed by the sound of the back door being unlocked. Footsteps approached his bedroom door. A metal key was inserted into the lock. *Click.* Billy knew their bedroom door had been unlocked. A few moments passed. *Click.* The other bedroom door down the hall was unlocked. His mind spun with questions before he finally drifted off to sleep.

10

Edward glanced at his gold pocket watch and noted the time as he gazed out of arched windows on the second floor located directly above their offices on the A wing. The garden was in full bloom. The white marble fountain gurgled. The orange and yellow daylilies had yet to open; it was too early in the morning. He turned to take his seat at the head of the table. "Good morning! It is zero six hundred." Edward scanned the large, hand-carved, ebony board room table that accommodated fourteen comfortably as he rapped his fountain pen on his coffee cup. Everyone was accounted for. "Let's get our leadership meeting underway. I know we all have a very busy day." He pointed his pen at the Chief Medical Officer, Dr. John Williams sitting next to him on his right. "Let's start with Dr. Williams since he and Dr. Leventhal have a full surgical schedule today."

"Thank you, Edward." Dr. Williams scanned his notes in front of him. "For the month of June, we operated on a total of seventy-two unique patients. We performed a total of eighty-four surgical procedures, meaning some of our patients required multiple or corrective surgeries due to unforeseen complications. Three patients died."

"That's very impressive for our first full month in operation," Alan Waxman, Chief Financial Officer, chimed in from across the table. He jotted a note in his notebook to include, date, time, topic, and presenter without looking up.

"I'm pleased." Dr. Williams shuffled his papers. "I've given Dr. Springer permission to provide community first aide classes to local firehouse number six. Our rationale is that if the firemen can be trained in basic medical management, those patients may have a better chance at survival when they reach us at the hospital."

"Are we charging them for these classes?" Alan raised his head.

"No."

Alan winced.

"We would like to start this as a pilot program, first. If it goes well, then let's discuss how to offset costs before we expand it to other fire stations throughout Atlanta."

"Don't forget, we can always organize a fundraiser for such a cause," Edward added.

"Why don't we just pass around an empty fireman's boot and take up a collection," Clyde joked. He poked Edward in his left arm.

Edward flinched. Typically, his gut churned with acid in the presence of Clyde, whose hiring had been a favor to a State Congressman's son. He listened to his gut. No gurgles or ripples this morning. "You know, Clyde, that idea isn't half bad." Edward mulled it over. "Alan, make it happen and include the boot thing, too." He turned back to Dr. Williams. "What else do you have for us?"

"Well, I do have a complaint to file against the McDaniel Brothers?"

"What do you have against our ambulance drivers?" Nurse Hartman sipped from her coffee cup.

"It appears that they are charging busy bodies to sneak peaks through our surgical theater windows."

Alan immediately took a liking to the idea. After all, money is money. "What's so bad about that?"

Annoyed, Dr. Williams squirmed in his chair. "Really? How would you like to be seen as a circus side show and have someone pay to see your gall bladder removed?"

"Well, as long as I got a percentage off the top." Alan chuckled.

The group, with the exception of Dr. Williams, laughed.

Lena rested her cup back in the saucer. "Why don't we just tape newspapers over the windows or soap them up like it instructs for at-home surgeries in our nursing text books?"

Dr. Williams's face turned red. He slammed his fist down on the table. Everyone jumped. The white bone china coffee cups with hand-painted gold rims and handles rattled. "This is not a joke. My two surgery suites are supposed to be the best in this city." He turned to Edward. "Do you want to run Sacred Heart like a top-notch hospital or a circus?" He pounded on his chest with the palm of his hand. "My reputation is at stake here!"

"Calm down, Dr. Williams. Of course, you already know the answer to that question." Edward placated. "Clyde, please talk with Brice McDaniel right after this meeting. Dr. Williams, please let Clyde know if you have any further problems."

"Thank you, Edward." Dr. Williams reshuffled his papers

and stood up. "If you'll excuse me, I need to scrub in for my first case." Dr. Williams excused himself and left the room.

"Let's move on. Nurse Hartman, what is going on with the nurses and the nursing school?"

"We're doing well with course instruction and are on track with their lessons. I've got two students on probation."

"It isn't Opal, is it?" Edward appeared concerned.

"Heavens no. Alice Fein and Isabelle Esposito are lagging behind a bit. But, not to worry, Nurse Scott is working closely with them. We don't want to see them fail." Lena added, "My students will be working with Dr. Williams and Dr. Leventhal in the surgical suites this month. I'm crossing my fingers that we don't upset the apple cart. Our first observation is scheduled for this afternoon."

"Leave him to me, Nurse Hartman." Edward pointed his pen at Clyde. "What news do you have for us?"

"No updates or changes to note since our last meeting regarding day-to-day operations. However, we do have a new working relationship with the Holy Cross Orphans' Asylum. Father Preti and his sister, Ida, run a home for homeless and orphaned boys."

"Great. I'm glad to know we can help get those boys get off the streets. I had a talk with my friend, the chief at the Atlanta Police Department, the other day at our Masonic meeting. There has been a rash of young boys being murdered. They are finding their bodies in alleys, washing up in creeks, and one young lad was even found floating in the lake at Stone Mountain by quarry workers the other day."

"How tragic!" Oliver Lewis, the Chief Operating Officer for Alexander Hall, said.

"It is. He has assigned a special detective to the case, Detective McGee. I told him if we overheard anything from our patients, we'd pass it along. I have the detective's business card on my desk downstairs." Edward pointed at the floor.

Shelby Lee Maddox leaned forward over the table to capture Edward's attention.

"Ah, yes! Tell us about the pharmacy this morning, Mr. Maddox."

"I've been collaborating with Dr. Williams, Dr. Leventhal, and Dr. Springer to make sure I have been stocking their specific medication requests. In addition, I'll be working with Nurse Hartman's nursing students next month to teach them about pharmacologic agents, administration, and dosing in pediatrics and adult patients."

Lena interjected, "The nurses have been learning a little bit about medication in class and while working with their nurse mentors in the hospital, but Dr. Maddox will be delving into the topic on a much deeper level."

Edward and others nodded.

Shelby reached for a small worn, black, leather notebook tied with a tan cord lying on the table. "I would also like to work with the doctors to develop some natural methods of curing and managing diseases."

Edward pointed at Shelby's book. "What's in the book, son?"

"These are my notes and recipes that I've collected over the years, passed down from my great-grand mother, a Creek Indian."

Edward noted his blonde hair and blue eyes. He saw traces of Shelby's Native American ancestry in his high cheek bones.

"I'd like permission to start a small botanical and herb garden. Come, I'll show you where I'd like to put it." Shelby stood up and walked over to the window. The others followed. He pointed to the side yard of the nursing school, a patch of land between the school and the dirt road the ambulances used that circled around the back of the Sacred Heart and Alexander Hall properties.

"I don't have a problem with it? Do you, Nurse Hartman?" Edward walked back to his seat.

"I sure don't. In fact, why don't we add this to the nursing student's studies next month? We can all pitch in and help you cultivate your medicinal garden. It'll be good for them to understand the genesis of medications."

"Great! Please ask Joshua to help you with this project." Edward looked at his pocket watch, returning it to his burgundy vest pocket. "We can borrow a mule and a plow from a local farmer and get that area up and running in no time."

"I'll procure the plants and seedlings," Shelby said enthusiastically.

"I calculate that we could probably save hundreds of dollars by developing our own medicines." Alan wrung his hands four times before picking up his pencil and scribbled away in his notebook.

Edward looked at Oliver. "How's the construction going at Alexander Hall?"

"The project is right on track, still slated to open in two and a half years." He ran his hand over his smooth bald head. His wiry white moustache wiggled as he spoke. "No further updates or hiccups to report."

"Excellent job, everybody." Edward clapped his hands together. "As my daddy used to say, 'Let's get to it and just do it!'"

Clyde mouthed the coined phrase as Edward spoke.

Edward caught Clyde mocking him out of the corner of his eye. His gut churned.

MONDAY AFTERNOON, SIXTH WARD

"Line up over here, ladies." Nurse Hartman instructed the students to form a single file line against the wall outside the surgical theater doors. "Once we are inside, please have a seat on the front row. Don't make a peep. Remember, you are nurses. Remain stoic and unfazed by what you see. Your job is to remain calm. If you think you are going to pass out, please stay seated and drop your head between your knees." She thought about saying something regarding if they fell out of their chair, then thought otherwise. She didn't want to scare them anymore. Simply being in the presence of Dr. Williams and Dr. Leventhal while they were performing a high risk surgical procedure was scary enough. Dr. William's nerves were already running high after this morning's leadership meeting. She opened the door. The nurses filed into the first row and took their seats in the theater. Behind them sat a variety of men, who Lena assumed were either local physicians or medical students, with perhaps even a reporter or two sprinkled in. She knew how Edward liked press, good or bad. The large arched windows to the courtyard outside showed no signs of any onlookers — the spectators that Dr. Williams complained about.

The double doors on the opposite side of the room parted. The patient was wheeled in on a surgical table, naked and draped with a white sheet. The surgical nurses locked the wheels into place. Dr. Williams and Dr. Leventhal walked into the room towards the patient, dressed in white with masks as they held their rubber-gloved hands in the air.

"Nurse, please administer the anesthesia." Inhaled ether was the drug of choice. "Ladies and gentlemen, this afternoon, Dr. Leventhal and I will be performing a very risky surgery to remove a mass from this woman's abdominal cavity. There will be a lot of blood, but today we are trying out a new piece of equipment. Instead of using a hand-cranked suction machine, we are going to use the latest electrical device." He pointed towards the machine before turning his back to the audience. "Let's begin."

The other nurse pulled back the sheet, exposing the body of a middle-aged woman, her abdomen distended, giving her the appearance that she was pregnant. Dr. Leventhal assisted Dr. Williams in the dissection process. Skin, layers of fat, and muscles were pulled back. Retractors helped to expose the mass. Blood seeped out of the wound and began pooling on the floor. Addie was amazed how the physicians and nurses remained clean.

"Suction, please." Dr. Williams ordered the nurse to turn the machine on.

She stepped into a small puddle of blood as she flipped the on the machine. The electric lights dimmed immediately and she began to shake uncontrollably. Her eyes rolled back and foam gurgled from her lips. She seemed unable to move.

"She's being electrocuted!" A man jumped up from behind Nurse Scott's seat and pushed past her, toppling chairs in the front row before leaping over the knee-high wall that separated the audience from the surgical area. He reached down, unplugging the machine from the wall.

Startled by the man's unexpected outburst, Dr. Leventhal nicked a major vessel in the patient. Blood arched in the air, splattering all over the operative staff. Horrified, various members of the audience jumped up and ran out of the room, screaming.

"HELP, NURSE HARTMAN AND NURSE SCOTT!" Dr. Williams lowered his voice. "All hands on deck. I need for you to operate the hand pump STAT!" Dr. Williams remained in command of the scene, barking orders. He pointed to the man who had unplugged the machine. "Are you a doctor?"

"Yes." The man turned pale as he adjusted his spectacles. He took off his black suit jacket. "I work at Saint Joseph's Hospital."

"Please attend to our nurse." Dr. Williams frantically worked to save his patient from bleeding to death, grabbing hemostats off the silver tray stand next to him. He clamped off the vessel.

The nurse at the head of the bed palpated for the woman's pulse in her neck. "She has a pulse, Doctor, but it's weak and irregular."

The visiting doctor pulled the unconscious and cyanotic nurse, named Nancy, to the side of the room. The doctor punched on her chest, repeatedly. He felt for a pulse in her wrist and neck areas. Nothing. The stench of body fluids and burnt flesh filled the air. Dr. Leventhal ran over and confirmed with a shaking of his head; she was gone. He ran back to assist Dr. Williams.

Dr. Williams looked up at the audience while Nurse Hartman and Nurse Scott feverishly operated the hand-cranked suction machine. He saw a young lad furiously making notes in his flip pad and called out to him. "Hey! You there, are you a reporter? Vacate my premises at once! I swear if I ever see you in my operating room again…"

Scout didn't have to be told twice and vanished out a side door.

"How can we help?" Addie called over to Nurse Hartman and Nurse Scott.

"Please calmly direct the rest of the class back to the dorms and go and be of help to our fallen sister."

Addie grabbed Opal by the arm and together, they ushered out the students who were too afraid to leave their seats. Retrieving another stretcher, they placed Nancy on it. They reverently covered her with a clean sheet and took her down the back elevators to Dr. Payne in the morgue.

Edward and Clyde rushed in the room. Blood spatter was everywhere.

"What can I help you with, Dr. Williams?" Edward avoided stepping too close to the patient.

"Please see the rest of our audience out so we can focus on this woman."

"I can't seem to find her pulse anymore, Doctor." The nurse at the head of the bed sobbed.

Dr. Leventhal felt for pulses in her neck, feet, and wrists while Dr. Williams grabbed his stethoscope, placed the bell upon her left breast, and listened. He watched Edward and Clyde shoo out the remaining viewers. Her heartbeat was absent.

Dr. Williams removed the stethoscope from his ears. "Please

note the time of death." He looked over at the clock on the wall. "Sixteen thirty-four."

"Confirmed, Doctor," Nurse Hartman said. She and Nurse Scott stopped operating the suction machine.

"Will you please help me by closing her up, Dr. Leventhal?"

"Yes, sir. It would be my honor."

Dr. Williams removed his mask. "I know what went wrong."

"What?" Dr. Leventhal unclamped the hemostats and threw them on the metal tray containing a variety of surgical instruments. *Clang.*

"Next time, we need to tape metal strips along the backs of our legs and over our wooden shoe heels." He removed his blood-spattered mask. "We forgot to remain grounded."

Outside of the surgical suite, Moira caught wind of the news from various hospital staff as they scurried by her desk. After piecing the details together, she picked up the phone and promptly dialed Charlie at *The Atlanta Dispatch*. "Hey, is it sunny out?" she whispered. "I've got some shocking news for you today."

11

THURSDAY, JULY 23, 1914, FIRST WARD

Billy collected old issues of *The Atlanta Dispatch* stacked by the sofa in the living room of the orphanage with his left hand, tucking them under his sling. He counted the days until he got his cast removed. His chores around the house included cleaning and washing dishes, fetching eggs from the hen house, helping Miss Ida with laundry, and anything else she or Father Preti asked of him. One very hot and humid day last week, Ida even asked Billy to rub her feet with a homemade astringent liniment while she rocked in a white wicker rocker on the front porch. He cringed at the thought of her hammer toes, ragged, thick yellow toenails, bunions, and cracked skin. He thanked the good Lord above that none of the older boys were home to bear witness to the gruesome task. The younger boys were with Father Preti tending the garden in the backyard. *Shocking Tragedy Strikes Sacred Heart Hospital* was the headline from the paper lying on the top of the stack. He scanned the article; a nurse died after being electrocuted in the operating room a few weeks ago.

His granny taught him to read and write at an early age. He

was a quick learner. He was often called on by the hobos to read stories to them at night. Homer's *Iliad* and *Odyssey* were their favorites. The boys enjoyed hearing the epic and heroic tales about Greek gods and adventures battling mysterious monsters like the cyclops and the six-headed Scylla and her counterpart, Charybdis, a sea monster that created whirlpools. He kept his book out of sight from Father Preti and Ida. It was his only treasured possession, a gift he'd received from Granny before she passed away a few years ago. He never met his mother or knew his father. He was thrown out on the streets after Granny died, left to fend for himself.

"Quit your dawdling, boy!" Ida smacked Billy on the back of the head as she walked by. "What are you reading?" She swiped the paper out of his hand.

"Nothing, ma'am. I was just looking at the pictures. I can't read," he lied.

"Come on, we don't have all day. I need your help to peel potatoes after you finish cleaning up in here." Ida waddled towards the rear of the house. "I'll be back in a jiffy, gotta fetch the bushel stored in the garage." She opened the screen door. *Screech. Slam.*

"Yes, ma'am." Billy knew until he heard that noise again, he could rummage through the house. After his roommate, David, disappeared in the night, Father Preti told the boys the next morning that he was adopted by a loving family. Billy's suspicions grew. He hoped and prayed to be adopted by a loving family of his own. However, his chances of being picked were slim. Childless parents preferred infants and toddlers over school-aged boys.

Scanning the living room, he spotted a dark brown ledger

book tucked away on the bookshelf by the fireplace. Setting the newspapers down, he ran over and pulled the book off the shelf. He flipped it open. Listed on the first page were names of boys, ages, adoption dates, and the last name of the adoptive family. He skimmed the pages. Twin brothers, Landon and Logan Farmer, were the next to last hand-written entry. The name of the adoptive family was blank. The last entry read *David Connley*. There was no adoptive family listed by his name either.

Screech. Slam.

Billy hastily shut the book, and returned it to its proper place on the shelf, making sure it was lined up perfectly with the others next to it. He collected the papers and hustled to intercept Ida in the main hallway. "When I finish tying these into small bundles for the fireplace, I'll be ready to start on the potatoes." Billy darted out the back door.

Screech. Slam.

THURSDAY AFTERNOON, SIXTH WARD

Sacred Heart's medicinal and herb garden was under development. Shelby had procured mature plants and herbs so he could begin utilizing them in his cure-alls. Wooden tongue depressors stuck out of the ground, marking the plants. The labels were all skillfully hand-painted by Opal. Addie concluded there wasn't anything Opal couldn't do perfectly. Joshua crafted a two-foot high picket fence around the perimeter of the garden to prevent local rodents, deer, and other wildlife from devouring the vegetation. This afternoon, Bertie was helping Alice white wash the fence.

Nurse Hartman assigned the students to work with Shelby on a rotating basis. They were eager to help the handsome bachelor. This outdoor activity was a welcome diversion after the debacle in the operating room. Counseling sessions were enacted to counter the psychological effects on the students after the incident. It was a good life lesson, Lena concluded. "Life is the most respected teacher of all," she told them. It was becoming her mantra.

Addie wiped perspiration from her brow before picking up the tin watering can and sprinkling a green herb in front of her. She leaned over and squinted to make out the name of the plant. Afternoon shadows cast by the nearby maple and rays of the sun prevented her from making out all of the white hand-painted letters on the tongue depressor. "What's this used for?" Addie pointed towards the sign, directing the question to Shelby, who was tending a patch of parsley a few feet away.

"Hoarhound. It's a member of the mint family. The juice of that herb can be combined with honey and is a great remedy for those who have a cough. I can also mix it with milk and administer it to those patients with advanced cases of consumption."

Opal stuck the last tongue-depressor into the ground. It read *Shepherd's Purse.* "What about this plant?"

Shelby looked over at Opal and nodded. "That one is an annual. We'll have to replant it every year. It can help those with flux, jaundice, inflammation and even help relieve pain in the ear.

"Why are we growing cabbage leaves? Aren't they better suited for a vegetable garden?" Bertie asked, moving her paint brush up and down the picket.

"Cabbage is a key ingredient in a cough medicine, helps to heal bruises, is used to counter the effects of mushroom poisoning, and can even be used as a laxative. Boiled cabbage leaves are an asset on the maternity ward and can be used on women with inflamed breasts."

Opal squatted down by a stalky plant with tiny purple flowers. "Lavender?" She pinched off a few florets and crushed them between her fingers. "I used to help Ms. Mattie, our mammy and Joshua's mother, plant this in our herb garden at home. I love its fragrance." She smelled the oil expressed on her skin.

"Momma uses that oil for almost everything that ailed her," Joshua said as he made adjustments to the gate with his wooden-handled screwdriver.

"Correct." Shelby was impressed. "Lavender Hyssop is often referred to as a 'holy herb' because it is mentioned in the Bible, especially the Old Testament."

"Really?" Opal stood up, placed her hands on her hips, and arched her back.

"Do you remember in the book of Exodus the passage that describes God instructing Israelites to mark their doorways with lamb's blood so the angel of death passed over them?"

"Yes, Mother loved reading that chapter to the family around Easter time."

"They were told to use hyssop as a paintbrush."

Joshua chimed in, "It's also referenced during the crucifixion of Jesus when they soak the sponge with wine and lifted the sponge on hyssop stalks for Jesus to drink."

"That's correct." Shelby stopped digging. "I heard you preach at a local AME Church on Sundays."

"Yes, sir. I have a church and a congregation that I tend to in the Second Ward just a few blocks down from Armstrong Street. That's how I know about the references to hyssop in the Bible."

Shelby plunged his wooden-handled trowel back in the dirt. "Actually, lavender is one of my favorite and most versatile plants in the garden. It's also related to the mint family and is used to help alleviate wheezing, minimize bruising, and heal wounds. The oil can kill lice and mitigate itching."

Addie scratched at her scalp. Opal, Bertie, Alice, and Joshua followed suit.

Shelby laughed as he scratched as his head. "Just mentioning those tiny blood sucking pests makes my head itch, too."

"Be careful when you work on the pediatric ward, tomorrow, Addie. Those kids have a tendency to harbor those miniscule creatures." Alice shivered and shook her arms, splattering paint on Bertie's face.

"Hey! Watch what you are doing, Alice!" Bertie flicked her paint brush at Alice's face. A few white speckles landed on Alice's nose and cheeks.

Bertie wound back with her paintbrush hoisted in front of her like a sword. Alice did the same. The duel was about to begin.

Ding. Ding. Ding. Ding. Ding. Ding. The dinner bell rang. Maybelle silenced the iron triangle that hung from the back porch of the nursing school with her hand and released the metal beater, which was secured by a piece of twine. She waved at the crew toiling in the garden.

"Saved by the bell." Bertie resigned.

"What does that even mean?" Alice replaced her paint brush in the bucket and handed it to Joshua.

"You've never heard that expression, Nurse Fein?" Shelby inquired. He watched Alice shake her head. He stopped manicuring the plants to explain. "The phrase 'saved by the bell' originated as an expression referring to people being buried alive. The idea was that, if someone was comatose and accidently pronounced dead and interred, in the event they awoke, they could ring a bell that was affixed above ground and be saved."

"Is that true?" Alice was suspicious. "You're pulling my leg." Unsure if they were joking, she stormed off. Bertie pursued.

Shelby remained on his hands and knees, laughing at the exchange as he resumed pruning the parsley.

Addie and Opal gathered their belongings and put them in Opal's basket.

"Have a great evening, Mr. Maddox." Opal stepped over his feet as she made her way towards the garden gate Joshua was holding open for her and Addie. "Good night, Joshua."

"And, to you, Miss Opal and Miss Addie." Joshua removed his straw hat and bowed his head as they walked by.

"Ladies, have a great night," Shelby called out from under the plants.

Addie teased Opal on the way back to the school. "Have a great evening, Mr. Maddox," she mimicked.

Opal nudged Addie with her basket. "Oh, please! What about you? Courting *two* men, I see?"

Addie reared back. "What the devil are you talking about?"

"I'm not blind, Addie. I see the way Dr. Springer looks at you when you're not looking at him. And, let's not forget about his dashing roommate, Mr. Firefighter."

"Are you crazy?"

"Not at all. It seems to me like you have got your hands full."

"I'll tell you what you're full of, Nurse Alexander."

"Why, Nurse Engel, you wouldn't dare."

"I'll race you to the supper table." Addie took off running.

Opal took off after her. "You can't run away from love, Addie. You're bound to get bitten by the love bug one of these days!"

12

"God, it's hotter than Hades out here." Detective McGee stood up, took off his hat, and wiped the sweat off his head and face with his handkerchief. Perspiration rolled down his chest; his heavy navy blue suit stuck to his back.

"Did you hear the news, sir?" The officer pulled back the kudzu and continued to examine the lifeless boy's body lying behind a row of red-tipped Photinia bushes about two miles south of the red brick buildings of the Fulton Bag and Cotton Mills, a complex on the eastside of Atlanta in a neighborhood called 'Cabbagetown.'

"What? That we've got another dead boy on our hands or about Germany declaring war on Russia?" He scanned the surrounding area. He had driven down Boulevard past Oakland Cemetery and Grant Park to get to the crime scene. He looked back towards the mills. The smokestacks belched plumes of dark smoke into the partly-cloudy sky.

"The war, sir."

"Yes, I read about it in the paper this morning. It's an unfortunate state of affairs over there. One thing is going to lead to another. I fear it won't be long before we get dragged into that mess."

Not one for small talk, he probed, "Whatcha' got for me so far?"

"Well, it appears that this fair-haired boy is between nine and eleven years old. There are ligature marks around his wrists and ankles." He retracted his pen from under the right leg of the boy's dungarees and flicked off a few maggots. "Based on the kudzu growth, which is about a foot a day, bloating, blistering, marbling of the skin, bloody foam around his nose and mouth, and the maggot mass around an apparent abdominal wound, he's been out here for a few days." The pile of bugs was in constant motion. "The maggots are boiling. Since they only have one orifice that they eat, breathe, and excrete from, they have to work their way up from the bottom of the pile to breathe and excrete before going back down to feed on the body again." He pointed his pen at some very large maggots. "See these larger ones here? Some of these guys look like they are about ready to migrate away from the corpse and transform into flies."

"So, we've got a dead lad and no reports for a missing child or runaway at the APD as of this morning. "

"My best guess is that he is either homeless or an orphan."

"That would be my hunch, too, Officer Walters. There are so many kids living on the streets in this town. I refer to them as Georgia's invisible children. There's no one to care about them and no one to notice when they go missing. It's despicable how we treat our future generation; it's like they're disposable. God has a special place in hell for people who mistreat and kill kids.

It's my job to make sure they get there." McGee dabbed at the beads of sweat popping up over his upper lip with the back of his jacket sleeve. The foul, sweet smell of putrefaction was over-whelming. The weather was taking its toll on the decomposition process. An iridescent-colored beetle crawled over the tip of his black boot. The detective knocked it off. "God, I hate bugs."

"Who doesn't? They're like our co-workers—pesky creatures. The boys are going to have to be careful handling this body. It hasn't burst yet."

McGee wrinkled his nose. He was taking a liking to APD's newest recruit from Augusta. Walters had a sense of humor, a key characteristic to staying sane on the job. The gruesome scenes they encountered while on duty were hard to erase from the mind. Time was a faithful friend that managed to blur the images in his memory as the years passed. While some officers chose to mitigate the visions with alcohol, drugs, food, or sex, he chose nicotine. "I think I need a smoke." He turned to walk away, making a mental note to check in with some of the children's charities and orphanages in town.

A voice called out from a pine thicket a few yards away, "Hey! Detective, over here! We've got another one. I think it's his twin brother."

"Damn it."

13

Detective McGee steered his police car past the white wooden sign on his left. *Holy Cross Orphans' Asylum* was painted in cobalt blue cursive letters. He pulled up next to the Galloway and set the brake before turning the engine off. He evaluated the white house and property. This was his last orphanage to visit as he methodically made his way across the city of Atlanta. He had visited with officials who represented all kinds of children's charities. McGee even met with the Jewish leaders who operated the Jewish Orphan's Asylum. The meeting took place at the Progressive Club, a new club established last year by Russian Jews who felt unwelcome at The Standard Club, a longstanding social club founded by German Jews.

He noted a garage or storage shed in the back. Father Preti emerged from behind the structure with three young boys in tow. He was carrying a hoe. Billy and Ida stepped out onto the front porch.

"My, what a welcome." McGee removed his hat and walked towards Ida.

She teetered down the steps, her arms outstretched for balance. Billy thought she looked like Humpty Dumpty from behind. He opted to stay on the porch and observe.

"Good morning, Detective McGee. To what do we owe the pleasure of your visit this fine morning?" Father Preti leaned on the hoe.

"Can I talk with you in private, Father?"

"Of course." She handed the hoe to one of the boys. "Jimmy, you and the others finish the weeding," she directed.

"Yes, Father."

"How can I help you? Do you have a boy for us today?" Father Preti watched the boys run back to the garden located behind the garage.

"No, not today, Father. It seems that I've got my hands full. Someone is killing Atlanta's children, namely homeless or orphan boys. It's already bad enough we've had a serial killer on the loose in the city for the past three years. We can't seem to catch a break."

"Are you referring to the Atlanta Ripper? I believe it was in the spring when I read in the paper that firemen were finding hand-written notes pinned on their fireboxes around town with the killer's promise to kill Negro women."

"Yes. One of my colleagues is running that investigation. I've been put in charge of the murdered children investigation." McGee analyzed Father Preti's reaction, facial expressions, body language, and response. Out of the corner of his eye, he noticed the boy with a broken arm pacing back and forth on the porch like a caged animal.

"Okay. But I'm not sure what that has to do with my sister and I."

"Well, I wanted to see if you had heard anything? Do you have any boys that have run away or gone missing in the past few months?"

"Why heaven's no, Detective. My sister keeps excellent records. The only boys that are no longer here are those that have been adopted into a loving and caring home."

"Good to know. May I see those records?"

"N-now?" Jo stammered.

"Sure. Now is good. You know, while I'm here?" McGee turned to walk towards the house. The pacing boy stopped moving.

"Let me run ahead and get my sister to bring our ledger book out to you on the porch. I'll bring you a nice glass of iced lemonade." Jo ran up the front porch steps and into the house before McGee had a chance to respond.

"Good morning, son. How'd you break your arm?" McGee took a seat in one of the white wicker rockers.

Billy noticed it was the same one that Ida sat in when he had to rub her knotty feet. "I broke it in a fight." He opted to leave out the details.

"I'd hate to see the other guy?" McGee laughed. "When do you get your cast off?

"Today, sir. I'm supposed to go back to Sacred Heart Hospital this afternoon."

"I bet you're looking forward to that."

"Yes, sir." Billy pointed at McGee's Colt, a double action revolver, in his holster. "Ever fire that thing?"

"Yes, son. But, only in self-defense from very bad people who break the law and are trying to hurt me, other officers, or someone else."

"Oh."

Jo returned, carrying a glass of lemonade. "My sister will be out in a jiffy. It seems that I caught her in the middle of washing the breakfast dishes." As she handed the glass to the detective, she said, "Billy, why don't you run inside and help her. I'm sure Detective McGee has a busy schedule. We don't want to keep him waiting."

Billy stalled. He wanted to see the officer's response to the blank spaces in the ledger under the column that read Adoptive Family next to the Farmer brothers' and David Connley's names.

"Go on, Billy." Jo shooed him away. "I think we'll have to get Sacred Heart's pediatrician to clean the wax out your ears this afternoon after he takes off your cast. Please don't make me ask you twice."

"No, Father. Sorry, Father." Billy excused himself and went inside. He found Ida scribbling feverishly in the ledger book with her pencil while she sat on the sofa. He took a seat next to her.

He watched her fill in the blank spaces with two surnames, Martin and Davis.

"What are you gawkin' at, boy?" Ida stopped writing, stuffed the pencil behind her ear, and slammed the book shut.

"Nothing, ma'am. Perhaps one day you will teach me how to read and write?"

Ida cackled. "I don't think so, boy. As soon as you get that cast off, we're sending you out to the textile mill to start earning a wage. Boarding, clothing, and feeding you boys is mighty expensive. But we're on a mission. We're doing the Lord's work." She vanished out the front door.

Billy ran up to the front door. Anxious to overhear their conversation, he carefully opened it, hoping not to attract any attention.

Ida pointed at the book. "Detective, as you can see, all our orphans are accounted for."

McGee appreciated his personal space. If he turned his head left for any reason, he would have been smothered by Ida's bosom. Out of his periphery, he noticed she had a pencil tucked behind her right ear. It wasn't there when she had first greeted him.

He flipped back and forth through the pages, reviewing names and dates. Two names caught his attention. "Landon and Logan Farmer." He tapped his index finger under their names, moving his finger to the last column. It read *The Martin Family*. The writing appeared fresh, not smudged and worn like the other entries. The entry below also appeared similar. He said nothing, but waited to hear what Father Preti and Ida had to confess. He continued to tap his finger by their entries, watching for a reaction. There wasn't one from Father Preti. However, Ida leaned in closer. He felt her breasts resting on his left shoulder. The stench of garlic was on her breath.

"Those were the cutest brothers. The Martin family was so happy to get those twins."

"Really? What color was their hair, if you mind me asking?"

"They had hair the color of corn silk, didn't they, Father?"

McGee immediately regretted turning his head.

"Oh!" Ida cried out.

Billy shut the door, ran over to the sofa, and buried his head in a pillow to suppress his giggles. After composing himself, he rummaged through Ida's sewing basket sitting between the sofa and the oak end table. He found a tiny pencil. Picking up an old issue of *The Atlanta Dispatch*, he found a page with some blank space under an ad for men's clothing at Rich and Brothers. He ripped out the paper and wrote, *Landon and Logan Farmer—not adopted by the Martins. David Connley—not adopted by the Davises.* He replaced the pencil in the basket, folded the piece of paper, and tucked it under the palm of his cast. He watched Father Preti and Ida through the sheers as they waved to the policeman driving away. He ran out of the living room, through the kitchen, and out the back door.

Screech. Slam.

"Shit!" Billy mumbled under his breath.

"Billy? Billy?" Ida called out.

"Yes, ma'am?" He listened to her response through the screened door.

"Get back in this house and get washed up. Father is going to take you uptown to the hospital within the hour. We want you to look your best."

"Yes, ma'am." He stepped back inside the kitchen.

She smacked him on the back of the head as he walked by. "No dawdling."

Billy wanted to take a swipe at her with his cast. Instead, he remained unfazed. "Yes, ma'am."

WEDNESDAY AFTERNOON, SIXTH WARD

Addie sat at the nurse's desk in the pediatric ward and wrote in the child's chart marked, *William Slopes. Date of Birth. February*

5, 1908. Patient in good spirits. She stopped writing for a moment and reflected on Nurse Hartman's constructive feedback about her patient charting after she received her monthly report card for July.

Cleanliness, Work—C; Cleanliness, Person—B; Reliability, Patients—B; Reliability, Records—C; Economy—B; Adaptability—A; Observation—B; Industry—B; Disposition—A; Executive Ability—B.

'Addie, you must be concise in your charting. Cease writing long narrative entries. Note any observed changes in the patient's condition. You must record a patient's urination and defecations when they occur; never trust your memory or your patient's word. May I suggest that you keep a notebook for convenience? At the end of the day, those notes recording a patient's temperature, pulse, weight, respirations can be converted to the permanent chart at the end of the shift. Remember, children's charts are not hung from the end of their beds since kids are apt to destroy them if they are within their reach. Parents and visitors will also be inclined to read those notes. Charts should be taken to the beds just before staff rounds and collected immediately afterwards.'

Addie scratched at her hairline at the base of her neck.

Father Preti stuck his head into the ward and looked around. "Good afternoon, Miss." Billy was by his side.

Addie stood up. "Good afternoon, Father." Addie rummaged through the patient charts and pulled one out. "Billy Swanson, I presume?"

"Yes, ma'am."

"Come with me, I'll escort you to our treatment room around the corner. Father, may I ask that you have a seat in our waiting room? We'll bring Billy out to you after the procedure is over."

Addie walked over to nurse mentor, Rita Connors, to let her know she would be assisting Dr. Springer with the case. She exited the unit with Father Preti and Billy.

"I'd really like to stay with Billy, if you don't mind," Father Preti pressed.

"I'm sorry, Father. It's hospital policy." Addie directed him to the nearby waiting area.

Addie and Billy stepped into the treatment room where they found Dr. Springer reviewing Billy's chart.

"Good afternoon, Billy. Are you ready to get that cast off?"

"Yes, sir. My skin is so itchy, it's driving me nuts at night."

Dr. Springer laughed. "That's the worst, isn't it?" He laid out his plaster knife, shears, and a cast spreader on a rolling cart and wheeled it next to Billy. Addie helped Billy out of his sling and boosted him up on the stretcher. Billy watched Dr. Springer fill a glass container with warm water and peroxide. Addie retrieved a stack of white cotton towels and laid them on the stretcher. She unfolded a few of them and placed them across Billy's lap.

"Nurse Engel, please apply small amounts of this water mixture to Billy's cast using this bulb syringe." Dr. Springer handed Addie a white rubber bulb. Addie squeezed the air out of it, inserted the tip of the bulb in the water, and slowly released the base of the bulb. It sucked up the water. She expressed small amounts along the outer side of the cast. "This is going to help soften the plaster before Dr. Springer cuts it apart with his plaster shears."

Billy watched her every move.

"Addie, I'll be right back. I forgot to pick up a salve from Mr. Maddox in the pharmacy."

Dr. Springer left the room.

Billy suddenly remembered he had tucked away his note in the palm of his cast. He dug under his cast with his left hand, retrieving the folded piece of newspaper.

"What have you stuck up in your cast?"

"Nurse Engel, I don't have much time. Here, this is for you." He shoved the folded paper into her apron pocket. "I think I'm in trouble."

"Whatever are you talking about, Billy?"

"I think our orphanage is not quite right."

"I'm not sure I'm following what you are saying."

"I think that boys are leaving our home, but Father Preti and his sister aren't being truthful about where the boys go."

"Aren't they being adopted?"

"I'm not really sure, ma'am. There's something fishy going on there. Please give that note to a police officer named Detective McGee. He'll know what to do with it. Please don't tell anyone else my secret. Promise me. Please?" Tears welled up in his eyes.

"Sure, Billy. I promise." Addie patted her pocket.

Dr. Springer returned carrying a small blue jar. "This stuff is pure magic. Rub this on your skin when it starts to itch. Don't scratch at your skin. You're going to have tender, baby-like skin when I take this cast off. It's going to take some time for your skin to toughen up again."

"Yes, sir."

"Are you ready?"

Billy stiffened his lower lip. He blinked. A tear ran down his cheek.

Addie raked her fingernails through her hair: her scalp itched.

WEDNESDAY NIGHT, SIXTH WARD

Exhausted, Addie stripped off her clothes and put them in the laundry bag. She slipped into her nightgown. It was too hot to wear her robe. She opened the laundry chute door and released her grip on the bag. While she overheard some of the nurses talking downstairs, she refrained from joining them, opting for a good night's sleep. Addie slipped into her bed and pulled up the covers. She closed her eyes, recounting the events of the day. Her head itched; she scratched. *Garrett's pebble. Billy. His note. I forgot to clean out my apron pockets!*

Addie jumped out of bed and scurried down the back dorm stairs, passing Opal along the way.

"Where's the fire?"

"I forgot to clean out my pockets of my uniform before I sent the laundry down the chute."

"Well, shoot!"

"Cute! Nice play on words." Addie opened the basement door that led to the Greene tunnel. Locating the laundry bin, she opened her bag marked with her initials: *ARE. Addie Rose Engel.* She dug through the clothes and retrieved her apron. She pulled out Garrett's pebble and the folded piece of newspaper. She shoved her uniforms and undergarments into the bag, closed it, and set it back on top of the pile. Walking up the stairs back to the dorm, Addie unfolded the note and read it. *Landon and Logan Farmer—not adopted by the Martins. David Connley—not adopted by the Davises.*

Addie opened her locker and put the pebble and note on the

top shelf, above where her uniforms and cape hung. *I swear. I'm getting so forgetful. I need reminder notes for my notes to help keep me on track. One day, I'm going to forget to put on my underwear!*

Addie returned to bed and closed her eyes. *What was I supposed to do with that note? Who was it supposed to go to? What was the officer's name? Fiddlesticks! I can't recall. Nurse Hartman will know what to do with it. I'll just give it to her in the morning.* Her scalp itched behind her right ear. She scratched and fell asleep.

WEDNESDAY NIGHT, FOURTH WARD

"Gentleman, must I always remind you, I'm the best card player in this house!" Garrett laid his cards down in front of him on the kitchen table. "I believe my ten, jack, queen, king, and ace of hearts will beat your full house tonight, Lieutenant."

Lieutenant Jones toppled his pile of red, white, and blue chips. "Fu…."

The firehouse alarm sounded. A firebox a few blocks south had alerted the dispatcher that there was a house fire on Antoinette Street. Chips and cards flew as the lieutenant, Garrett, and the others ran down the back stairs, threw on their gear, and hopped on the firetruck. Moments later, they pulled up to find the two-story structure ablaze. A young man wearing a singed nightshirt waved his arms frantically at the crew. Garrett, first out of the vehicle, ran over to him. The distinct smell of burnt human hair caught his attention. Parts of the man's long beard were broken off and scorched.

"I got Maw out!" He pointed to an elderly woman huddled in her white nightgown under a pecan tree in the side yard. "My brothers, Runt and Peanut, are still inside!" he yelled.

"What's your name, sir? Are you or your mother hurt?"

"My name's Butter Bean. No, we're not hurt. Just got licked by the flames, that's all."

Garrett ran back to Lieutenant Jones. "Sir, we got two men trapped inside. Names are Runt and Peanut. This here is Butter Bean." Garrett pointed over his shoulder. "His mother is safe. She's sitting under the tree. They're not hurt."

"Butter Bean, Peanut, and Runt. Gotta love Southern nicknames." Lieutenant Jones reached for his ax, handing one to Garrett as both raced behind the firemen towing the firehose through the front door.

Yellow, orange, white, and red flames climbed the walls in the living room. The lieutenant motioned Garrett to stay close behind him.

"Help! Help!" Two men shouted from over the upstairs banister. "Up here!" They waved their hands. The small spaces between the boards in the stairs glowed red.

The lieutenant directed the hose to be sprayed on the steps. The men doused the staircase, sweeping the water back and forth. He knew it was just a matter of moments before the entire stairwell was engulfed, trapping the brothers. He raced up the stairs and pushed the smaller of the two down the stairs first, followed by the slightly larger but shorter one. They were drenched in water on their rapid descent. Garrett escorted the men out the door, down the front steps, and into the awaiting open arms of their brother.

"The house is too far gone to be saved," the lieutenant shouted to his men. "Time to leave, now!"

Pieces of the ceiling collapsed behind them as they retreated to the front yard. Lieutenant Jones turned to see the entire foyer engulfed in flames. An unexpected explosion rocked the back of the house, sending timbers flying hundreds of feet in the air. The men scattered, running in every direction.

"Must be our tanks of gasoline in...." Peanut never felt the piece of wood impale him in the head. He was gone before he hit the ground.

Maw screamed and fainted. Runt froze.

"Jesus Christ!" Garrett shouted, ducking and holding on to his helmet.

Butter Bean ran back and scooped Peanut up in his arms. "No!" He buried his head in his brother's chest and sobbed.

Debris and ash fell from above as the firefighters secured the family in a safe place across the street. The lieutenant offered to carry Peanut, but Butter Bean insisted he be the one to lay him on the lawn and cover him with a blanket provided by one of the firefighters.

Grady's ambulance sped through the street, pulled up to the curb in front of the small crowd, and carried away Peanut. It was hours before Garrett and the other firefighters managed to contain and extinguish the fire.

Memories of Addie's parent's house fire flashed through Garrett's mind as he swept the fire hose over the smoldering remains of what was left of the family home. He wondered what Addie was doing. It had been so long since they last spoke. He heard from Dr. Springer that Addie was tough and smart. She was becoming an excellent nurse. Although their studies were unrelenting, Addie was beginning to see small improvements on her report cards. Too busy to call or write, Garrett promised himself he would make a surprise visit to her on his next day off. The scent of lilacs still lingered throughout his aunt's house, reminding him that she wasn't that far away. Garrett looked forward to seeing her radiant smile and golden strands of hair glowing in the sunlight.

The night sky faded, ushering in the dawn and hope of a new day.

14

Clip. Clip. Clip. Addie felt the cold stainless steel shears against her scalp. Healthy, auburn locks that once cascaded down her back now fell one by one to the floor in clumps, gathering by her feet onto a white sheet that covered the black and white tiled floor in the dormitory bathroom. Squinting, she tried to make out the dark, foggy images of the people outside the frosted glass window, who were walking away from the flickering red and orange flames in the backyard below. Irritated, Addie turned her attention toward her evolving image in the mirror. She stared deep into her green eyes in an effort to speak to her soul. She blinked back tears. Addie connected with her inner self and spoke silently. *I've shed so many tears. Some were at the hand of my father. Others were for his death and Maw's suicide. Many have been for Sissy, and my little brother, Ben, who left this world way too soon. My childhood memories of our family farm in Hope are fading and are being replaced by new ones here with my sisters at Sacred Heart. I've got so much to learn about diseases, medicine, life, love, this world, and myself.* Addie blotted a falling tear off her right cheek. *Who is this frightful and scared young lady looking back at me in the mirror?* She wiped away another tear. *I don't think I recognize myself anymore.*

Nurse Hartman slathered shaving cream on the tortoise shell-handled, boar hair shaving brush. "This is going to be cold."

Addie shivered as chills ran through her body and goose bumps popped up on her arms.

"I'm so sorry about that." Lena was apologetic as she brushed the velvety cream all over the top of Addie's head.

It smells astringent, like menthol. Addie plunged her right hand into her apron pockets. She felt around until her fingers touched the familiar round object. *Garrett's pebble.* She recalled the conversation they had over a year ago in the guest bedroom of the Darling house as she packed her grip to relocate to Atlanta to care for his widow aunt following the tragic death of her parents. Their conversation echoed in her ears. *'Do you remember when Miss McGowan read to us about how penguins picked out a special pebble to present to their mate?'* Addie continued to roll the stone between her fingers. *'I handpicked this particular stone because the specks of Fool's Gold radiate like your hair in the sunlight.'*

Well, my hair used to….

Lena picked up the straight razor from the white porcelain sink counter and scraped it over Addie's scalp, removing the shaving cream methodically row by row. Periodically, she'd stop, rinse it under the faucet, and dry it off on a white, linen towel before proceeding.

Addie pulled out the stone and glanced down to look at it.

"Nurse Engel, please hold still. I do have a sharp implement in my hand and I surely don't want to cut you." Lena manually tilted Addie's head to the desired position.

"Sorry about that." Sparks of gold caught her attention out of the periphery of her right eye. *He used to tease me about turning into a town mouse. We've been through so much together. He was my first love. He was my first kiss. I miss seeing him. I miss talking to him.* Addie bit her bottom lip. She reached up and slid her left index finger over her wet crimson lips. Addie's chest and neck flushed with red blotches. She closed her eyes, placed the rock back into her pocket, and then reopened them as tears continued to stream down her face. *What would Garrett think of me now? I don't think I could bear it if he saw me like this.*

"Buck up, Addie, dear. This is just one of many of life's lessons." Opal's white capped head popped into the reflection on the bathroom wall. "Just think how much time we will have on our hands now that we don't have to wash and style our hair… at least for a few months. You know, until it all starts to grow back. I've even read an ad about a special formulated tonic in *The Atlanta Journal* that promotes hair growth. We could give it a whirl. What do you think about that?" Opal started to slap Addie on the back and promptly retracted her arm as soon as she realized that Nurse Hartman still wielded a straight knife in her hand as she hovered over Addie's ear.

Addie's emotions and thoughts stirred while her outward presence remained still. "No, thank you. I've had my fair share of bad encounters with tonics. I've sworn them off." Memories flashed through her mind of the debacle with Lester and Doc Gray's tonic. The drama had spilled out all over the front pages of Atlanta newspapers for a few weeks last year. Eventually, the story evaporated and was replaced with good news. She read about women-led organizations that were popping up in

Georgia, charged with making a difference in this world. Addie racked her brain to remember the names of the new groups. *The Girl Scouts* and *The American Red Cross*. Unable to contain herself any longer, Addie squirmed in the hard-back chair.

"Nurse Engel, I know it must feel like your nerves are coming unglued, but you've got to remain still. You are learning that we are not always in control of what happens. It is how we choose to react to our circumstance that defines us." Lena bent Addie's ear forward and carefully shaved behind it. She peered up for a moment and looked at Opal. "You were so brave to go first, Nurse Alexander."

"As my granddaddy use to say to my father, 'Let's get to it, and just do it!'"

Lena stopped, held up the razor, and laughed. "Oh, now that is so true. You father loves to toss that saying out at all of our leadership meetings. He truly has a 'can do' attitude about all things in life. I think that's what drives him." Lena flipped the tip of the razor towards the mirror and watched a blob of shaving cream obliterate Addie's and Opal's reflections. Smudging it into the shape of a circle with the palm of her right hand, she dotted two eyes and drew a smile with her index finger. She stepped back and admired her finger painting. "There, now don't we all look like dream boats!" Lena placed her cotton-capped head next to Addie's and Opal's as they laughed together at the sight.

"I think I would have rather been bitten by the love bug," Addie joked.

Bertie burst into the bathroom. "This is not a joyous occasion. What are y'all laughing at?" Her lips pursed and her rosy, cherubic cheeks crimsoned as she put her hands on her wide hips. "I'm not at all amused." Unable to contain herself at the sight of Addie's new bald head, Bertie's plump, pink lips popped open to let out a roar of laughter. "Oh my goodness gracious!" She clapped her hands together. "We're going to look just heavenly at the hospital Christmas party in four months. I'm sure we'll have a line of suitors a mile long just waiting to dance with us!" Bertie scratched at her bare scalp where her black, uncontrollable curls used to be.

Lena applied a generous amount of lavender oil followed by warm paraffin on Addie's head and wrapped it in a white, cotton cloth, making a cap. "Well, hair grows approximately a half of an inch every month. We all should have at least two inches of hair by then, more or less!"

Addie stood up and stepped into Opal's and Bertie's outstretched arms. She buried her head in their shoulders. Tears mixed with laughter. "I'm such a mess. This is quite a humbling experience. I've never given much thought to losing all of my hair until now."

The girls patted each other reassuringly on the backs as they departed from bathroom to join the other young ladies, who sat in small groups of two and three on their beds in the dorm. All were fussing over each other and their coiffed cloth head coverings.

Lena joined them. She surveyed the room, taking pity on them. "Ladies, I know this is not an ideal situation. However, this is the hand that has been dealt to us, and we need to adapt and move forward. Now, tomorrow morning we will gather in the bathroom at six to remove the cloth coverings. I want you to wash your heads with soap and water. We will continue this treatment daily. Please put your clothes and linens in the special bin that Mr. and Mrs. Wu provided. They will continue to tend to all laundry matters and burn the linens daily until this problem is resolved. As our hair and the hair on the affected patients begins to grow back, we will use a tooth-comb soaked in vinegar to be sure everyone is free from infestation and infection."

"Ped-icu-losis cap-i-tus!" Lexie tripped over the words in her thick Scottish accent.

"Gesundheit! God bless you!" Belle chimed back.

Lena said sympathetically, "Good, Nurse Carmichael. I can see you have been reading ahead in your communicable disease textbook. While we haven't delved into this discussion yet, I guess there's no time like the present to get a bit of a tutorial on the matter at hand. There's nothing like life experience as the most respected teacher of all. Can someone tell me how head lice are spread?"

Deborah's left hand shot up. Her dark eyes caught Lena's attention.

"Yes, Nurse Owens?"

"Direct contact."

"Correct. Humans serve as the host for these little lice. The female louse lays eggs, called nits, and secures them onto a shaft of hair near the skin. In about six to nine days, the nymph hatches and goes through three growth phases before it reaches its adult status in a week's time. They immediately feed and thrive on human blood. Their life cycle is about thirty days." Lena noticed everyone scratching at their caps. She chuckled to herself, recalling when she had contracted lice in grade school as a child growing up in Macon. "This is the second time I have been bald in my lifetime. Please remember, our hair doesn't define who we are. Our actions, spirit, and determination will get us over this small hurdle." Mary Margaret raised her hand. Lena shifted her attention to the slight girl with freckles two beds away. "Yes, Nurse O'Malley?"

"I read in *The Atlanta Dispatch* that head lice are becoming a pandemic problem, especially amongst the soldiers overseas." Mary Margaret wrung her hands.

"Yes, with the war going on in Europe, I'm sure head lice will be the least of those military men's problems." Lena bowed her head and gazed outside the second story window. She watched a groundskeeper dressed in blue coveralls scoop out the leaves and debris floating in the fountain at the center of the boxwood and floral garden. Inhaling deeply, she took comfort in the smell of the lavender oil that had diffused throughout the room. "I fear that it won't be long before this country will need to intercede into this horrible war." She turned her back to the window that framed the late afternoon sky. "I can feel it in my gut." As she touched her abdominal area, she witnessed the young, innocent faces reflect her worry. Lena decided to change the subject. She picked up her gold watch pendant pinned to her apron. It showed 5:30 p.m. "Alright, it's time to focus on assignments and duties."

Addie raised her hand as she nudged Opal in the ribs. "Nurse Hartman? Nurse Alexander and I will volunteer to be the nit nurses."

Opal shot Addie a look. She whispered to Addie, "What in the heck are you thinking? Why would we want to do that?"

"Great! I'll update the schedule posted on the bulletin board outside of your dressing room. I appreciate your willingness to do so." Lena exited the dorm room.

Opal was still waiting for a response from Addie as she scratched at her cap.

Addie turned to her and smiled. "Come on. Where's that can-do spirit you are always talking about? At least it will give us a break from bed pans for a few days."

"You think of everything, don't you?"

Lena reentered the room with a brown, wooden clipboard in hand. She flipped through the pages and cleared her throat a few times. "Okay, listen up, ladies. This will be the adjusted ward assignments for the next four days. Our nit nurses for the wards will be Nurse Engel and Nurse Alexander." She spoke directly to Addie and Opal. "I expect you to screen the patients methodically, beginning with pediatrics and the nursery. I will inform Dr. Springer that you will be on his unit by zero seven-thirty." The other nurses sighed.

"He's so dreamy," Bertie mumbled under her breath, causing the girls around her to giggle.

"Did I say something humorous, Nurse Jones?"

"Why, no ma'am." Bertie shifted around uncomfortably and coughed into her hand.

Lena continued, "I want you to proceed with your nit nurse duties on the maternity ward, followed by the medical-surgical unit. The TB ward on the second floor will be last on your rounds." Lena paused for a moment. She loved the funny saying the nurses adopted for the tuberculosis ward located on 2-B of the hospital, but she would never admit it to them. "After you've assessed the patients, please report to me the names of those patients with positive findings. I will work with their ward physicians and assigned nurses to address their issues." Lena directed her next comment to a short statured student who had once had thick brown hair. "Nurse Esposito, you will report to the pediatric unit." Belle nodded. "Nurse O'Malley, I'm placing you in the nursery."

"Oh, yay! I love those little babies." Mary Margaret clasped her hands together and beamed.

"Nurse Jones, you are being assigned to work in maternity. Nurse Kessler and Nurse Fein, I will need you on the medical-surgical unit." Susan and Alice winked at each other. "Nurse Owens, I will need you to assist Dr. David Leventhal in the surgical suite."

Unaffected and apathetically, Deborah shrugged her shoulders. "What kinds of cases does he have?"

Lena flipped through the papers on the clipboard. "Tomorrow, he's got three cases; an umbilical hernia repair on a six-month old baby boy, followed by an excision of a testicular mass in a thirty-two-year-old man, and a possible amputation on a septic ring finger on an eighteen-year-old lad. Be mindful that anything may be brought in through the emergency room or that any patient's status could change on any of the units and require emergency intervention."

Deborah inhaled deeply through her nose and slowly exhaled.

Lena noticed. "Nurse Owens? Is there anything you'd like to say?"

"No," Deborah chirped.

Addie watched Deborah's exchange with Nurse Hartman. *I can't figure out for the life of me why Lena would have picked Deb-*

orah for a position in this nursing school. She must have turned on the charm and borrowed someone's personality when she interviewed with her. Or perhaps her daddy offered a generous donation to the hospital foundation. I don't think she has a compassionate bone in her body, not even if one was surgically implanted into her. I bet she was an arch-back baby! We're three months into nursing program and I still don't know her. Actually, come to think of it, no one really does. I wonder if I try what I will find out? Addie shrugged. *Time will tell.*

"Ladies, it's time for supper. Let's proceed downstairs, where Miss Maybelle has prepared a delectable meal for us tonight." Lena motioned her students to follow her down the back stairs.

"What's on the menu tonight?" Bertie inquired as she followed the procession down the staircase.

"Miss Maybelle said she has cooked up a batch of chicken mull for us."

Lexie turned back to Addie as she descended the stairs. "I love chicken mull. It's perfect and hearty."

Mary Margaret and Alice both grimaced.

"I'm still having a difficult time eating chicken, or any kind of meat for that matter, especially after our anatomy classes with Dr. Payne. Remind me, what's in this stew?" Alice questioned Addie.

Reflecting back on Maw's recipe, Addie recited the ingredients from memory. "It's made with a boiled chicken, milk or cream based broth, butter, and seasoned with salt and pepper. Sometimes Maw would add a pinch of parsley for color. To thicken the broth, she would add rice or crumbled soda crackers."

"Yummy! I'm starving," Mary Margaret added as she rounded the bottom stair and made her way into the kitchen.

The students filled their bowls and sat down at the kitchen table to eat their meal.

"It's an honor to have you eat with us tonight, Nurse Hartman," Belle commented.

"Thank you, Belle. Usually, about this time, I am riding my bicycle back to my apartment on Ponce." Lena took her place at the head of the table. "Tonight is a different night. I believe we all need each other for moral support right now. Please bow your heads for the blessing." Lena began coughing. Picking up her water glass, she sipped from it and regained her composure. "Heavenly Father, we thank you for the food that has been prepared for us. Keep our minds, bodies, and hearts strong so that we can do your work here on Earth. I ask that you bless each one of these girls at the table tonight." Lena touched the cotton covering on her head. "I know this is a test of our will and inner strength. We shall adapt and overcome so that we can humbly care for the wounded, the weak, and the infirmed. It is in your name we pray and say, Amen."

The students replied in unison, "Amen."

15

After completing their morning rounds, Addie and Opal stood in the hallway outside the TB ward and tallied their findings of affected patients with head lice.

"There are no infants, three children, no expectant mothers, two men in the medical-surgical unit, and four more TB patients with lice." Addie tapped her lead pencil on the paper as she rechecked her notes on the pine clipboard.

Opal peered over Addie's shoulder. "That's a total of nine more patients since the weekend. Wow! Nurse Hartman isn't going to be pleased with that news."

Addie winced. "I know. Those little buggers really know how to wreak havoc in a hospital. Come on, let's go to her office and give her our report."

Moira swung around as soon as she heard Addie's and Opal's footsteps on the travertine floor behind her. Her eyes opened wide, and her mouth followed as she let out a gasp. "Oh my heavens, girls! What happened to your hair?" Moira clutched at her dark, brown ringlets.

"I thought you of all people knew about the outbreak of lice in the hospital," Addie replied.

"What? Lice? No, I've not been privy to that bit of news until now. Are you kidding me? Lice?"

"Does it look like we're kidding?" Opal pointed to her wrapped head and then down the hall of 1-B to the nurse's desk where Susan sat, charting on her medical-surgical patients.

Moira observed the white cloth around Nurse Kessler's scalp, where straight strands of light brown hair were usually secured into a chignon. "Oh, my God! What has happened to y'all? Y'all had hair last week!"

Opal threw her hands up and smiled. "I know, right? Hair today and gone tomorrow."

"It's highly contagious. We have to shave the infected patients' heads and the Wus are burning the clothing and linens out back. We've just finished our rounds on the units." Opal approached the desk. "Would you like us to check you for lice, too?"

Moira retreated to the opposite side of the circular desk and threw her hands out in front of her in protest. "Oh, no! You can stay away from me. I'm sure my head is completely lice free. In fact, I just washed my hair last night and I didn't notice anything unusual." Moira stopped to think. "In fact, what should I be on the lookout for anyway?"

"Well, if your scalp starts itching or you notice tiny, white eggs about the size of a pin head at the base of your hair shafts, then you will need to seek out treatment from the medical team." Addie watched Moira disappear underneath the desk. She returned with a red, silk scarf that she retrieved from her pocketbook.

Moira secured the scarf around her head and tied the ends together in a knot under her chin. "There, that should protect me from those pesky cooties!"

"Yeah, good luck!" Addie joked as she and Opal continued past the desk, making their way to Lena's office.

Moira carefully watched Addie and Opal knock on Lena's office door and disappear inside before she picked up the phone receiver and asked the operator to ring *The Atlanta Dispatch*.

"Charlie Finch's office, please." A few moments passed before she heard the senior reporter's voice on the other line.

"Hey, this is Charlie Finch. With whom am I speaking to?"

Using their code phrase, Moira asked. "Is it sunny out?"

"Clear blue skies for as far as I can see. Whatcha' got for me today, Moira?"

"Well…." Like a periscope, Moira stood up, pivoted in a circle to make sure her conversation wasn't overheard, and then sat back down in her chair. "There is an outbreak of head lice here at Sacred Heart. I mean it's rampant throughout the hospital," she whispered into the black microphone, pressing the receiver close to her left ear.

"Do you have them?"

"Heavens, no! What kind of woman do you take me for? I keep myself very clean. I've even covered my head with a scarf. That will protect me…I think? It will, won't it?" Moira scratched at her head.

"I have no idea. I'm not a medical expert on this matter. I have heard that it is becoming a big problem in Europe amongst the soldiers. By the way, define 'rampant.'"

"It seems that all of the student nurses had to shave their

heads last night. Even the nursing superintendent, Nurse Hartman, is bald. Can you believe it? I saw the nurses rounding on the patient wards this morning to count the infested."

"Holy crap!" Charlie began scratching at the sparse hair on his head. "How many people are you talking about?"

Moira made up a figure and blurted it out. "Fifty."

"Fifty? Fifty people? Are you sure? Sacred Heart is only a 40-bed facility."

Moira fudged the numbers. "Yes, fifty people have lice. That figure includes the nursing students and medical staff, too."

"Jesus, Mary, and Joseph! That sounds like an epic problem over there."

"You know, I noticed they were having a lot of bon fires in the backyard lately. I just thought they were burning leaves. Little did I know, they were torching infested linens and clothing. By the way, you can't catch them by inhaling the smoke, can you?" Moira ploughed on. "God, I hope not. Well, that's why I called you. You always want to know the inside scoop and I'm delivering it to you on a silver platter."

"Moira, do me a favor and take a breath, would you?" Charlie thought for a moment. "Well, this is definitely newsworthy. I appreciate the heads-up on this one. I'm going to put in a call into the other hospitals like Grady Memorial, Wesley Memorial, St. Joes, Georgia Baptist, and the Piedmont Sanitarium to see what's going on inside their four walls, too. It might turn out to be a substantial article, fit for the front page."

"Stick with me, Charlie. You mark my words, I bet you'll have Sam Sloan's chair within the year if you keep uncovering big stories in Atlanta."

"Just as long as I can stay out ahead of *The Atlanta Constitution* and *The Atlanta Journal*." Charlie scribbled notes on his notepad in front of him. "Hey, thanks for the call and keep 'em coming."

"Will do, Charlie dear. I'm keeping a tally of all of the stories I've been giving you. Let's meet up at the end of the month so I can give you my bill."

"Sounds wonderful. We're long overdue for a visit. I'll be in touch, Miss Sunshine."

"Oh, Charlie, you know how I love that nickname. It's so fetching. It's so me!" The sound of fingers tapping the concierge desk startled Moira. She looked up to find Alan peering over his gold, wire spectacles down at her. She spoke into the receiver. "Yes, sir. Congratulations on the birth of your baby boy." She flushed and quickly set the receiver into the holder before placing the phone back down on the desk.

Alan studied her. He waited for her to speak first.

Flustered, Moira stammered. "G-Good morning, Mr. Waxman. It's a mighty fine day, isn't it?"

Alan gazed down at the phone and then back at Moira in her red scarf.

"Oh, that was Mr. Everett. He was checking in on his wife and baby boy." She reached up and touched her scarf. "Hey, by the way, did you hear about the outbreak of lice here in the hospital?"

Alan's face grew pale as he clutched at his leather binder and stepped away from the desk. "Is that why you are wearing your scarf indoors, Miss Goldberg?"

She adjusted it, making sure it covered her ears. "Yes. You haven't noticed the student nurses' shaved heads today?"

Alan glanced frantically around the hallways. He noticed now. He hated germs, diseases, contagions, and people. "I'm going back to the safe haven of my office, where I prefer to keep company with my accounting books, ledgers, and numbers." He wiped his hands four times on his trousers as he retreated down the hall and returned to his office. He closed the door and leaned up against the frosted glass. Relieved to be out of the main corridor, he opened up his leather notebook. Removing the pencil from its holder, he wrote an entry next to his daily notes from meetings and phone calls. *Moira Goldberg, Concierge. Lied about phone call. Overheard her saying how she loves being called 'Miss Sunshine.'* He flipped back through the pages to an entry labelled *Wednesday, May 20, 1914: the grand opening and ribbon cutting ceremony for Sacred Heart Hospital. He glanced at his notes. Moira Goldberg, Concierge. Overheard her on a phone call asking, "Is it sunny out? Of course not, it's very cloudy right now." She promptly hung up the receiver. Weather note: Cloudless, sunny day.*

MONDAY NIGHT, FIRST WARD

Mr. Chang flicked his pointy nails in the air while he and Jo reclined on a red velvet banquette. Jo, wearing only an embroidered black silk kimono, toked on a long, curvy hand-carved pipe made from ivory. It resembled a dragon. The heroin was taking its effects. Jo swore she saw the dragon move and breathe fire.

A group of three Chinese women entered the Red Room at Mr. Chang's Opium and Massage Emporium. The low-lit, over-ly-decorated room featured two soapstone 'foo dogs'—which guarded the hand-carved, pecan, arched doorway. Embroidered lotus flowers on silk set in black frames adorned the walls along-side wood panels with intricate carvings depicting the Great Wall, village scenes with cherry trees, and warriors embroiled in battle. Ceramic vases, a variety of jade dragons and Buddhas, gold platters, and burning candles and incense sat atop various end and coffee tables and ornate red and black cabinets. A large Oriental carpet covered the floor beneath a black chandelier. Ten dragon heads circled the top while their long torsos interwove below. Red tassels attached to round green jade medallions hung from the base of the fixture.

Jo carefully watched the women, noting their dainty, swaying gait. Her heart panged. She was the antithesis of a delicate wom-an. Diagnosed with hirsutism as a teenager, Jo tried everything to hide and minimize the male-patterned hair growth, deep voice, and pimples. Her six-foot two-inch frame and large hands and feet quickly became topics of whispers and hushed comments from on-lookers. Instead of fighting it, she chose to embrace her new image when she and her sister left their home in New York, traveling to places where she could be anyone. Choosing the ho-liest of professions, she blossomed.

Jo continued to admire the ladies dressed in red silk robes. They took short strides as they swayed towards the couch. "They have a funny kind of walk," she blurted out.

"They have Golden Lotus." Mr. Chang indicated in Chinese that he and Jo wanted their feet massaged. The Chinese women complied.

"What the heck does that even mean?"

The woman poured a concoction of warm milk and herbs into porcelain basins, setting them at Mr. Chang's and Jo's feet. Rose petals were added. Sitting on the edge of the couch, Mr. Chang and Jo immersed their feet.

"It is our custom to bind feet in order to give women a better life. Having foot in shape of lotus petal very erotic and desirable."

"Really? To whom?" Jo watched the women shuffle in their lotus shoes, silk slippers custom made to accommodate their re-shaped feet. "Their feet are so tiny."

"Small is good. Ideal size is three to four inches."

Jo hoisted up her size eleven feet in the air. "How is that even possible?" She tumbled backward. One of the Chinese woman grabbed her hand, pulled her forward, and helped her place her feet back in the perfumed liquid.

"Start with young girls in winter when feet cold and numb. Makes process less painful." Mr. Chang indicated with his hands and broken English that they soaked the feet in a mixture of an-imal blood, warm water, and herbs to soften the skin before for-cibly bending the toes under, breaking the second through fifth toes in the process. The foot was drawn straight down in align-ment with the leg; the manipulation caused the arch to break. The foot was bandaged in a figure-eight fashion, the cloth sewn closed to prevent the young girl from unwrapping the binding.

Jo grimaced and winced. "You've got to be kidding me."

Mr. Chang continued, "The feet are unbound, washed, and toenails cut. Sometime infection set in. That a good thing. Makes bones soft and toes fall off. Sometime glass or broken tile put between toes to make infected."

"How barbaric! Why on earth would you do that?"

"Sometime girls lose foot or die. We think it gives them a better life. Tradition goes back for centuries. Wealthy women don't need feet to work. Stay home. But, China just banned practice two years ago. Some people still do it."

Jo shook her head.

"What? You no like?"

"No. I see it as torture. It's a way for a man to dominate a woman and restrict her activities. It prevents her from interfering with his social and political life."

"Interesting." Mr. Chang cackled, bearing his pointy bottom teeth. He flipped his long braid.

"What? You don't like hearing my opinion?"

"Interesting, you don't see problem. You sell boys to me, but these women bind feet out of respect and to have a better life. Like you, you want to make money." Mr. Chang pointed his index finger at Jo. "You want a better life. With money, you a dragon, with no money, a worm."

"What kind of saying is that?"

"Ancient Chinese proverb. These women just like you. They want to be perfect and beautiful just like lotus flower that grows and blossoms out the mud and murky water."

"Isn't that what you are doing for the boys? Giving them a better life? Better than one on the streets?"

Mr. Chang wagged his finger. "Yes, my hope is to give all my little lotus flowers a chance to be reborn, blossom, and be perfect. When they stray or become disobedient, that's when the dragon strikes." Mr. Chang swiped at the air with his claws, making a hissing sound.

Jo recoiled. "I hope I never encounter the dragon."

"Well then, how about having an encounter with me?" Clyde said as he entered the Red Room.

Jo squealed in delight, her heart flipped, and emotions stirred. For the first time, she felt as beautiful as a lotus flower.

16

The Atlanta Dispatch office was buzzing. News was coming in over the wire that the Oceanic, a transatlantic ocean liner built for the White Star Line and the sister ship of the Titanic, just sank off the coast of Scotland yesterday.

Charlie puffed on his cigar while he spoke into the phone receiver. "I understand that the ship was commissioned, serving in the Royal Navy. How did this converted armed cruiser run aground off the coast of the Shetland Islands? Uh-huh. You don't say. Calm waters, clear skies. Uh—huh. What do you mean you don't want me to run the story? People have the right to know the truth." Charlie pulled out his cigar and snuffed the end in the ashtray. "Morale? Embarrassing? I would agree with you that it's embarrassing to have a naval ship run off course and wreck on a reef."

There was a knock on the door.

Charlie covered the mouth piece. "Come in."

Scout entered the room, shut the door behind him, and took a seat in the empty chair in front of Charlie's desk.

"Look, I know is a complete mess over there. You've got Germany declaring war on everyone. Great Britain, Japan, and others declaring war on Germany, I'm sure it's just a matter of time before the United States steps into the center ring of that circus. Just let me go to press with something. Uh-huh. Fine, Sam." Charlie slammed the phone down on the desk before hanging it up.

Scout squirmed in his chair. "Do you want me to come back another time?"

"No," Charlie growled. "My editor is such a dick. We've got a great lead thrown in our laps with the sinking of a well-known ocean liner, but the owners of the paper are being pressured to not run the story by the President. It has something to do with maintaining diplomatic relations. Blah, blah, blah."

"Why?"

Charlie pulled on his suit lapels, sat up straight in his chair, and mimicked a British accent. "The Royal Navy wants to keep a stiff upper lip about the incident and keep it hush-hush. It's embarrassing for them to admit that one of their ships wrecked on its own. There's no great combat story to accompany it." Charlie slouched back down.

Amused, Scout nodded his head. "Oh! I get it. It's all about politics!"

"Once politicians get in the middle of real news, it has the tendency of becoming a three-ring circus. I love the clowns, just not the circus!"

Scout laughed and slapped his knee. "That's funny, Charlie."

"Twain had a saying about that. Something about not letting the facts get in the way of a good story?" Charlie shuffled a pile of papers in front of him. "So, what do you have for me? Any more lice outbreaks at the other hospitals? Murdered kids? Ripper news?"

"Seems that the hospitals are on top of the lice, no more updates about the murdered twins, and the APD doesn't have any leads about the Ripper. However, I'm hearing reports that the streets in towns around the city are piled up with bales of cotton. Something about the war in Europe is affecting the markets here. Is that true?"

"Kid, it's true. The markets overseas and major cotton exchanges across the country are closed. It's taking a catastrophic toll. Cotton prices are falling and the South's economic wheels are grinding to a halt. *The Atlanta Journal* published an editorial a few days ago encouraging a movement called 'Buy a Bale of Cotton.' They plan to have everyone who can purchase a bale store it in their garage, front porch, or wherever they can to help these poor bankrupt farmers. I also read where they are asking the farmers to grow more food crops next year instead of cotton. I hope their plan works."

"I hope it does, too."

"And, I hope Atlanta can cough up something interesting for me before my five o'clock deadline."

"I'm sure you will find something to write about, Charlie. You always do."

Charlie shook his head, shooed Scout out of the room, and relit his cigar.

His phone rang. He picked up the receiver. "This is Charlie Finch." Charlie grinned, picked up his pencil, and started taking notes.

WEDNESDAY AFTERNOON, SIXTH WARD

Addie sat alone on a bench in the garden, relishing her thirty minute break. She watched three large flatbed trucks filled with bales of cotton drive down the back road behind the hospital toward the garage. The fountain gurgled and bubbled while the geraniums nearby waved in the warm breeze. The gardens were a beautiful escape from her hectic morning working in the emergency room. She bowed her head to pray for a boy found at the city dump with third-degree leg burns. While rummaging through the garbage piles, he fell through to the incinerated refuse smoldering below the fresh pile. According to her pediatric nursing textbook, burns in children covering over one-third of the body could result in death because they were susceptible to infection, shock, and fluid instability, along with a host of other concerns.

Dr. Springer and Dr. Williams discussed two burn treatment options. Paraffin dressings, which consisted of spraying on a thin layer of wax, or a proprietary substance called ambrine, and wrapping the affected areas with fine cotton batting and bandages; or picric acid-soaked gauze bandaging. The concern for sepsis was overwhelming; the antiseptic, picric acid dressings were used. Because the boy slipped in and out of consciousness, they weren't able to learn his name to notify family. They would have to give him time to rest. *Dear God, please send your angels to be with this boy. Help us find his family. Please give the doctors and nurses the strength and courage to do what is best for him. I ask that you ease his pain and suffering. In your name I pray. Amen.*

"Boo!" a male voice called out as someone tapped her on the left shoulder.

Addie shrieked, jumped up, and turned around to see her life-long childhood friend. "Garrett!" She threw her arms around his neck.

He drew her close. She didn't smell familiar. The aroma of lavender filled his senses, not lilacs. He noticed her head covering. "What has happened to you? What happened to your hair?"

Embarrassed, Addie turned away. "Oh, Garrett. I hate that you are seeing me like this." She touched her cap.

"Addie, it's just me." Garrett motioned for her to sit beside him on the bench. The familiar hands beckoned, the distal part of his right index finger missing.

Addie knew him so well and how he sustained every scratch, scar, and injury over the years. Garrett, at the age of thirteen, caught his finger in the sharp edge of a brass buckle on the bridle of a spooked mule. Farm life was always taking its share of flesh and blood.

"Lice. Lice happened to me, some of my nursing colleagues, and even to some of the patients."

"I've been reading in the papers how it's running rampant through the soldier's camps overseas. Randall has been giving me updates about you, but he failed to mention this."

"I made him promise not to tell you. I thought you might think less of me."

"How could I think any less of you? You are more to me than just your looks and your hair. You should know that by now, Addie." Garrett paused, and then laughed. "Nicknames are big at the firehouse. I could always call you *Thumb*." Garrett held up the back of his thumb and rubbed the top of it with his fingers.

"That's not funny." Addie tried to suppress her laughter and punched him in the upper arm. "So, what's your nickname?"

Garrett extended his right index finger in the air. "Lieutenant Jones dubbed me *Plug*. He said since I can't pick anymore with this finger, it can only be used for a plug." He jammed his finger into the hole in his left fist, between the index finger and thumb.

Addie smacked his hands down. "Really, Garrett?" She shook her head, eager to switch the topic. "What brings you here, Plug?"

"You. I promised myself that I would come and visit you on my next day off. I asked Randall to look at your schedule for me and he called to tell me when your break was today. Voilà! Here I am."

Addie reached out to touch his face. *No boyfriends allowed.* The clause in her nursing contract popped into her head like a warning bell, reminding her that fraternizing was not permitted. The penalty was termination. She withdrew her hand.

"Randall has been keeping me updated about you, too. I know you've been so busy. He tells me you have been through some rough periods, especially after bearing witness to such horrible tragedies. I know what it's like." She wrung her hands, blotches popping up on her neck and chest.

Garrett noticed but refrained from reaching out to comfort her, mindful that a physician was standing nearby.

"Oh, I've got a question for you. Randall asked me about a secret room in the basement of your aunt's house."

"You mean your house. It's your home now, Addie."

"I know. I miss her."

"I do to."

"Has Randall asked you about it yet?"

"No, he hasn't. We've been on opposite schedules these past months." Garrett peered over his shoulders. He lowered his voice. "I've been meaning to tell you about that room. No better time than the present."

Addie glanced at her watch. *I have twenty more minutes to be in his company.*

"I know you don't have much time. I have a few secrets to confess to you about my family. My uncle and aunt used that room to hide run-away slaves. Have you ever heard of the Underground Railroad?"

"Of course. I heard rumors when we were young kids in Hope that there were a few safe houses in our community. Maw used to tell me that they hung quilts on the laundry line outside the farms depicting specific landmarks or used lamps in the windows to direct the slaves to the next location."

"That's true. Doc Gray felt compelled to help and excavated that room himself. He even made the floor of sand to prevent their footsteps from betraying their location under his house. My uncle wanted to help provide them safe passage on their journey up to the Hannah House in Indianapolis, ultimately making their way across the border to Canada. I heard him tell heroic and horrific tales, including an overturned lantern causing a handful of slaves to perish in their secret hide-away at the Hannah House. That was such a terrible tragedy. My uncle and aunt put themselves at such risk, but they knew their mission was important to humanity."

Addie took a moment to process the information. "Probably best not to broach the subject with Randall. If he asks again, just tell him it was used as a tornado shelter."

"That seems to be a reasonable explanation. I was going to say something about it being used as a root cellar. However, I like your explanation much better." He elbowed her in the ribs.

Addie saw Randall waving at her from the back porch landing. "I've got to go. It seems that Dr. Springer needs me for something." She looked at the time. "And, my break is over." She stood up. "I can't thank you enough for surprising me today. Your visit absolutely made my day." She beamed. "Even if I don't look my best." She touched her head dressing.

"You'll always be beautiful to me, Addie." Garrett stood and waved back at Randall.

"Duty calls."

"Yes, it does." Garrett watched Addie scurry towards the back entrance of Sacred Heart. His stomach fluttered. The thought of Addie being in nursing school until Spring 1917 pained his heart. A poem written by English poet Alexander Pope in the early 1700s sprang to mind.

Hope springs eternal in the human breast;
Man never is, but always to be blessed:
The soul, uneasy and confined from home,
Rests and expatiates in a life to come.

Garrett remembered finding the book, *An Essay on Man*, on his late uncle's bookshelf. Pope wrote that no matter how imperfect and chaotic the universe appeared to be, its functions were in accordance with the natural order and laws that represent the perfect work of God. Everything was as it should be, at this moment, at this time. He took comfort in knowing that this was God's will.

17

"Here, let me show you how to wrap these bandages properly. Don't be afraid. You're not going to hurt him. I've given him a sedative." Randall placed his hands around Addie's hands to guide her as she wound the loose-fitting dressing around the patient's right thigh.

Addie's neck and chest flushed. Amorous emotions arose. *Oh my stars! His hands are touching my hands! It's making me quiver inside. He is so refined, smart, gentile, caring, and compassionate. He's not Garrett. I dare not look him in the eye. I'm afraid he'll see what I'm feeling.* She tried to quell her feelings. *Focus on the patient, Addie. This poor little boy needs your help and care. Focus!*

Dr. Springer continued the bedside lecture. "These daily dressing changes, although extremely painful, are important. We've got to be vigilant about removing the necrotic tissue. The formation of cicatrices, or scar tissue, must be guarded against."

"Shall we continue to give him intravenous fluids via the gravity method?" Addie reached for the graduated glass flask with red rubber tubing that lay on the bedside tray.

"Yes, please make sure the temperature of the saline solution is 100 degrees Fahrenheit."

"Yes, Doctor." Addie reached for the glass thermometer.

There was a knock on the pediatric ward room door.

"Come in." Dr. Springer stepped out from behind the white cotton-cloth screen to greet the visitor.

"Dr. Springer?" A policeman, carrying his hat under his arm, entered. He glanced around the ward at the small children lying in beds. He lowered his voice to a whisper. "My name is Detective McGee. I work at the APD and am running the investigation for a missing child. I am looking for a boy by the name of Stuart Harvey. He is fourteen years old. Have you encountered anyone by that name lately?"

"The name doesn't ring a bell. Have you checked with the emergency department? They have all kinds of kids that flow through that place. Better yet, check with Moira Goldberg, our concierge. She maintains our patient admission and discharge logs."

"I did and they directed me to you."

"Well, I just have a Johnny Doe. He is about that age." Randall pointed at the screen. "What is Stuart's description?"

McGee pulled out his notebook. "Dark brown hair, brown eyes, and his mother said he has a scar over his right knee. He gashed it while he was climbing over a fence a few years ago."

Randall's eyes widened. "Sir, I need for you to come with me. But, first, are you okay with seeing a child in a medically fragile condition?"

"Doctor, I'm sure it pales in comparison to what I've encountered over the years working the streets of Atlanta."

"You're right. I never want to assume. Between the nurses, doctors, firefighters, and police officers, we tend to see tragic events."

"I call those the 'unmentionables'."

"Exactly." Randall removed the screen that shielded the boy from McGee's view.

McGee referred back to his notes, then back to the child in the bed. "I believe that's him."

"Addie, this is…" Randall looked at the brass name plate on McGee's suit lapel. "Detective McGee. He is investigating a missing child case."

"How do you do, sir?" Addie refrained from shaking his hand. She was holding the glass vessel and tubing that infused liquids into the boy's vein in the antecubital space in his right arm.

McGee. McGee. Why does that name sound so familiar? "Have we met before?"

"Not to my knowledge, Miss."

Addie couldn't place the name. "What is it you do exactly at the APD?"

"I'm in charge of the missing and murdered children cases." McGee chose not to talk about the discovery of the Farmer twins. As a result of his last encounter with Father Preti, Ida, and her buxom bosoms, he was working closely with his Chief to launch an undercover investigation into Holy Cross Orphans' Asylum.

"Oh, my stars! How could I have forgotten? I have a message for you. It was given to me by a young boy." Addie fidgeted. "Dr. Springer I need for you to get another nurse to hold this for me. I need to get something from my dorm locker. I'll be back in a jiffy. Please excuse me."

Dr. Springer motioned Bertie over to take Addie's place. Addie ran down the back stairs, through the Greene tunnel, and up to the second floor of the dorm dressing room. She retrieved the folded newspaper note located on the top shelf of her locker and sprinted back to the unit.

Winded and panting, Addie handed the note to McGee. "This was meant for you. I forgot all about it. I'm so sorry. I promised Billy I'd get this to you. I didn't know what to do with it and was going to give it to my nursing superintendent. I stashed it away on the top shelf of my locker and completely forgot about it. Please accept my humblest apologies."

McGee unfolded the note. *Landon and Logan Farmer—not adopted by the Martins. David Connley—not adopted by the Davises.* "Where did you get this?"

Addie stuttered, realizing Billy gave it to her in confidence. "Fiddlesticks! One of our patients, Billy Swanson, was being treated for a broken arm. He stays at a local orphanage in the First Ward. Father Preti brought him in to get his cast off. Billy stuck this note in my pocket while Dr. Springer stepped out of the treatment room. He said that something fishy was going on at the orphanage. He specifically asked me to give this to you." Tears streamed down her face and hives erupted around her neck and chest. "Oh, goodness! I'm so sorry. Please excuse me." Addie ran out of the room and down the hall. Unable to catch her breath, she thought she was going to faint. She clung on to the rim of Moira's desk before darting out the back doors.

Detective McGee and Dr. Springer pursued her. Moira stood up from her chair.

"Which way did she go?" Dr. Springer asked Moira. She pointed towards the back doors.

"Oh, this ought to be good. One of Sacred Heart's nursing students being chased by an APD policeman and a pediatrician," Moira muttered to herself. She continued to observe the three-way exchange on the back porch, unable to make out the conversation behind the closed doors.

"Addie, stop running. You didn't do anything wrong." McGee grabbed the back of her arm before she could take off down the back stairs towards the garden.

Addie nearly collapsed. Dr. Springer and McGee guided her to have a seat on the stairs. They sat beside her.

McGee let Addie catch her breath before continuing. "Look, I need your help. Actually, I need to enlist the both of you. I've got an investigation going on and based on this note, I need to talk to Billy in a safe environment. Someplace that won't draw any attention to him. I can't talk with him at the mill where he works now, nor can I speak with him at the orphanage. I can't go into the details. I want you to call the orphanage and schedule a follow up appointment for his broken arm here. Tell them whatever you need to in order to get them to bring Billy here. Can you help me?" He pleaded, "Will you help me?"

Randall thought for a moment. "You need to run your plan by my medical director and the founder of the hospital. You're going to need their approval, first."

McGee nodded. "I understand. All I want is to have a safe place to talk to this boy. Somewhere that is away from the prying eyes and ears of Father Preti and his sister. The boy's welfare may be at stake."

Addie stiffened. "Oh my stars!" She buried her head in her hands and sobbed. "What have I done?"

Randall offered to comfort her, but McGee stepped in. "Addie, please stop crying and listen. I didn't mean to make it sound so dire," he reassured her, swallowing the lie. He pulled out a handkerchief and handed it to Addie. "I will need your full cooperation in order to pull this off. Do you understand me? Will you help me?"

Addie blotted her tears. She looked at Dr. Springer before answering. He nodded his head. "Yes, sir."

"Good." McGee stood up and brushed off the back of his pants with his hat. "Please point me in the direction of your administrative offices."

Randall directed him to speak with Moira at the concierge desk. "Thank you both for your time. And, more importantly, it seems that we may have an identity for your Johnny Doe. I'll be in touch."

Randall watched McGee step back inside the hospital before he erupted. "Addie, why didn't you tell me about Billy and his note?"

Addie shook her head. "I don't know. I thought I could take care of it myself and give it to Nurse Hartman."

"You know that Detective McGee is going to have a nice chat with Dr. Williams and Edward. We're both going to be put in the hot seat for his one." Randall fumed. "You could be jeopardizing our careers with this oversight. Did you ever think about that?"

"It was an honest mistake. I completely forgot." Addie stammered, "I almost had the note laundered with my uniform. With all of my classroom and bedside lessons, my head is about to burst. I'm forgetting the simplest of things."

Randall looked up to find Moira's face pressed to the glass of the back door. "God, that woman is such a busybody." He made a face at her. She quickly disappeared.

"I'm truly sorry, Dr. Springer."

Resigned, Randall shrugged his shoulders. "This occurrence is out of my hands, Addie. It will be up to Nurse Hartman to decide what the repercussions will be for neglecting to pass along a crucial piece of evidence to a police officer." A moment of silence passed. "Oh hell, Addie! It could always be worse."

Addie blew her nose. "How can things get much worse?"

"Well, at least you didn't accidently give the wrong medication to a patient and kill them."

"How can you joke about something like that at a time like this?"

"It's called perspective." Randall helped Addie stand up. "And, I wasn't joking around." He stammered before confessing, "That… that actually happened to me in medical school. Like you, I got so caught up in my studies and hospital work that I got careless. I actually gave a patient a medication that was contraindicated for his condition. As a result, he passed away from complications and side effects of the drug." He hung his head. "It haunts me to this day." He picked his head back up to look into her green eyes. "Errare humanum est. To err is human. I believe that is what my medical professor said to me. It taught me an invaluable lesson about how not to gloss over details and to stay focused and vigilant when caring for my patients. This is one of many of life's lessons. What you choose to do about it and how you chose to react and respond to your punishment is completely up to you."

Addie couldn't bear looking at him any longer. She lowered her eyes.

He reached out and lifted her chin; their eyes met. He knew her life's dreams hung on a heart-shaped collage on the back of her bedroom door. "Life hasn't been easy for you. Learn to grow from these challenges. It will make you stronger and you'll be a better nurse for it. Remember, diamonds are created from enduring high pressure and heat. And, in order to get a pearl, you need a little grit."

Addie dried her tears. "I get it. I need to buck up and take responsibility for my actions. Life is full of many tests, isn't it?" *Dear God, I put my fate in your hands.*

"Yes, it is." Randall reached out to Addie. "Come, we've got to get back to our patient. When he awakes from the sedative, I'll try talking to him and calling him by the name of 'Stuart'. Will you help me?"

"Yes, Doctor. I will help you." Addie shoved the handkerchief in her apron pocket and took his hand. *P.S. God? I hope I don't get expelled from school. It's all I have left in this world. It's all I am.*

FRIDAY NIGHT, FIRST WARD

An impatient, portly man with greasy brown hair knocked on a black door in the alley. Thunder rumbled overhead and raindrops speckled the shoulders of his brown, windowpane jacket. The first three raps were slow and steady. *Knock. Knock. Knock.* The last two were rapid fire. *Knock. Knock.* The door opened. He was greeted by Gang and escorted down a long and narrow dark hallway. The men stopped in front of another heavy wooden door. Two large gold dragons were painted on the front. A tiny slot within the door slid open. Gang spoke four words in Chinese. The door slid shut and the main door opened. Gang motioned for the gentleman to walk inside. The man nodded and bowed. He proceeded into the next room, which was filled with women of all shapes and sizes. He watched as they lounged on a variety of couches scattered along the periphery. Some called out to him and undulated to attract his attention while others were fondling and kissing their clients, male and female. Crushed red velvet wallpaper covered in images of lotus flowers was affixed to the walls. Incense burned, filling the room with the fragrance of sandalwood and roses. The door shut and locked behind him.

A middle-aged Chinese woman wearing a yellow silk dragon gown emerged from the group, took him by the arm, and walked him toward the stairs. Her jet black hair was piled high into a tiny bun on top of her head. Two gold hair sticks with yellow tassels on the ends were inserted in a crisscross fashion in the top knot. She knew this room did not contain anything that would interest him. "Any special requests tonight?"

The gentleman ran his fingers along the teeth of the black, ornately carved dragon's head at the end of the banister. The scaled body ran the entire length of the staircase to the second floor. "Will you deliver some lotus flowers to my room?" She knew he liked young boys and laughed to herself at the use of the code word. "Two."

"Yes, sir. They will be delivered to your room in fifteen minutes. Is there anything else I can do for you?"

"No. That will be all. Thank you." He ascended the stairs.

18

"Good morning, everyone." Edward walked into the Sacred Heart conference room and took his seat at the head of the table. He watched the others take their seats. "We've got a lot to cover in our leadership meeting this morning. So, let's get to it." He opened his leather notebook. "But first, I feel compelled to kick off the discussion." Edward looked at Dr. Williams. "I know you typically go first, and you have another busy surgical schedule today. However, I need to talk with y'all about a few things, and I need everyone's approval before moving forward."

"I hope it won't take long," Dr. Williams grumbled under his breath.

"Y'all are aware that it has been my life's dream and passion to build this hospital. I did so with a long-term vision in mind. Growing up in the Catholic Church, I embraced all of the lessons I learned, that Jesus' physical heart represented his divine love for all humanity. In concert with those teachings, I hope that Atlanta will dissolve the segregation ordinances. I also am keenly aware that we will never bear witness to it in our lifetime. Our non-disclosure pact binds us and passes along the Alexander Hall's secret to the next generation, planning for the day when the bricks will be removed from the future colored hospital, revealing the travertine tile underneath. The walls will also come down around the property and between the colored and white nursing schools so that all of the travertine-built facilities will merge into one entity, allowing the medical facility to care for all Georgians as one Sacred Heart." Emotions welled. Edward paused to clear his throat. "While the architectural plans and accounting ledgers fleshed out the details so nicely on paper, the unpredictable behaviors of people, pathogens, and politics needed to be factored in. As a result, I knew our course was set for uncharted territory."

"Isn't that the truth?" Clyde snickered.

Edward's gut churned. Ignoring Clyde, he continued, "We have experienced unforeseen accidents and lost a fine nurse in the process."

"God rest her soul." Nurse Hartman made the sign of the cross on her chest.

"Our poor nursing students, my dear daughter, Opal, Nurse Hartman, and Nurse Scott, along with countless others have had to shave their heads because of the lice epidemic." Edward paused and rubbed his forehead.

Oliver shuddered and scratched his bald head.

"Edward, speaking of epidemics, please remind me to give an update about the pellagra problem," Dr. Williams interjected.

"Will do." Edward picked up his fountain pen and jotted *pellagra* on his notepad. He pointed his pen at his leadership team. "On Friday afternoon, I was briefed by Detective McGee at the APD about an incident that occurred in our hospital."

"Isn't he the detective you spoke of in our meeting on…." Alan flipped through his notes. "It was on July sixth. He's the one in charge of the missing and murdered children investigation."

"Yes, that's correct. Evidently one of our pediatric patients who resides in a local orphanage passed a note to one of our nursing students when he was here getting his cast removed. That note needed to be brought to the attention of Detective McGee. However, the nurse forgot about the note and failed to let her supervisors know of its existence. It wasn't until the officer came to our hospital in search of another missing child did the topic of the note surface." Edward paused, setting his pen back on the table. "Nurse Hartman and I had a long conversation with this student and Dr. Springer since he was the attending physician for this child. We unanimously concluded it was an honest oversight on her part. She is truly sorry about it."

Clyde interrupted. "I think you should expel her."

"Actually, that's not your call to make, Clyde. May I continue?"

"Yes, sir." Clyde sat back in his chair and folded his arms across his chest.

"Detective McGee needs our help, the help of our student nurse, and Dr. Springer in an undercover investigation."

"What is he investigating?" Clyde squirmed in his seat. "Who is he investigating?"

Edward's face turned crimson. "Jesus, Mary, and Joseph! Can I finish talking without being interrupted?"

"Yes, sir. Sorry, Edward." He skimmed his slicked-back black hair in an attempt to appear cool and composed.

"While the officer debriefed me about the case, I swore to

keep the details confidential." Edward eyed his leaders. "I wanted to lay all of the cards out on the table so I can have your understanding and approval as we move forward to assist the APD." All heads nodded. "Good. As for the consequences of the student's actions, Nurse Hartman and I have agreed that her poor judgement will be reflected on her report card. We already have two nurses on probation because they may lack the skill set and fortitude required for the job. We have lost another one to electrocution. Do we really want to lose a good nurse because of one act of forgetfulness? Haven't we all forgotten to do something at one time or another because we've been overwhelmed or been pulled in a myriad of directions?"

"I, for one, have forgotten...." Clyde stopped, realizing it was a rhetorical question, not an invitation for confession.

Edward's gut ached and rumbled. He reached inside his green suit jacket pocket and retrieved a tiny white pill. He discretely popped it in his mouth, chewed, and swallowed it. "Now that I have debriefed you on this important matter, I will let you know when the investigation concludes. I will not be sharing any details until that time. The detective is afraid that if anything about this case is leaked, it could put lives at risk. Actually, children's lives may be at risk." Edward looked at Dr. Williams. "Please, Dr. Williams, give us your updates to include the update about the pellagra epidemic."

"Thank you, Edward." Dr. Williams referred to his notes. "In the month of August, we had eighty-one unique surgical cases, eighty-nine surgical procedures, and thirteen deaths."

Alan wrote on his ledger pad. "Why were the deaths so high last month?"

"The pellagra epidemic is running rampant throughout the South."

"What is pellagra?" Alan patted his leg four times.

"It's a condition commonly seen in mill workers, poor farming families, orphans, prisoners, and those locked away in asylums. We first started seeing cases emerge when I was in private practice. Five years ago, a colleague and I attended the international pellagra conference in Columbia, South Carolina. Since then, we have been corresponding about his research efforts at the Spartanburg Pellagra Hospital, which was established to help find the root cause and cure. There were over a thousand deaths in our state and over thirteen hundred in South Carolina last year. With a mortality rate of almost forty percent, Georgians are at high risk for acquiring this condition. In fact, many of our adult patients have had to be transferred to the local mental asylums because the individuals are so affected by the disease."

Edward raised his eyebrows. "Two questions for you. First, how do these patients present to us at the hospital? And second, how are you managing these patients?"

"We don't think it's contagious in nature."

"Well, that's a huge relief." Alan wrung his hands four times.

"Patients typically present with the three Ds—diarrhea, dementia, and dermatitis in the form of scaly skin and sores. Their mucosal linings tend to be inflamed. They can be easily agitated, and sensitive to light. Males present with sores on their scrotal areas."

Alan crossed his legs.

"Regarding the milder cases, I'm working with Nurse Hartman, Mr. Maddox, and Maybelle to manage their illness. There are a lot of theories as to the cause that range from toxic corn to a certain insect or to bad water. The doctors in Spartanburg are following a hunch that pellagra is caused by a poor diet, but only through objective analysis and experiments can they prove their theory. I am relying on the nurses to obtain a thorough dietary history. If we find that the affected patient's diet is heavy in corn, rice, starchy vegetables, grits, biscuits, cabbage, or mash, then we are providing them with a balanced meal to include proteins, dairy, and legumes. We have even adopted the research center's slogan to help us teach those patients about how to lessen their chances of acquiring the dreadful disease."

"What's the slogan?" Alan uncrossed and crossed his legs again.

"'Own a cow'. The officials in Spartanburg feel that if the individual can purchase and own a cow, they can use the milk produced by that cow to stay healthy."

Clyde howled in laughter. "Why not own a chicken, or how about a pig? We're coming up on hog killing season. Every bit of that animal is edible from snout to tail."

Dr. Williams couldn't tell if Clyde was joking or not. "Well, for one thing, you can't milk a chicken or a pig."

Lena covered her mouth to prevent herself from laughing out loud.

Dr. Williams pressed on. "Once you've slaughtered the animal, then what? We're talking about people who, for whatever reason, don't have access to meats and other forms of food. Why do you think the prisons and mental institutions feed that crap to the inmates and patients?"

"The cereal-based diet is cheap, Clyde," Shelby added.

Sensing the group was sharpening their claws and was about ready to pounce on Clyde, Edward was eager to move the discussion along. He held up his hand. "Listen, Dr. Williams. I know your time is precious and we've got a few more items to discuss. Why don't you reach out to Sam Sloan, the editor at *The Atlanta Dispatch*, and have one of his reporters write a feature article that profiles the work y'all are doing to combat this problem, quote your friend's research, and promote that slogan of theirs. More importantly, we could use some good exposure to help us in our upcoming holiday fundraising. When we have to go to potential donors and solicit for additional funds in the future, those articles are helpful to have on hand."

"Great idea, Edward. I'll make some time in my schedule this afternoon to talk with Sam." Dr. Williams collected his belongings and left the room.

"Milk a chicken or a pig." Shelby was tickled by the image. He began to giggle. He tried to contain his laughter, but the more he tried to suppress it, the more he realized it was hopeless.

A contagious laughter broke out around the table. Edward let go too. He roared and slammed his hand up and down on the table until tears ran down his cheeks. He couldn't recall laughing this hard in ages. It had been a stressful few months. His heart filled with joy. He was proud of all that his team had accomplished to date, and took comfort in knowing that Opal was happy, pursuing a career that she loved, and that he had built the hospital of his dreams. That's all he had ever wanted.

MONDAY AFTERNOON, FOURTH WARD

Addie's happiness—that's all Garrett ever wanted now. Gazing out of the second story window of the firehouse, he watched the afternoon autumn breeze blow crimson, amber, and umber-colored leaves from the trees as he sat at a desk and began to pen a letter to Addie. He hated seeing her upset about the loss of her hair and worried about her appearance during his recent visit. That's not what mattered to him. She was all that mattered to him—her happiness and her safety. *Ding! Ding! Ding! Ding!* The dispatcher summoned the firefighters after receiving the notice via telegraph from a fire alarm box. Garrett dropped the pen, ran to the brass pole, and slid down to the first floor. He donned his gear and quickly boarded the firetruck as it pulled out of the station.

Moments after the truck disappeared, the dispatcher picked up the telephone. "Operator, please connect me to Sacred Heart's ambulance service. Thank you."

"Sacred Heart ambulance service. This is Brice. How can we help ya?"

"Brice, it's Matt down at fire house number six. We had a call come over the wire a few minutes ago at 36 Magruder Street, a block from the Inman Park area. They'll need your services. A few people are suffering from burns and smoke inhalation."

"Thanks for the 'eads up, dear man. We'll be there in a jiffy before Grady can get their units on the scene. Hey, I gotta good hose dragger joke for ya. A fireman 'ad two sons. What did he name 'em?"

"I have no idea."

"HoseA and HoseB." Laughter crackled through the receiver as Brice hung up the phone.

As the firetruck pulled up in front of the house, light white smoke rolled out of the open front door and two open front room windows. About a dozen people, all dressed in their Sunday-best attire, were huddled together, consoling each other on the front lawn.

"Well, that's a good sign, fellas." Lieutenant Jones grabbed his ax.

"What do you mean by that?" Garrett secured his helmet as he watched a few of the firemen enter the house with a hose. Another darted off to tend to the burns on an elderly man's palms. Garrett observed that the gentleman's white shirt and cuffs were singed.

"It's important to read and assess the smoke, Plug. It can quickly tell you about the type of fire you have on your hands. Look at the volume, velocity, density, and color. Smoke follows the path of least resistance. To put it simply, find the fastest smoke emitting from the smallest opening—typically, that is where the fire is. What do you see here?" The lieutenant paused and waited for Garrett's reply.

"Slow, rolling, light white smoke from both the entryway and first floor windows."

"Good, Plug. White smoke indicates there is a lot of moisture. When you see brown or tan smoke, it tends to be a wood fire."

Garrett tried to remember the color of the Engel's house fire. He couldn't recall.

"Thick, turbulent smoke is a sure sign of a pending ignition or flashover. Fast-rolling, dark black smoke, or 'black fire', tends to be closer to the source, whereas light, slow moving smoke is farther away. Black smoke is just as dangerous as the flames. Temperatures can reach up to 1,000 degrees. It can be destructive, cause structural damage to metal buildings, and is extremely toxic. Once inhaled, it can render one unconscious quickly. Death occurs within minutes. Remember, Plug, fire is as fickle as a woman." He patted Garrett on the shoulder. "Tomorrow, we'll review the different odors that certain fires have after Dr. Springer's first aid class."

Garrett and Lieutenant Jones watched the firemen exit the house carrying a smoldering closed coffin.

"Oh, poor Aunt Ida!" One frail lady fanned herself with her hand fan and swooned.

A few of the gentlemen caught her and sat her down on the grass.

Garrett overheard an elderly woman cough and whisper to a tall, younger woman standing beside her, who wore a black, broad-brimmed hat with netting covering her face. "It wasn't Ophelia's turn to faint yet. It was mine."

Garrett and Lieutenant Jones joined the others around the coffin.

The elderly man's voice quivered as he spoke. "My poor Ida. Found her in the 'mater patch two days ago when God called her home."

"Praise Jesus!" one woman called out.

"Uncle Buster, here...." He pointed to a middle-aged man with a scruffy white mustache and beard. "He was smokin' his cigar while payin' his respects. A few of his ashes fell into the coffin. Before ya know it, Ida was smokin' and flames were poppin' out of her casket."

"Lord have mercy!" Another woman threw her hands in the air and sobbed.

"I threw my glass of sweet tea on her, but that only squelched the flames for a minute. I ran to the dining room, came back, and threw the whole darn pitcher on her. Flames were lickin' up the sides of the casket. I tried to get my Ida out." He turned his hands over. His skin was bright red and blistered.

Lieutenant Jones examined his palms. "You're going to need to see a doctor." He eyed one of the firemen, who stepped over to the casket. "Best to keep it closed, Winkie. We don't want to shock the family, nor do we want air to reignite the excelsior."

The elderly man appeared confused. "What? She ain't carrin' no sword."

The lieutenant bit his lower lip. "No, that's *Excalibur*. Excelsior is thin pieces of wood used under the satin lining in a coffin to help pad, fluff, and lift the body up inside the casket for viewings. The smaller the person, the more excelsior you need for good visibility. The larger the person, the less you need." The lieutenant turned his head towards the sound of an ambulance siren a few blocks away. Upon hearing additional sirens coming from the opposite direction, he turned his head and chuckled. "This is going to be interesting." He walked back towards the truck.

Sacred Heart's ambulance pulled up in front of the house. *Sacred Heart Hospital Ambulance Service. Reliable. Reputable. Responsive* was hand-painted on both sides of the vehicle. Twin ambulance attendants got out, one with red hair, the other with strawberry-blonde locks. "Don't believe we 'ad the pleasure of meetin' ya yet. I'm Tim McDaniel and this 'ere is me brothah, Jim." Jim waved as he retrieved a rolled up cloth stretcher out of the back of the ambulance. "What 'ave we 'ere, Lieutenant?"

"This poor man suffered second degree burns on the palms of his hands. He tried to lift his wife out of a burning coffin. It caught fire from Uncle Buster's cigar ashes."

"Jesus, Mary and Joseph!" He lowered his voice. "I guess the joke's on her. I hope she didn't think she was burning in 'ell," Tim chided.

Grady's ambulance drove up. They turned off their siren after seeing that Sacred Heart had beaten them to their next customer. The driver flipped a bird out the window as he sped off down the road.

"Such a sore loser, that bastard," Tim muttered. "So, we only 'ave one patient?"

"Yes, it appears that everyone else is okay." The lieutenant motioned for the elderly man to go with the ambulance attendants.

Tim belted out a hymn as Jim secured the elderly man in the back of the ambulance bed.

"What a friend we have in Jesus, all our sins and griefs to bear! What a privilege to carry everything to God in prayer! O what peace we often forfeit, O what needless pain we bear, all because we do not carry everything to God in prayer."

"Why are you singing?" Lieutenant Jones unfastened the chin strap on his helmet.

The baritone opened the driver's side door. "When people ask me why I sing, me story is always the same. When I was a wee lad, I remember our Presbyterian minister telling us 'He who sings prays twice.' I figure I'm doublin' up on me prayers for the sick and dying. I sing to make 'em happy on their journey, wherever they may end up. And, I don't want to be haunted by any ghosts of the disappointed if you know what I mean." Tim winked, closed the door, and turned the engine over and the sirens on. They drove off down the street. His brother joined him in song, harmonizing the second verse.

19

The Negro congregation at the AME church sang the new two-year-old hymn. The music filled the rafters of the small white-washed church with a red door located a few blocks down from Armstrong Street. "So I'll cherish the old rugged Cross, Till my trophies at last I lay down, I will cling to the old rugged Cross, And exchange it some day for a crown."

Mrs. Glover, a frail, elderly woman dressed in a tan dress with a white lace collar and a brown hat, played the upright Steinway, a gift to the church from the Alexander family. At the conclusion of the song, she dramatically lifted her arthritic fingers off the keys and raised her hands up to the ceiling. "Praise Jesus!" She shook her hands in the air.

Reverend Goode closed his red hymnal. "Thank you, Mrs. Glover. That was beautiful." He took his place at the pulpit and cleared his throat. Spotting his mother, Mattie, in the fourth pew on his right, he winked at her. Sitting next to her was a new guest, Maybelle. It warmed his heart to see both of their faces beaming as he began his sermon titled "We are all servants of God!" Twenty minutes later, he concluded, "There is a joy in doing what God created you to do, even if you find the notion scary. I want you to find your courage in the face of that fear. Remember, fear is just the Devil telling you, 'You're no good. You can't do it.'"

A white-haired woman wearing a lavender hat jumped up two rows up from Mattie and Maybelle. "Go away, ya nasty Devil!" She swatted her pink ostrich hand fan at the air around her.

Her husband, a slight fellow who sat on her left, winced and ducked out of her way.

Startled, a young gentleman leapt up and yelled, "Holy Jesus!" He darted towards the center aisle in the opposite direction. A few of the children's giggles were hastily hushed by their parents.

Joshua grinned and continued, "Learn to overcome your trials and tribulations with prayer. Lift your prayers to Him." He lifted his Bible in the air. "For we don't know what the future holds, but we know who holds the future! He is our Lord and Savior and we are his servants. Can I get an amen?"

"Amen!" The congregation erupted.

"Mrs. Glover, let's conclude this service with 'Ye Servants of God.'"

Mrs. Glover gracefully placed her crooked fingers on the ivory keys. Beginning in the key of D, she played a short prelude to the hymn.

Mattie said a silent prayer. Her heart fluttered and skipped a few beats as she asked the Lord to quell the noise inside of her. The secret she had kept from Joshua. The secret that could be revealed if one looked too closely at Joshua's and Edward's eyes. The secret she and Edward swore to take with them to the grave.

Mrs. Glover paused and nodded her head, signaling the congregation to join in.

The congregation, belting out the first verse, sang, "Ye servants of God, your Master proclaim, and publish abroad his wonderful name; the name all-victorious of Jesus extol, his kingdom is glorious and rules over all."

SUNDAY AFTERNOON, SIXTH WARD

"My heart is racing. I'm so nervous." Addie shook out her hands, pacing back and forth in the treatment room. Hives broke out on her neck; her cheeks flushed. She started fanning her face with her hands.

"Calm down and take a deep breath." Randall looked at the clock on the wall. It read two fifty-five. "They are going to be arriving here with Billy any minute. The detective is getting changed into a white doctor's jacket. In order for this interview to be successful, you need to get a hold of yourself. Remember, it's just business as usual." Randall took Addie's trembling hands in his. "You can do this." His tone reassuring. "*We* can do this."

"Nurse Hartman said if I make one more mistake, I'm going to be put on probation. This is all I have. I don't want to mess this up again." *My less-than-stellar September report card came early. Cleanliness, Work — C; Cleanliness, Person — B; Reliability, Patients — F; Reliability, Records — D; Economy — D; Adaptability — B; Observation — B; Industry — D; Disposition — B; Executive Ability — F.*

Randall squared Addie in front of him. "You won't fail again. You are a great nurse. Believe me when I say you're a natural. Don't let this one mistake spiral out of control and turn into your ultimate demise. I promise you that you can do this, and you will see great improvement on your next report card." He glanced at the closed door. "It's time for you to get out there and bring Billy back here for his follow-up appointment. The detective is depending on us." He adjusted his coat as he walked to the door. Placing his hand on the knob, he twisted it open. "Nurse Engel, our next patient, if you please?"

Addie smoothed out her white apron and fiddled with the white cap covering her month's worth of hair growth. "Yes, Doctor Springer." She stepped out in the hall and walked cautiously toward the concierge desk. Moira was already checking in Father Preti and Billy. Addie watched the priest fold up his umbrella and shake the rain drops from his coat.

Upon seeing Addie, Billy removed his cap. "Good afternoon, Nurse Engel. I'm here for my check up."

Addie forced a smile. "Good afternoon to you both." She reached out to take Billy's hand. "Father Preti, if you don't mind, please take a seat in our waiting room."

"I'm not sure about this. Why are we here again?" Father Preti slipped out of his raincoat as he walked behind them.

"It's just a follow-up appointment with Dr. Springer. He wants to be sure Billy's arm is healing. Rest assured, it's all routine."

"Billy's already back at work. That's why we asked if we could be seen today, because he earns wages that help support the orphanage. He's even pulling his fair share of chores at the orphanage."

"It's customary to do another x-ray to be sure the bones are healing in place," Addie fudged, and then added, "Dr. Springer is going to evaluate the amount of callus the bone has laid down around the fracture site and to see how much absorption has taken place to date."

Father Preti flipped his hand in the air. "Now you are getting a bit too technical for me. I'll be in here if you need me." Jo walked into the waiting room and took a seat in the walnut chair against the wall.

"Come, Billy. Dr. Springer is waiting for us in the treatment room." Addie and Billy walked down the hall and into the treatment room. Addie closed the door behind her. Billy hopped up on the exam table and kicked his feet back and forth. Addie knocked on another door that led to the physician's room.

Dr. Springer opened the door and entered the room. Detective McGee, dressed in a white doctor's jacket, followed behind. "Good afternoon, Billy. Thanks so much for coming in today."

He pulled up two rolling stools. Dr. Springer sat on one. The detective sat on the other. Addie locked the treatment room door and leaned against it.

While McGee reached in his pocket and unfolded the note Billy slipped to Addie, Billy pointed to him. "Hey! I know you. I've seen you before. You came to the orphanage." Confused, he asked, "Aren't you a police officer, mister? What are you doing dressed like a doctor?"

McGee lowered his voice to a whisper. "Billy, yes, I'm a police detective. My name is Detective McGee. I have a few questions to ask of you."

"You didn't answer my question. Why are you dressed like a doctor?"

McGee stammered. "Look, I'm not used to getting interrogated by a child."

"Billy," Addie interjected, "Detective McGee wants to talk with you about the note you gave me at your last visit. He's on a secret mission and dressed like a doctor to blend in with the rest of us."

"I love secret missions!" Excited, Billy's feet swung back and forth faster. "Is it like one of those adventures I've read about in the *Iliad* and the *Odyssey*?"

Randall reached out to prevent Billy from kicking Detective McGee in the face while Addie put her index finger to her lips.

"Oh! Sorry, mister." Billy stopped moving his legs. He dropped the volume of his voice to match the detective's. "So, I'm not here to get an x-ray of my arm?"

McGee wanted to say aloud that they were on a quest to hunt monsters, but refrained. Instead, he waved the note. "No, son, not today. Why did you write this? What does this mean?"

He read the note. "*Landon and Logan Farmer — not adopted by the Martins. David Connley — not adopted by the Davises.*"

Billy fidgeted. "I'm afraid that Father Preti and his sister aren't telling you the truth. When you came to the orphanage, I watched Miss Preti write in the log book right before she showed it to you. The spaces that listed the adoptive family were blank. She wrote in those names while you sat on the porch." Billy anticipated the detective's next question. "Don't worry, mister. They don't think I can read or write."

Randall watched the clock and eyed Addie. "Detective, please move this along. You don't have much time."

"What happened to those boys? Where did they go?"

"I'm not sure. I saw Father Preti come in our room late one night and carry out David Connley. They locked us in our rooms and they took the truck. They were gone for a while and then they returned. I heard them unlock our bedroom doors after they got home."

"Did David go willingly? Did he try to fight off Father Preti?"

"David was asleep. He fell asleep pretty soon after we were tucked in our beds."

"What about the twin boys?"

"I didn't know them. I was told they were adopted by some nice family before I arrived."

"Who told you that?"

"Father Preti."

"Billy, what made you think that something was wrong with the orphanage or the Pretis?"

Billy started swinging his legs again.

McGee recoiled, pedaling his feet to roll the stool backwards.

Billy's leg swings immediately ceased. "Oh! Sorry! I'm trying to think." He twisted his mouth. "I can't put it into words, exactly. It's a feeling I got in my gut. Who adopts kids in the middle of the night? Who adopts older boys? Families always want the young ones, the babies. Not kids my age." Tears welled in his eyes. "I didn't ask for this life. My grandma raised me. I got thrown out on the streets after she died. I always hoped for a family of my own. My granny taught me to read and write." He pounded his chest. "I'm a smart boy. I'm a good boy. I just want to be loved."

Overcome, McGee turned to wipe away a tear. There was a knock on the door. Everyone jumped.

"Is Billy done yet? I've got to get him back for evening chores. My sister will have my head if we're not back within the hour." Father Preti grew impatient as he twisted the handle of the door and found it locked.

McGee popped up. "Billy, don't utter a word about our conversation. Promise?" He rolled the stool to the far corner of the room.

"Yes, I promise. It's our secret mission. Gotcha." Billy gave him an exaggerated wink.

The detective darted through the doctor's door and carefully closed it behind him as Addie unlocked the treatment room door. Father Preti entered the room as Randall jumped up and took hold of Billy's left arm.

"Dr. Springer, how's Billy's arm healing?" He observed Randall examining the left arm. "Doctor, I'm no expert. But, Billy broke his right arm."

"Of course he did. I must always examine the contralateral extremity during my evaluation."

"You've lost me on your medical jargon, Doctor." He tapped his umbrella on the floor. "By the way, I'd like to see his x-ray. I think it would be interesting to see a picture of someone's bones."

Billy looked at Dr. Springer. His eyes widened.

Dr. Springer turned his back to Father Preti and pretended to flip through Billy's chart on the counter. He mouthed "Shit!" He turned and grabbed a hold of the counter behind him as he looked at Addie. His complexion paled.

Oh, my stars! Dr. Springer is scared. Think, Addie. You can salvage this situation. What needs to be done? Nurse Hartman said in our counseling session that she is trying to teach me how to think, not what to think. I'm teaching you how to handle a big problem. I need for you to tap into your critical thinking skills. If you do something, what are the potential consequences? What needs to happen next. And after that? Prioritize, act, analyze, evaluate, and reprioritize.'

With complete authority, Addie responded, "Doctor, I'll fetch that x-ray for you. If you'll excuse me, I'll be right back." She retreated through the side door into the physician's room. There was no sign of Detective McGee. The white coat he was wearing was draped over an office chair. Addie ran over to the desk and flipped through a stack of patients' charts and put her hands on the first set of x-rays she came across that said 'Fracture' in the diagnosis. She grabbed the radiograph and returned to the treatment room, handing it to Dr. Springer.

Dr. Springer held it up to the light and gasped under his breath. He adjusted his grip on the film to hide something from view.

Father Preti leaned over Randall's shoulder. "What am I looking at, Doctor?"

Realizing Father Preti had no idea what he was looking at, Randall pointed at the film. "See this long white bone, here?" The priest nodded; his eyes followed Dr. Springer's fingers. "See the thin black line through this bone? That is where the bone was broken. The white areas here and here are what we call callus. The body is remarkable about healing itself. The bone forms a patch around the injured area and over time, this extra bone is absorbed." Before Father Preti had the chance to examine the x-ray further, Randall hastily removed it from view and placed the film on top of Billy's chart. Redirecting the priest's focus, he said, "Feel Billy's arm." Father Preti touched the place where Billy had broken his right forearm. "Feel that bump?" Father Preti nodded. "That is the callus, or bone patch, that will eventually go away."

"That's pretty neat, Doctor."

"My pleasure, Father. There won't be a charge for today's visit and, of course, the educational lecture was also free." Randall laughed nervously. His cheeks rosied.

"So, we're done for today?"

"Yes, Father. You both are free to go." Randall shook Father Preti's hand. "Nurse Engel will escort you out."

"Oh, there's no need. We've been here plenty of times. We know our way around here by now. We'll see ourselves out." He and Billy departed, closing the door being them.

Addie promptly locked the door and watched Randall collapse on the stool. He ran his hands through his blonde hair. "Holy, shit!" he mouthed under his breath; he started laughing. "That could have gone so horribly wrong."

Addie walked over to the x-ray and held it up to the light. Randall rolled out of her way and gazed up at the film. "Well, everything you said to Father Preti was the truth, Doctor."

He looked at her. She looked at him. Her heart raced.

"Except for the part that this x-ray is not Billy's." Randall watched Addie retrieve the other rolling stool and plop down next to him.

She covered her mouth. Before the nervous giggles overtook both of them, she managed to eke out, "No, it was a forty-eight-year-old woman's broken leg!" She waved the x-ray. "You did a great job covering up the foot!"

"What a pair we make!" Randall leaned in close; she smelled of lilacs, once again.

20

"Today, we are going to start our morning leadership meeting with a prayer. In honor of President Wilson's declaration of a National Day of Prayer for Peace to help in the effort to end the Great War, may I ask that you bow your heads? There are those among us who practice a variety of religions, so please take a moment for silent prayer and reflection." Edward bowed his head and closed his eyes. He said a prayer for the soldiers abroad and that the political leaders could see their way clear to finding mutual resolution soon, before the casualties became too great. Or worse, before the United States of America was eventually dragged into the conflict. "Amen." Edward opened his eyes and looked around the table.

Lena wiped her eyes. Oliver offered her a handkerchief; she declined.

Edward looked at his notes. "I've got a few updates for you."

"Does it include progress on the undercover investigation?" Clyde's boot tapped nervously on the oriental carpet beneath him.

"No." Edward refrained from divulging that the detective had met with the orphan boy who handed Addie a note, remaining mum about the investigation already underway by the APD. "However, it is a bit of good news. The boy that was recovered from the smoldering refuse pile has been reunited with his family."

"Our Johnny Doe patient?" Alan inquired.

"Yes, his name is Stuart Harvey. The family asked that he be transferred to Grady where they can properly care for the severe burns on his legs. Our ambulance is transferring him later this morning."

"Good. At least we know now where to send his medical bill." Alan wrote Harvey in his notebook.

"Actually, I'd like for the hospital to cover those costs," Edward corrected.

Alan balked.

"Listen. This family has endured enough pain. This boy is lucky to still have his legs, thanks to Dr. Williams, Dr. Springer, and our fine nursing staff."

"It would have been easier to amputate, but we chose to salvage his limbs instead," Dr. Williams added. "His rehabilitation and recovery will be painful. He's lucky to still be alive. He's not out of the woods yet."

"Alan, we have saved his life and reunited him with his family. Let the burn specialists at Grady do their part. We're entering into the holiday season and charitable stories such as this are good for the papers, don't you agree?"

Alan reluctantly agreed. "It will help on the back end with fundraising efforts."

"There's the spirit!"

Oliver raised his hand. Edward acknowledged him with a nod.

"Nurse Hartman and I have heard that Grady has opened their Municipal Training School for Colored Nurses. I would like to set up a meeting with their new superintendent, Ludie Andrews."

"We'd love to meet with her to find out how their enrollment is going and learn from her as we move forward with the opening of Alexander Hall and our Colored Nursing School in a few years. We want to establish a collaborative relationship with her. I'm sure she'll impart some sound advice." Lena was eager to hear Edward's response.

"I actually had that on my list to discuss with you both today." Edward crossed through the talking point on his notepad with his pen. "I think it is a splendid idea. Oliver and Nurse Hartman, please keep me posted on the outcome of your meeting."

"Yes, we will, Edward." Oliver said reassuringly.

Lena beamed, looking forward to meeting Mrs. Andrews. There was a knock on the conference room door.

"Come in," Edward replied.

Moira entered the room and immediately ran to Edward. She whispered something in his ear.

The color washed out of his face. "Clyde, I need for you to take over this meeting." Edward stood and buttoned his suit jacket closed. "If you will excuse me, there seems to be a family medical emergency."

Dr. Williams stood up. "Do you need for me to go with you?"

"Yes, that would be most kind of you, Dr. Williams. We could use your expert advice. The rest of you, please carry on."

The three departed. Dr. Williams and Edward chose to take the back stairs while Moira took the elevator back to her desk.

Edward walked in on a commotion in one of the emergency department's treatment rooms.

"We can't keep her here. I can't treat her. She needs to go to the Negro hospital in the Fourth Ward," the emergency room doctor huffed.

"What do you mean? You can't? Or, you *won't?*" Joshua pleaded as he watched the doctor nearly collide with Edward on his way out.

Mattie struggled to catch her breath. Her lips were cyanotic and she slipped in and out of consciousness. Trudy, Edward's wife, stood beside Mattie, holding her swollen, blue hand.

"Edward, darling, I'm so sorry. Mattie passed out at the house. I called the Sacred Heart's ambulance to come and pick us up and bring her here straight away." Trudy wiped her tears and blew her nose on a baby blue, lace handkerchief. "She confided that she hasn't been making water for the past few days, now."

"Mother, don't leave us," Joshua begged. "We're going to get you the best medical care."

"Step aside, son." Dr. Williams pulled out his black stethoscope from his doctor's bag. "Quiet everyone." He placed the silver metal bell over Mattie's left breast and moved it carefully around her chest. He pressed on her cold, blue nail beds. There was no capillary refill; they remained blue, not pink. He examined her swollen legs and abdomen. He pressed his thumb on the top of her foot. His thumb indentation remained. "She has pitting edema." He removed his stethoscope and folded it, returning it to the pocket of his lab coat. He whispered to Nurse Scott, who stood in the corner of the room.

"Yes, Doctor." Claire turned to unlock the medicine cabinet behind her and retrieved a vile and a glass syringe and needle.

"We're going to give her something to pull the fluid from her lungs and out of her body. It's going to be a temporary fix." He put his arm around Joshua as they walked to the opposite side of the room. "Son, I need to have a frank discussion with you."

Edward walked over and took hold of Mattie's other hand, patting it reassuringly. Tears streamed down his face. Trudy watched in anguish. Nurse Scott administered the injection.

Joshua began crying. "Your mother has dropsy and is in end stage heart failure. Her heart is not pumping blood efficiently through her body anymore. Fluid and toxins are building up inside and her organ systems are shutting down."

"You mean she is dying?" He wiped his eyes and nose with his hands.

"Yes, son. She doesn't have much time." Dr. Williams looked at Edward and Trudy. "We will keep her here. We won't transfer her. I think it's best that she be surrounded by family." He directed his comment to Joshua. "Is there any family that needs to be notified?"

Joshua shook his head. "It's always just been Mother and me. And, of course, the Alexanders." He pulled out a handkerchief from his back pocket. "We're all the family she has."

Edward spoke to Claire. "Nurse Scott, would you please fetch my daughter?"

"Yes, sir. She is working in the nursery today. I'll be right back." Claire left the room.

"Trudy, where is Trip and Pearl?"

"Trip is at school. I left Pearl at home. You know how fragile she is."

Edward rubbed his forehead. "Our delicate little flower."

Minutes later, Opal burst through the door and ran over to join her father beside Mattie. "Oh, Miss Mattie!"

She threw her hands around Mattie's neck and buried her head in her bosom.

Mattie made a few gasps, exhaling for the last time.

"MOTHER!"

Edward immediately reached out to Joshua, quickly joining Joshua's hand with Mattie's. Edward stepped back.

Trudy noticed something for the first time. Edward's amber eyes. Joshua's amber eyes. She dropped Mattie's hand and swayed. Dr. Williams caught her, setting her down in a chair in the corner of the room.

Edward raced over to Trudy. He studied her face. The secret he and Mattie swore to take with them to their graves had been revealed. He'd hoped and prayed the truth would never come out. But it had. She knew. Beads of sweat popped up on his forehead and upper lip. He bolted to the far corner of the room and threw up in the metal trashcan.

Dr. Williams hustled across the room to tend to Edward.

Edward pushed him away. "GET AWAY FROM ME!"

"Whatever you say, Edward." Dr. Williams backed away.

Edward propped himself up against the wall with his right hand and bent over, vomiting again. He spun around and grabbed the edge of Dr. William's white coat, startling him. Edward's bloodshot eyes narrowed. Through gritted teeth, he growled, "I demand that you go after that emergency room physician and fire him right now."

"But Dr. Putnam is one of my best."

"I DON'T GIVE A SHIT!" Edward drilled his right index finger into Dr. William's chest. He hissed, "Get that son-of-a bitch out of my hospital. I don't want that kind of attitude or intolerant, poisonous mentality here. GET RID OF HIM, NOW!"

Dr. Williams remained calm. He knew the traumatic event had gotten the best of his friend. He was accustomed to seeing people react to the death of a loved one. Some people get quiet, while others are immediately filled with rage and anger. Some break down in hysterics and tears; others fall to the floor and curl up in the fetal position. And sometimes people become impulsive, irrational, and throw up. "Yes, Edward. I'll take care of it right now." He pivoted on his heels and exited the room.

Edward had never raised his voice in anger publically. Trudy buried her face in her handkerchief, wailing, "Oh, Edward! How could you!"

"Father, really? What has gotten into you?" Opal left Mattie's side to comfort her mother.

Nurse Scott opted to stay in the corner of the room, hoping she was invisible.

Joshua glared at Edward. "In the name of all that's Holy, please leave this room at once." He pointed towards the door.

Edward hung his head. He exited the room and walked out into the hallway. Doctors, nurses, patients, and visitors stared at him. They stood motionless. "WHAT THE HELL ARE Y'ALL LOOKING AT?" He waved his hands wildly in the air. "GET ON WITH YOURSELVES!"

The bystanders scurried along, clearing a path for him as he burst out the side door, stormed through the garden, and up-ended one of the picnic benches on the side lawn. He buried his head in his hands and wailed. "Dear God! I'm so sorry! Please forgive me!" Edward tore off his suit jacket. He ran his hands over his head as he paced in circles. He stopped, fell to his knees, and looked up at the white clouds billowing overhead. Rays of sunlight illuminated the large maple tree's yellow and orange leaves. Leaves abscised in the chilly westerly wind, falling like confetti around him. With arms outstretched towards the sky, he begged, "Forgive me, Father! Please, forgive me!"

21

"Captain, I'm begging you to let me look into the Holy Cross Orphans' Asylum and their adoption practices," Detective McGee pleaded, rising up out of the oak chair in front of his captain's matching desk. He nearly knocked off the brass name plate engraved with the name Captain Phillip Summers.

"Sit your ass back down in that chair and listen to me." Captain Summers rolled a toothpick from one side of his mouth to the other. He pulled it out and stabbed it repeatedly into the papers on his desk as he spoke. "Mayor Woodward is up my ass about getting results and said to focus on the dead boy's investigation, not the orphans."

"But I believe that there is a link between the dead boys and the orphanage."

"You need more proof. More evidence." The toothpick splintered under the pressure. "So, you've questioned one of the orphan boys. Kids make up stuff all the time. How can you possibly believe the word of a child?" He threw the fragments into the waste paper basket beside his desk. "Have you spoken with the other participating hospitals yet?"

"No."

"Have you verified that these adoptive families are legit?"

"I've attempted to follow up on that information and it's a dead end. It's as if they don't exist."

"Now, I must admit, the link between the twin boys and the orphanage piqued my interest, but understand me when I say you better have all the facts and this case buttoned up tight before we open up a formal investigation. You're dealing with a priest, a man of the cloth doing God's work."

"I believe what Billy told me and I have a bad feeling about that asylum. You know…." McGee balled up his hand in a fist and touched his abdomen. "It's that thing in the pit of your stomach that tells you something isn't right."

"Look, McGee, you've got an impeccable track record. Let's not fuck it up on a hunch and something twinging in your stomach. How do you know you don't have gas?" Captain Summers chortled as he reached behind his right ear and pulled out another toothpick, popping it into his mouth. "Come back to me when you have something…." The toothpick twirled and flipped up and down.

McGee grew impatient. "More?"

The toothpick came to rest on his lower lip. "Indisputable."

WEDNESDAY AFTERNOON, SIXTH WARD

"Will you hand me the rake, Opal?" Addie reached out over the knee-high, white picket fence surrounding the hospital botanical garden.

"Sure thing." Opal handed Addie the wood-handled rake. "What did you think of Dr. William's lecture this morning? I must admit, I got a little grossed out. I didn't think I could take any more if it." She shuddered.

"What? What have those little black leeches ever done to you?" Addie bent over, picking something out of the dirt from under a fallen leaf. "Speaking of little slimy things, what do you think of him?" A reddish-brown earthworm squirmed between Addie's fingers. "These are great for fishing." Addie tossed it at Opal.

"Hey! That's not funny!" Opal jumped out of the way. It landed on the top of a pile of leaves behind her.

"At least it wasn't a leech. He would have stuck to you like glue!"

"When Dr. Williams reached into his pocket, pulled out that silver metal box with tiny holes in it, and slid it open, I thought Mary Margaret was going to faint!"

Addie howled in laughter as she raked leaves into a pile.

"I can't believe doctors use medicinal leeches to restore circulation in extremities. Once he explained how the leeches have anticoagulant properties in their saliva, it all made perfect sense. I wonder who the first brave soul to figure that out was."

A big black crow swooped down, picked off the earthworm, and flew off.

"Death comes quick, huh?" Opal shielded her eyes, watching the crow take roost on a large limb in the big maple tree.

"Speaking of death, how was Ms. Mattie's funeral on Wednesday?" Addie bent over and picked up a handful of leaves, tossing them over the side of the fence.

"Nice segue, Nurse Engel." Opal bristled.

"Oh, I'm sorry. I didn't mean to sound so callous."

Opal picked up a few leaves and threw them at Addie. "Oh, don't worry. I need to learn to lighten up about such things. It was just so unexpected. I mean, you would think we would be used to seeing people dying. But when it is someone you know and love dearly, it comes too soon."

"Oh, I know only too well." Memories of her family's tragic death flooded Addie's mind. The Engel farm had been nearly lost to the bank but was bought by the city with the help of Garrett's father, Mr. Darling, and converted into Hope's Guardian Angel Cemetery. Addie tearfully realized a visit to Hope was long overdue. The strict school requirements prevented such travel. She yearned for her Maw's embrace and to hear the laughter of her little brother and sister again. *I'll rejoin them someday in heaven, God willing.*

"Mother didn't attend the funeral with us. Father said she was overcome with nerves. She left on the train for the Greenbrier Hotel on Tuesday. I've seen her succumb to nerves before. Once, she had a miscarriage before she got pregnant with Tripp. I was a teenager then. I remember that she packed her trunks after the funeral and left to go spend time with her sister in Florida. She was gone for months. If it wasn't for Ms. Mattie to keep the household together, I swear we would have just fallen apart." Opal reached in her coat pockets and donned her red wool mittens. "That was a tough time for Father."

"How's Joshua doing?"

"He did a marvelous job preaching at her service. He's quite a remarkable man. Did you know that he's sweet on Miss Maybelle?"

"What? Wherever did you hear that?"

"I saw it with my own two eyes. She was at the funeral and…" Opal lowered her voice to a whisper. "I heard that she's been attending Joshua's Sunday sermons, sitting right alongside of his momma in the pew."

"Oh, Opal. You have an active imagination. That's how rumors get started."

Opal held up her right hand and touched her heart. "I swear, Addie Engel. It's the gospel truth."

The big black crow swooped down and began pecking at the ground near a patch of peppermint.

"Shoo! Shoo!" Addie began making her way over to him. He flew around in a circle over her head and perched on the picket of the gate. "Wow! This one is a brave little bird, isn't he?"

"He reminds me of someone else I know!"

"Hey! I've got an idea. Do you know what this garden is missing?"

"Corn? Potatoes?"

"No, silly. We need to make a scarecrow to keep these pesky birds away."

"That's a great idea! I know where we can get some clothes. We can use pine straw instead of hay for the stuffing."

"Wonderful! I'll run over to the construction site at Alexander Hall to see if they have some scrap lumber from which to hang him. I'll meet you back here."

Opal looked at the late afternoon sun. "We best be quick about it. We've got about two hours of daylight left."

As the sun set, hues of orange, yellow, red, purple, and navy blue washed across the evening sky; Addie and Opal stepped back to admire their work. The scarecrow wore overalls with black and green paint stains and a red plaid shirt. A matching red bandana and a straw hat completed the look. Upon hearing footsteps shuffling through the grass behind them, they turned around.

"He looks mighty fine, ladies." Dr. Springer surveyed their work. "I believe the straw hat is a very nice touch. Wherever did you find those clothes?"

"I got them out of the hospital lost and found box in the basement. Mr. and Mrs. Wu keep it inside of their laundry room."

"I've got to hand it to you, ladies, you are the most resourceful nurses I know."

The dinner bell rang. Miss Maybelle waved at them. They waved back.

"Opal, I'll meet you inside. I've got a question I need to ask Dr. Springer."

Opal winked. "Sure thing. Have a great night, Dr. Springer. I'll see you on the ward tomorrow."

"What's on your mind, Addie?"

"Have you heard anything more about the investigation?"

"Not a word. Mr. Alexander promised to keep us in the loop should he hear anything more from the detective."

"Okay. I just worry about Billy. If what he says is true, he and the other boys could be in some real danger."

"Don't let you imagination take flight, Nurse Engel."

The black crow flew past them. Upon seeing the scarecrow, he veered away from the garden and sought refuge in a nearby pine tree.

"I won't. I remember what you taught us on the pediatric ward." Addie counted off on her gloved fingers. "Be objective. Be observant. Don't jump to conclusions."

"Good, Nurse Engel. I hope your grades reflect your improvement this month."

"Oh, they did. I was pleased that some of my failing scores have risen above 'C' level." Addie lowered her voice. "And, I'm off probation next month, provided I don't mess anything else up."

"Good for you! That's excellent news. Please continue to keep your head above water and stay out of trouble." Randall loved seeing a spark return to her emerald eyes. "You know, I must admit, I put in a few good words for you with Mr. Alexander and Nurse Hartman after the detective questioned Billy. I let them know how invaluable you were to me." He thought of saying more, but refrained.

Addie shivered in the cool night air. "Oh, thank you so much. I truly appreciate all of your support. And, more importantly, I promise not to get into any more trouble."

Laughing, Randall touched her arm. "Best be getting along, Nurse Engel. Supper waits."

"Good night, Doctor."

Resisting the impulsive urge to kiss her, he patted her on the arm instead and turned to walk back towards the hospital. "Good night, Nurse Engel."

22

"Mr. Chang, the phone for you." The mamasan of his emporium, Mrs. Lee, handed him the black receiver and hand-held mouthpiece. "It's Customer #313. He sound upset."

Mr. Chang's long fingernails coiled around the neck of the phone like claws. "Hello?"

Frantic, the caller asked, "Is this Mr. Chang? This is Mr. …"

"Customer #313. Yes, I know who you are. Your name not important. Remember the rules, Customer #313."

"My apologies, sir. I hope you can help me?"

"What kind of help do you need? Did you receive your flower delivery? I hope your lotus blossom was to your liking?" Mr. Chang watched Mrs. Lee, dressed in a cobalt blue silk robe that had a red dragon embroidered on the back, pour him a cup of hot green tea from a black tea pot as he lounged on a red leather banquette.

"I think my flower is…dying."

"Oh, so you overwatered your plant?"

"Uh, yeah." Customer #313 sniffed. "I guess I did. I don't think it will…survive. It's…turning…blue."

"Pity. It will cost extra." Mr. Chang hated losing a young boy to a customer's carelessness with drugs. However, there were plenty of other "lotus flowers" in his garden.

"When would you like to pick up your…." The voice on the other line cracked; he began sobbing. "Plant? We can be in the Second Ward within the hour." Mr. Chang despised grown men who cried, especially, high powered, wealthy ones. What would their stockholders think? "Pull yourself together. Turn off all lights and unlock the back door. We take care of the rest. Probably best that you leave the premises for a few hours."

The caller abruptly blew his nose in the receiver.

Mr. Chang recoiled, withdrawing the earpiece from his ear, and hung up the phone. "Mrs. Lee. Please have my men make a pick-up at Customer #313's estate. Be sure they don't go to Stone Mountain. It's Saturday night. I'm sure all kinds of lovers near the lake." He waggled his index finger as he spoke. "Too risky. Make them go to another ward far from here."

Mrs. Lee took the phone from Mr. Chang, exchanging it with a Chinese red porcelain tea cup that had a hand-painted gold dragon circling it. She bowed, turned to part the red velvet curtains, and disappeared as they closed behind her.

SATURDAY NIGHT, FOURTH WARD

The firetruck took a sharp left turn out of the station and sped down Boulevard Avenue, disappearing into the darkness towards the Third Ward. The call came over the telegraph wire at ten fifty-five. Garrett and his fellow brothers hung on for dear life as the engine roared down the road. A few blocks south of Grant Park, they found a house engulfed. Gold, red, and orange flames licked up the sides of the structure and out of the broken windows.

Hastily, Garrett exited the vehicle and surveyed the building. Chipped white paint and kudzu vines spiraling up the columns of the front porch indicated that the place was either poorly kept or abandoned. He hoped for the later. In his peripheral vision, he saw a man running towards him. He turned.

A middle-aged, stocky white man with black hair, dressed in his striped pajamas, a navy blue cotton robe with white pipping, and tan leather slippers, ran up to Garrett. Breathless, he managed to say, "I made the call to the station. My name is Mr. Grover."

"Who lives here?" Garrett had to know.

"No one. It's been abandoned for a year and a half now. We see vagrants come and go from the premises, but I keep a keen watch on my neighborhood. We don't want no trouble 'round here."

"How long has the house been burning?"

Crack. Crack. Crack. Boom!

Everyone stood motionless, watching the roof collapse.

Mr. Grover, fixated on the dancing flames, said, "I heard a big bang that startled me out of a deep sleep. Lad, our little terrier, barked incessantly after that. I knew something wasn't right. So, when I peeked out of the window, I saw the house on fire. That's when I called y'all."

"Thank you, Mr. Grover. Best you run on back to your home. I don't want this cold night air to be the death of you. We can handle it from here." The man nodded as Garrett ran over to Lieutenant Jones. "Sir, one of the neighbors reported that the house has been unoccupied for over a year. He mentioned seeing vagrants every now and again."

"I pray no one was sleeping in there on this cold night." The lieutenant clapped his gloved hands together and shouted orders. "Alright, men, this is an abandoned home, but be mindful there may be a drifter inside." He had run across similar fires, where hobos had created campfires inside of empty buildings in an effort to stay warm during the fall and winter months. Left unsupervised, the wood-burning fires would burn through the hard-wood floors and spread. It also wasn't uncommon for bums to die from smoke inhalation and carbon monoxide poisoning from poor ventilation or closed windows. Cherry-red, not cyanotic lips, were a key indicator of that kind of death.

The firemen worked diligently to contain the blaze throughout the night, letting the home burn to the ground. When there was nothing but black, burnt timbers, and areas that puffed out tiny plumes of white smoke, the lieutenant ordered the men to rummage through the periphery of the rubble.

The lieutenant poked at a smoldering pile that appeared to have an iron curtain rod in it. He scanned the area. "Men, be aware that there still may be some hot spots that could flare up, so watch your step. We're also not sure if this place had a basement. As long as I have breath in my body, I don't plan on losing any of you." He prodded the mound of debris in front of him. "This place went up fast. You said the neighbor heard a loud boom?"

"Yes. What are you thinking? That there was an explosion of some sort?"

"Perhaps. It would have been great to know what color the initial smoke cloud was after he heard the boom. White smoke is indicative of dynamite. When TNT is used, the smoke can be black or gray. An easy way to remember the difference in smoke colors is that if it's white, it's dynamite," he rhymed.

"If I were a bad guy, I would rather use TNT over dynamite. It's more stable. Even though the liquid nitroglycerine in dynamite is stabilized with sawdust and an antacid, such as sodium carbonate, heat, shock, or friction can easily set it off."

"Excellent, Garrett. You are now applying your lessons in the field."

Garrett moved the lieutenant out of his way. "Look here." Garrett pointed under a smoldering pile of timbers. "Do you see what I see?" He shook his head to clear his head of memories of finding Addie's parent's charred remains.

Lieutenant Jones knelt down and gently lifted a fallen piece of scorched lumber. "By the size of the body, it looks to be that of a child."

"Oh, God in heaven, not another one." Garrett knelt down beside him. "May we say a prayer for this poor innocent soul?"

"Of course." Lieutenant Jones patted Garrett on the shoulder. "You have a good heart, Garrett. Let me gather the others." The lieutenant directed his men to come over. They removed their helmets and bowed their heads in prayer.

23

Dr. Williams walked behind Edward and placed a copy of the Sunday edition of *the Atlanta Dispatch* in front of him. The headlines read *Charred Remains of Teen Boy Discovered*. Below that story was the article *Atlanta's Federal Reserve Opens in November*. Under international news, it read *By Means of Terror*, which highlighted the trial in Sarajevo that had commenced two weeks ago for the seventeen conspirators who plotted the assassination of Archduke Franz Ferdinand of Austria. Gavrilo Princip, the Serbian student who fired the fatal shots, admitted in court that his motivation for assassination was purely political 'by means of terror.'

"Do you have any updates for us from Detective McGee?" The decadent aroma of fresh bread, buttermilk biscuits, and coffee filled the room. Dr. Williams reached for a bran muffin from the silver bread basket in the middle of the table as he took his seat.

Edward folded the paper in half and placed it to the side; his affect was flat. "The only update I have is that Detective McGee met with his captain. For political reasons, he has to focus on these cases and find the perpetrator or perpetrators. Evidently, there is mounting pressure coming from the Mayor's office." Edward tapped on the paper. "I read the story yesterday. The boy's remains were found in the Third Ward during an abandoned house fire." Edward's thoughts drifted.

Sensing there was more, Nurse Hartman asked, "Is there anything else you want to share with us?"

Edward decided not to go into the affair he'd had with Ms. Mattie decades ago while his wife grieved over the loss of their unborn child. As a result, Joshua grew up not knowing who his father was. Edward thought the truth would remain hidden. He was so embarrassed for losing his temper and had since apologized to all involved for his outburst. While Sacred Heart and Alexander Hall were his pride and joy, his family was priority. After he and Trudy spoke at length on the phone yesterday, he was content to share, "I'm going to be taking a leave of absence starting Monday, November 1st, returning on Monday, November 30th. I've already spoken with Clyde about this." He looked over at Clyde. His gut rumbled and ached. He reached in his pocket, pulled out two sodium bicarbonate tablets, and popped them in his mouth. He chased them down with orange juice. "I'm leaving him in charge while I'm gone."

"Where are you going?" Genuinely concerned, Lena's brows furled.

"I am taking my family up to the Greenbrier. Of course, Opal will remain here in school. We need some family time together. The passing of Ms. Mattie has been very hard on everyone, especially Trudy. I spoke with her yesterday. She's already been up there for about two weeks now. We're going to join her." Edward choked back a tear. "Perhaps we'll spend a week there, and then we may take the train to the Carolina seashore."

"The ocean air does one good, Edward." Oliver sipped from his coffee cup.

"It surely does, Oliver." Edward saw the look of worry in their eyes. "Please don't be concerned. Our family just needs time together to grieve. When I return, everything will be as it was before I left. I already let the Sacred Heart Board members know, too. Trudy and I are also going to use this time to plan our annual Christmas party." With feigned happiness, Edward pointed at Lena. "Please know that the inaugural nursing class is invited. Make arrangements for their shifts to be covered at the hospital. I will pay the cab fare to and from the party." He paused, and then added, "Please put in a call to Rich and Brothers Department store to have them deliver some gowns for the girls to wear."

Alan looked up at Edward, wondering about the cost of an evening gown. He hastily concluded he could account for it under "non-patient supplies" in his financial ledger. He picked up his pencil and started to make a note.

Edward read Alan's mind. "Tell them to put it on my personal account." He'd find a way to have his accountant take it off on his personal taxes as a work-related expense.

Alan flipped his pencil over, erasing his entry.

"Oh, Edward! That is so thoughtful of you." Lena covered her mouth as tears filled her eyes.

"It's been a tough first year on y'all. Please be sure to get a new dress for yourself and Nurse Scott."

Lena was speechless and could only nod her head.

"Our census should be lower over the holidays. I'll work with Nurse Hartman to make sure that we plan our discharges accordingly." Dr. Williams penned a note to remind him in his notebook. "In addition, I'll work with the other surgeons to make sure we don't schedule any elective cases before Christmas. That should help decrease inpatient volumes, too."

"Thanks, Dr. Williams. I appreciate y'all working together on this." Edward stood and buttoned his black suit jacket. "If you'll excuse me, I have a meeting uptown with my attorney." He refrained from divulging that he needed to amend his will and have Ms. Mattie removed. Joshua would remain and stood to inherit much. He preferred to keep that information confidential. Even Trudy was unaware of the allocations in his last will and testament. "I'm going to turn the reins over to Clyde."

"Thank you, Edward." Clyde watched Edward gather his belongings and walk out of the room. As soon as the wooden door shut behind him, Clyde rose out of his chair and took Edward's seat at the head of the table.

Lena gasped under her breath.

Alan peered over his gold wire spectacles. "Son, do you really think that's a good idea?"

Clyde slammed his hands down on the table. Everyone jumped. "Look, it matters where one sits at the table if one is to run an effective meeting. Don't you agree, Alan?"

Alan despised being the focus of attention; he patted his leg under the table four times. "Please proceed, Clyde. We all have a busy day ahead of us." Clyde reminded him why he loved working with numbers, not assholes.

MONDAY AFTERNOON, SIXTH WARD

"Nurse Scott taught us in class last week that the essential qualification of a good pediatric nurse is to love children." Bertie batted her eyes at Dr. Springer as he stood across the crib from her and watched her collect a urine sample in a glass test tube from a thirteen month old boy who had a fever of unknown origin. "Do you know that I just love children? What about you, Dr. Springer?" Bertie lost her grip on the child's penis. A fountain of urine sprayed straight up in the air. "Oh, my!" Bertie hastily redirected the flow of urine back into the collection tube.

Randall tried to suppress his laughter, but couldn't. The look on Bertie's face was too priceless. "I'm sorry, Nurse Jones. Welcome to the unpredictable world of pediatrics. And, yes, pediatric medicine is my calling."

"Dr. Springer, your patient is ready for you." Addie rolled a silver tray to the bedside of a six-year-old young girl in bed number three. She reflected on last night's phone call—a much needed conversation with Garrett. She yearned to feel his touch, his skin on her skin, his breath on her lips, and his soft caress. She felt her body flush deep inside and cheeks become rosy. Unfortunately, their call was cut short by the sound of the station's fire alarm. Duty called. Duty always calls.

Dr. Springer walked over to the white porcelain sink mounted on the wall, and washed and dried his hands before making his way to attend to Addie's patient. The sedative he ordered for the child was taking effect. Her persistent cough was subsiding. "Are you feeling okay, Nurse Engel? You seem to appear a bit flushed."

Addie waved him off. "Oh, I'm just fine. I was simply rushing around trying to get everything ready for you."

"Well, thank you. I appreciate your steadfast dedication." He cleared his throat. "This test, called the Von Pirquet Test for Tuberculosis, is routinely done on children to aid in the diagnosis of TB. Do you have the alcohol and ether ready?"

"Yes, Doctor." Addie pointed to two small medicine glasses on the tray. "I've also collected the other medical supplies you requested." Addie pointed to each item. "We have cotton sponges, sterile gauze pads, tape, a sterilized scarifier, Koch's Old Tuberculin, forceps soaking in a five percent Lysol solution, normal saline, and a kidney basin."

"Excellent job, Nurse Engel." Randall walked around the bed, assessing the arms of the young girl. "The forearm is the best place to apply this test."

Addie watched as he took the young girl's left arm and cleaned an area with alcohol and ether. Their distinctive odors were pungent and wafted through the unit.

Randall dried the area with a sterile gauze pad. "I'm going to make three scarifications about one inch apart and then drop Koch's Old Tuberculin on two of the three incisions. Here, Addie, please hold the arm until it has dried."

Addie held the arm still.

"If there is a reaction, it will occur within twelve to twenty-four hours."

"What will the reaction look like?"

"The affected area will redden and there won't be a response from the control, the incision without the tuberculin."

"Nurse Hartman also taught us about another test in class

last week called the Mantoux Test that doctors also use to diagnose TB."

"Yes, that is another popular test. The difference is that in the Mantoux Test, the tuberculin is introduced intradermally under the skin using a twenty-six or twenty-eight gauge hypodermic needle."

Noting the child's arm was dry, Addie covered it with sterile gauze, taping it into place. She gathered the supplies and rolled the equipment cart across the room to the sink, where she washed and dried her hands. Dr. Springer did the same.

"If she tests positive, we'll have to move her up to 2-B."

"TB or not TB, that is the question!" Addie joked quietly.

Randall laughed quietly. "Precisely! By the way, that is the funniest thing y'all have come up with. I can't say 2-B without that silly saying flying through my head. I fear I may blurt it out in front of a patient!"

"By the way, I want to follow up on what Bertie asked you. I'm curious, too. What made you get into pediatrics?"

"When I was in medical school in New York, a former professor of mine had studied under a great mentor named Dr. Abraham Jacobi. Dr. Jacobi was one of the first doctors to teach the subject of diseases in children at New York Medical College. He's the founder of the American Pediatric Society and been dubbed the 'Nestor of American Pediatrics.' I guess my professor's enthusiasm rubbed off on me."

"Interesting, please go on." Addie, lost in his blue eyes, hung on every word. *Dear Lord above. He's so different from Garrett. How can I find myself having feelings for two men? How is that humanly possible?*

"Pediatrics requires attention to minute detail and the acute powers of observation. I loved that aspect of the field. I had to learn to care for the tiny patient based on presenting signs and symptoms, without a word of explanation or utterance of feelings. Children aren't little adults." Randall paused, gazed at all of the children in their beds and cribs, and then continued. "However, they are great gauges of humans and respond intuitively and quickly to the presence of an unsympathetic person. I appreciated that raw, pure, and innocent interaction."

"Well, you have the patience of Job and are so calm and faithful to detail." *Don't embarrass yourself, Addie. Please, don't accidently cut yourself. Remain focused, just like Nurse Hartman and Nurse Scott instructed. Focus on the patient. Focus on the doctor. Ugh! That's my problem.*

Addie carefully cleaned and sterilized the scarifier blades with alcohol, setting the spring-loaded device down on a sterile gauze pad to air dry.

"I had the opportunity to work at the first children's hospital located in Philadelphia, the first pioneer pediatric city of America. They opened the twelve-bed hospital in 1855." Randall paused again. "Come to think of it, foundling asylums date back to the year 787, but were built to care for illegitimate kids. Unfortunately, those abandoned children were put to death, so I really wouldn't consider that providing proper medical care, would you?" He raised his eyebrows, hinting at a smile.

"Heavens no!" Addie wrinkled her freckled nose. "I always wondered why previous cultures thought kids were to be disregarded, abused, or used as slave labor."

"I'm not sure. However, I believe that we can save the world by saving the children."

Bertie rushed over to the sink, overhearing every word of their conversation. She wrung her hands as she spoke. "Oh, that is the most beautiful thing I've ever heard, Dr. Springer."

"Why thank you, Nurse Jones."

The door to the pediatric ward swung open. Nurse Owens entered the room, scanning the room before making her way over to them. Her tone cold and prickly, she said, "Nurse Hartman assigned me here to work the evening shift."

A hand shot up from a little boy in the last bed. "Excuse me, Dr. Springer? May I see you for a moment?"

"Will you excuse me, ladies? I'm sure you want to give Nurse Owens a shift report before you leave for the day. Please be sure to have your charting completed. Remember if you didn't document it, it never happened." Randall walked over to the eight-year-old lad. "How are you feeling? Is your sore throat better?" Dr. Springer brushed the light brown locks off the child's forehead and placed the back of his hand against his skin. "It seems that your fever has broken. I'll have Nurse Owens take your temperature in a few minutes just to be sure."

The boy grabbed Dr. Springer's right wrist. "Oh, please, Doctor. Don't have her stick that thermometer up my butt!"

Randall covered his mouth with the back of his arm and faked a coughing spell.

"That's why I called you over here. I don't want *that* nurse to care for me." He pulled up the covers and discretely pointed at Deborah.

Randall raised a brow. "Why not?"

"She's mean. She says hateful things to crying children and tells us that the boogeyman is going to get us if we don't behave.

I think she even pinches that little baby in the crib over there to make it cry so she can give it sleepy medicine. He always cries after she changes its diaper. Then he falls asleep after sucking on some medicine from a dropper. She even told me I got a sore throat and a fever from telling lies."

"Really?" Randall was trying to process the information, unsure if the boy's active imagination was getting the best of him. The infant was prescribed medication for its colic and typically babies are content after their diapers are changed. He'd hated hearing that the parents abandoned the baby after the father secured a job in North Carolina. Regardless, he opted to keep a watchful eye on Deborah. After all, kids tended to be truthful.

"I'm not a bad boy. I don't tell lies. Mama threatens to wash our mouths out with soap if we do." He stuck out his tongue.

"I know you don't. How about I assign you a different nurse tonight?"

" Yes, please."

Randall pulled up the covers, tucked him in, and fluffed his pillow.

"Dr. Springer? I have one more request."

"What's that?"

"May I have some vanilla ice cream?"

"I don't see why not. I'll tell the charge nurse on the evening shift to allow it."

The little boy beamed. "Oh, thank you, Doctor! I think ice cream is the best medicine."

Dr. Springer winked. "I do, too."

24

"Oh, that's just wonderful news! Thank you, Moira. I'll let Father Preti know that the baby boy in the pediatric ward at Sacred Heart has been cleared to be discharged and will be ready to be picked up later this morning. Uh, huh. You don't say. That *is* dreadful that his parents abandoned him. Uh, huh. No children were allowed in company housing? My, oh, my. Perhaps they thought he'd have a better life with another family. Uh, huh. Oh, yes. I couldn't agree with you more. We'll have him placed in a loving and Godly home within a few months. I'd bet my last breath on that." Ida shifted her weight, causing the wood floors to creak underneath her feet. She lifted her nose in the air. "Oh my heavens! I have to go, Moira. I've got a pot of oatmeal burning on the stove." Ida threw the receiver in the holder and hastily waddled off to the kitchen.

Billy, a few of the orphan boys, and Father Preti opened the back door and walked into a smoke-filled kitchen.

"My goodness, sister! Are you trying to burn down this place?" Father Preti retrieved a rock off the back porch and propped the door open.

Clang! Ida dropped the cast-iron pot into the sink and poured water on the brownish-black blob. *Hiss!* A cloud of white steam rolled out of the sink. "Boys, grab some dish towels and start swirling them in the air to help clear out some of this smoke."

Billy ran to one of the drawers, pulled out a few towels, and handed them out. Billy swung one in circles over his head. The other boys did the same.

"I just got off the phone with Moira at Sacred Heart."

"Ah, so you two were up to no good gossiping, and that's why the oatmeal burned?"

Ida was adamant, placing her hand on her broad hips. "No. She called to let me know that there is a baby boy to be picked up this morning. It seems that the parents had to leave him behind so the father could find work at a local cotton mill in North Carolina. The company didn't allow children in their company housing."

"It seems like you found out a lot of information from that phone call," Father Preti chided.

"Oh, sister! Whatever do you mean?"

Jo turned around with a horrified look on her face. She quickly glanced at the boys, who were oblivious to their conversation and too busy making noises with their mouths as they flipped their dishtowels around.

Ida tottered out of the room, making her way down the back hallway to their bedroom.

"Boys, you're doing a fine job. Keep up the good work." Jo pursued Ida and closed the door to their bedroom behind her.

Ida was already sitting on the side of one of the twin beds, sobbing. "I'm so sorry, Jo. I am always so careful with my words. It just slipped out."

"Don't worry about it, sister. Those boys weren't listening to what we were talking about, let alone enough to notice an incorrect pronoun slip out." Pulling out one of the bureau drawers, she retrieved a pale yellow handkerchief and handed it to Ida. "I need you to get yourself cleaned up and prepare a crib for this new baby that I've got to pick up."

"Oh, will you please forgive me, sister?" She blew her nose with enough force that the tail end of the hanky stood straight out.

"Of course." Jo made the sign of the cross in the air over Ida. "You have been absolved of your wrong doing." She laughed.

Ida balled up the handkerchief and stuffed it into her chocolate brown dress pocket. "You are going to hell if you keep up that kind of behavior." Ida stood and turned to straighten out the cream matelassé. She glanced at her reflection in the dresser mirror and attempted to fix an unmanageable curl sticking out from the top of her head. It refused to be tamed. She spit on two fingers and wet down the lock. It only held for a moment before springing right back up again.

"Just face it, Ida, it's hopeless."

"Nothing is hopeless. I should just shave it all off and get a man's haircut like you did." Ida pulled out a hairpin from her pocket, pulled it apart with her teeth, and stuck it in her hair. "Or, I could get a bad case of head lice like those poor nursing students at Sacred Heart."

"So, that's why they wear those white caps? I thought they looked a bit odd and that was all part of the hospital's new uniform."

"No, sister. Moira told me all about it."

"Of course she did."

"Never cross her, sister. You're lucky you haven't run into her at Clyde's house during your late night rendezvous with him. She'd be a force to reckon with, for sure."

Jo straightened. "How do you know that's who I'm seeing?"

"Oh, please. It was so obvious after our first meeting with him that you two had a thing for each other. I mean, that your tastes for the exotic were similar."

Jo blushed. "He's an interesting sort."

"I'd say. I think he's a complete slimy bastard. But then again, who am I to criticize another for being just as ambitious as we are. These are tough times. We have to do our part to stay afloat and get ahead."

"Well, it takes one to know one, sister."

"Yes, it does."

"Speaking of slimy bastards, any news from Mr. Chang?"

"Not yet. When we made our drop a few weeks ago, his men mentioned that Mr. Chang would probably need another delivery within the week."

"Funny, we've not heard from him yet."

"He's probably keeping a low profile after they found that boy's burned body last month."

Ida's eyes widened. "You think he's involved with that?"

"I sure wouldn't put it past him. He's one scary man. I wouldn't want to double cross him. As he so eloquently put it when we first met, I don't want to be 'torn apart by the dragon.'" Jo snarled and bared her teeth.

"Oh, please. We're saints compared to him."

"Don't act like you're a saint, sister." Jo opened the bedroom door. "We're simply not."

TUESDAY LATE AFTERNOON, SIXTH WARD

Detective McGee parked his patrol car in the ambulance bay and walked into Sacred Heart Hospital using the side door. The sign on the door read, Emergency Entrance. Despite his captain's explicit instructions, McGee felt in his gut that the murdered boys and Holy Cross Orphans' Asylum were related. He had to find proof of the connection by going back to the source: where the orphanage procured their boys. After spotting Moira at her desk, he knew exactly who to start with.

Moira saw Detective McGee approaching the desk out of the corner of her eye. She turned to greet him. "Good afternoon, Detective." She watched him smooth down his light brown hair and unbutton his navy blue overcoat. "What brings you here today?"

"Actually, I'm here to see you." He leaned in closer to her. She stood up and leaned over the desk. "I think you're the brains of this operation and I don't think much gets past you."

Cautious, she took her seat and made herself comfortable. She flattened out her purple suit jacket and tugged on the beige lace sleeves. "I'm flattered you noticed, Detective. I do my job and I do it well. I'd like to see this place run without me," she huffed.

"That's exactly what I'm talking about. I bet they don't go out of their way to show their appreciation for all that you do for them."

"They sure don't. Mr. Alexander is too busy. Mr. Waxman watches me like a hawk. But, my boss, Mr. Posey, he takes real good care of me. He knows I do a good job 'round here. That's all that matters."

"Speaking of Mr. Alexander, is he in the office today? I don't have an appointment, but I was hoping to have a brief conversation with him."

"He sure isn't. He took a leave of absence for a few weeks. It seems that his nanny up and died and his wife is having a hard time with it." Moira glanced over her shoulders and lowered her voice. "I hear she suffers from nerves."

"Oh, I see."

"Well, who's in charge while he's gone?"

"That would be my boss, Mr. Posey, the hospital's COO, but he's not here either. He's got a meeting with Father Preti."

McGee decided to fish for details. "Father Preti? What church does he represent? Is he from the Shrine of the Immaculate Conception?"

"Oh, no. He and his sister run the Holy Cross Orphans' Asylum somewhere over in the First Ward. When we have kids that are abandoned or homeless, we call them to pick them up."

"Really? That's so nice that they do charitable work for the girls and boys in Atlanta."

"Oh, no. They just want boys—the babies up to a certain age." Moira drummed her nails on the wooden desk. "I can't recall exactly up to what age they take. I don't think they like the older boys, though."

"Oh, that's good to know."

"We also refer kids to the Hebrew Orphans' Home, the Georgia Baptist Children's Home, and the Home for the Friendless. However, Mr. Posey said the boys have to go to Holy Cross."

"Interesting. We make referrals for wayward and neglected kids to those other places, too. We try to get them off the streets, but it's an ongoing challenge."

Moira had to ask. "So, I don't mean to be forward, but I don't see a wedding ring. Are you single?"

McGee became flummoxed and speechless. "Wow. You are a bold one, aren't you?"

"Well?" Moira searched his deep blue eyes for an answer. "This girl has to know. I make it my business to be in the know, ya know?" She studied the emerging wrinkles around the corners of his eyes and mouth. She estimated he was in his mid-forties, although his tan skin seemed to age him a bit. He could be five years younger, give or take a year.

McGee surveyed his surroundings, always self-aware of his immediate exits, and evaluating people and the environment for threats. He watched the nurses, doctors, visitors walk by. He was in a safe place and chose to answer her honestly. "I used to be. My wife, Sandra, died a few years back from throat cancer. It's a nasty way to go."

Moira reached out to touch his hand. "I'm so sorry to hear that." She patted it until he slipped his hand out from under hers. "Well, I'm here if you need any…comforting." She searched her desk for a pad of paper and a pen. "Would you like my phone number? Perhaps…."

"I tell you what, why don't I give you my number and you can call me the next time you have a child going to Holy Cross. How does that sound?" He handed her his business card.

A young male attendant pushed a wooden wheelchair up to the front desk. In the wheelchair was an elderly man with an amputated leg. He wore a Confederate officer's frock coat with two columns of brass buttons down the breast of the jacket. A red sash surrounded his waist.

The caretaker tried getting Moira's attention. "Excuse me, ma'am. Mr. Simmons isn't feeling well and wants to see a doctor."

Mr. Simmons began to gag and dry heave. "God damn war! It took my leg!" He retched again. "Those Yankee bastards took my leg!"

Moira popped up. "Get him away from this desk and over to the Emergency Department." She pointed towards the left. "It's at the end of the hall down there."

McGee took the distraction as his cue to leave. He slipped out the back door and stepped out into the cool, breezy afternoon air. As he buttoned his coat, he opted for a walk through the garden to enjoy the fall afternoon and put some puzzle pieces into place before going back to his car.

By the time Moira had directed the ill man and his caretaker to the other end of the hallway, she turned around to find that Detective McGee had already left. She flipped his business card around between her fingers.

"What do you have there?" Clyde walked by as he shed his overcoat. He plucked the card from her hands.

"Hey. What's it any business of yours whose card it is?"

He read it and pocketed it. "What did the detective want today? Did he have any updates for me about the investigation?"

Moira looked genuinely confused. "What investigation? What are you talking about?" Moira reached out over the top of the desk and pulled on his coat. "What haven't you told me?"

As Clyde backed up, Moira's feet slipped out from under her

and flew up in the air behind her. She immediately released his coat and grabbed on to the top of the desk to prevent her from toppling over. He glared at her and hissed. "Ms. Goldberg, please get a grip on yourself. Remember where we are. Let's not bring any attention to ourselves, shall we?"

Once her feet touched the floor, she pleaded, "What investigation are you referring to?"

"It's nothing important. If it was, I would have shared it with you." He thought he better misdirect her rather than have the topic become pillow talk tonight. "It's about a lawsuit between a patient and his employer. Someone lost his finger in a meat grinder, or something like that." He acted put out. "I simply can't be bothered to remember all of the details."

"Oh, well, he didn't mention anything about that while he was here."

"What did he want?"

"He wanted to speak to Mr. Alexander, but I told him he was gone and that you were covering for him during his absence." She omitted telling the whole truth. "I told him you were busy in a meeting and couldn't be bothered."

"Did he say what it was regarding?"

"It had something to do with the Holy Cross Orphanage. He just asked to be called when we send another patient to them."

"You will do no such thing," Clyde snapped and then realized he needed to calm down and collect his thoughts. "Moira, darling, you are such a busy person and vital to this hospital that I will take that task on myself."

Moira softened. "Well aren't you a dear. I told him that you were the only one who truly appreciated me 'round here." She puckered her rouged lips at him. "He left before I had the chance to tell him that Father Preti came by this morning to pick up the baby boy who was abandoned by his parents."

"Don't you worry your pretty little head about it. When I get back into my office, I'll ring him to let him know."

"By the way, how'd your meeting go with him this afternoon?"

"Who?"

"Father Preti, of course."

"Oh, uh, that meeting, uh, went well. Thank you for asking."

Moira gave him a funny look. She nodded her head down repeatedly.

"What's wrong with you? Have you come down with some kind of nervous tick or something?"

"No, you fool." She mouthed, "Your trousers are unzipped."

Clyde quickly draped his coat in front of him. He reached underneath it and zipped up his pants. "Thank you, Ms. Goldberg. That will be all." He walked around the desk, making his way to his office.

"Good afternoon, Moira." Addie and Nurse Kessler walked past the concierge desk, carrying a tray full of medications.

"Is it?" Reticently, Moira sank slowly back down in her chair.

"What's with her?" Susan asked.

Addie rolled her eyes. "Who knows."

"I hear that she is quite the talker."

Addie stopped in front of the door marked *Medical-Surgical Ward* in black paint on the frosted glass. "I heard that, too."

Susan opened the door. They walked toward the medication and supply cabinet.

Nurse Owens intercepted them. "Here, I'll take that tray for you." She reached out and removed the silver tray containing various corked bottles of liquids, powders, and pills in a variety of colors—white, orange, green, pink, red, and brown.

"Oh, well, thank you, Nurse Owens." Addie was taken aback by Deborah's act of kindness.

"I know you two must be very busy helping Nurse Scott restock the medicine cabinets on the wards. I can take it from here."

"Great. We appreciate it. We've still got to get some medications up to the second floor." Susan took Addie by the arm. "Come on. If we finish early, we can get back to the dorm and get a jump on our studies."

"Aren't you the ambitious one!" Addie said as they left the room.

Deborah approached the medicine cabinet and set the tray down. She unlocked the doors with a set of keys and proceeded to inspect each bottle before placing it on its respective shelf.

"I'm almost done changing this dressing. Do you need any help?" Three beds away, Lexie placed a sterile gauze pad over the patient's abdominal incision. She pulled a strip of white tape from the roll and secured the bandage.

"No, I've got this. Thank you, Nurse Carmichael." Deborah turned her back to Lexie. She pulled out two wax paper pouches. She reached for *Strychnine Sulphate* in a brown corked bottle. She poured a few of the white tablets into the envelope, folded the edges over, and stuffed it in her uniform pocket. She recapped the bottle, setting it on the shelf inscribed *For Heart and Respiratory Conditions*. She stocked a few more medications before another drug piqued her interest—*Digitalis*, derived from the Foxglove plant. Deborah uncapped it, poured out a few of the pills in the other pouch, and sealed it before palming it into her pocket. She secured the lid on the bottle and placed it on the shelf next to the Strychnine. Mr. Martin taught them in his Pharmacy lecture last month how digitalis was used for patients with dropsy. Strychnine was used for cardiac conditions. However, if one administered too much of either drug, the consequences were deadly. She closed and locked the medicine cabinet, returning to care for the gentleman in bed number seven, who had sustained a fractured femur after being kicked in the left thigh by his horse.

25

Clad in a yellow silk robe with two green dragons scaling the back, Mrs. Lee pointed at the two APD officers in civilian clothes sitting on a beige and gold silk-covered couch in the "White Room," a private seating area decorated in white, cream, beige, and gold. Large white peacock feathers displayed in pale green-ish-white jade vases sat on octagonal tables in each corner of the room. "Come this way, Mr. Washington and Mr. Lincoln. Mr. Chang will see you now." She escorted the officers up the main stairs.

"I think I need one of these dragon banisters in my house," Mr. Lincoln said to Mr. Washington, caressing the hand railing as he ascended the stairs.

"I think its befitting the house of a former president," Mr. Washington joked. "It's funny how Mr. Chang thought to give you the name of Lincoln. I'm the tall and slender one with dark hair."

He poked Mr. Lincoln in his abundant belly.

"Hey! What the hell is wrong with you? Keep your damn

hands off of me. If you are that upset about your alias, then I'll swap with you."

Mrs. Lee stopped at the top of the stairs. "There will be no name swapping. Mr. Chang has his reasons for assigning each of you those names. Remember, this is his house, his rules."

"Must we remind him who's working for whom in this town?" Mr. Lincoln pulled back his brown wool suit jacket to reveal his gold badge and holstered Smith and Wesson revolver.

"Suit yourself." Mrs. Lee parted the heavy red velvet curtain.

The officers followed her into the room and found Mr. Chang sitting on a black leather couch with two women wearing only pale pink illusion robes. They were barely visible through the thick haze of smoke emitted by burning incense and pipe smoke. Black Chinese lanterns with red tassels that hung from the ceiling draped the room in a yellow-cast.

"Welcome, Mr. Washington and Mr. Lincoln. It's a pleasure seeing you tonight. Ladies, if you'll excuse us." Mr. Chang slapped the brunette on the buttocks when she stood up. The blonde popped out her rear end. He smacked her bare cheeks. He watched Mrs. Lee escort the women out. She, too, left the room.

"Thanks for seeing us on such short notice." Mr. Lincoln walked over to the red velvet, floral-patterned wallpaper and stroked it. "Nice stuff."

"My time precious, like sand in hourglass, I'm watching it slip by, grain by grain, as you pet my wall."

Mr. Washington snickered.

"Fine. I'll get straight to the point." Mr. Lincoln stuffed his hands in his pants pockets. "We caught wind that one of our detectives at the APD is sniffing around and asking a lot of questions about the murdered boys and the Holy Cross Orphanage. He thinks there is some kind of link. I hope and pray you don't have anything to do with those dead kids."

Mr. Chang pointed his right index finger at him; a long nail exaggerated his point. "None of your business what I do in this town. That's what I pay you for. Protection and information. In return, you get useful information about clients."

"Yes, but you've not been forthcoming about two people: Father Preti and Clyde Posey. We keep seeing them come and go from here. We see that as a clue. We're thinking that's kind of an odd coincidence. Don't you? You wouldn't want us relaying that kind of information, would you?"

Mr. Chang threw his hands up in the air. "What you two doing? Staking out my place?"

"Hey, you're the one who keeps us on your payroll for…oh, how did you phrase it? Oh, yeah, 'protection and information.' It's our job to be knowledgeable. Information is power." Mr. Lincoln strolled over to take a seat in one of the pair of leopard-covered chairs with daintily-curved ebony arms and legs.

Mr. Chang fired off, "That chair not for you, fat boy."

"Hey, it's not nice to throw insults at my partner," Mr. Washington interjected.

"All I say is those chairs not meant for big men, such as you. They meant for delicate asses." Mr. Chang patted his slight backside.

"Oh, for the love of God!" Mr. Lincoln huffed. He grabbed his partner's arm. "Come on, we're outta here."

"Don't say we didn't warn you, Chang. You're on your own with this mess."

Mr. Chang called out, "That's Mr. Chang to you. Don't you forget that, fat boy!"

Mr. Lincoln whipped around.

Mr. Washington grabbed the back of his partner's jacket and murmured, "It's not worth the risk. Let's not mess up a good thing. The pay is too good."

"Listen to your buddy, fat boy."

"What did you call me? I hope to the dear Lord above you keep your trap shut. If you don't, I'm gonna shut it permanently for you."

"Are you threatening Mr. Chang?" Mr. Chang moved to the edge of the sofa and discretely reached underneath it. "There are plenty of other APD officers that would love to be in your shoes. It's a privilege to work for the dragon."

Mr. Lincoln turned to his partner. "Take me outta here. If you don't, I swear to God, I'm gonna regret my next move."

Mr. Washington whispered, "The day will come when we'll need to slay this dragon. It's not today."

"Promise?"

"Promise."

TUESDAY EVENING, FOURTH WARD

"You promise you are telling me the whole truth about the investigation?" Moira batted her eyelashes as Clyde thrust himself inside her.

"Oh, for the love of God! Really Moira, you want to talk

about this now?" The phone rang. He groaned as he slid off of her and crawled over the crumpled blankets and bed sheets to the bedside table to answer it. "Hello?"

"We need to talk. The dragon very upset. We may have problem."

Clyde pulled up the green velvet coverlet. Moira reached behind her head, extracted an extra pillow, and handed it to Clyde. He stuffed it between his bare back and the pecan headboard. "What do you mean by *we*? Please explain."

Moira rolled over and brushed her dark curly hair out of her face. She adjusted the covers and closed her eyes.

"Two of my APD officers tipped me off about a snooping detective. The dragon don't like snoops. The dragon feasts on snoops."

"So, what does that have to do with me? Or, as you so eloquently put it, what does that have to do with us?"

"They mentioned seeing you and Jo coming and going from here."

Clyde stiffened. He pressed the receiver tightly against his ear so Moira couldn't overhear Mr. Chang's voice. "Why are they staking out your place?"

"That's what I say. They say they protecting me. But…"

"You know what you have to do." Clyde gazed over at Moira, watching the blanket gently rise and fall. "It's time to shut down that operation."

"But…"

"You have other resources. It's getting too risky for the both of us. You need to erase all traces that lead back to you and I."

"Both of them?"

"Yes, both."

"Okay. The dragon will take care of everything."

"Good." Clyde carefully returned the receiver into the holder and set the phone on his nightstand. He ran his hands over his head. He hated making such decisions, but in order to follow in his father's footsteps to the Georgia State Capital, his path needed to be kept clear of any obstructions. His mind raced. Slipping out of bed, he wrapped himself in his blue velvet robe and walked towards the bedroom door. He looked back at Moira. She was sleeping soundly. He carefully twisted the door knob, stepped into the hallway, and shut the door behind him.

Moira's eyes shot open.

26

Billy swept the dust and debris into a small pile and pushed it across the threshold of his bedroom doorway into the main hallway. He reached down with the white enamel dust pan. *Ring.* There was no sign of Father Preti or his sister. *Ring.* Dropping the broom handle and pan to the floor, Billy ran to answer the phone. "Hey, this is Billy Swanson. May I help you?"

Silence.

"Is anybody there?"

Ida swooped in, breathless, and grunted, "Give me that phone." She grabbed it out of Billy's hands and shoved him to the floor.

"Hello. Hello." Ida's tone was melodic and sweet.

Abruptly, the caller asked, "Ida? Is that you? This is Mr. Chang."

"Oh, yes, Mr. Chang. How can we be of service to you?" Ida glared at Billy, shooing him away.

Billy scrambled to his feet and slipped around the corner. Picking up the broom and pan, he tiptoed up the hall to overhear Ida's conversation.

"You want your men to come to make a pick up here? *To-night?* This is highly unusual, Mr. Chang. I was under the impression that…." The floor boards creaked and squeaked as she shifted her weight. "Look, Mr. Chang. You don't have to make any kind of threat. I was only trying to say that…." She hissed as she exhaled. "Fine. Nine o'clock it is. I'll pick the perfect boy for you." Ida was quiet for a moment. "Hello? Mr. Chang, are you still there?" She slammed down the phone.

Billy heard footsteps storming his direction. He scurried back down the hallway towards the baby's room, resuming his chores.

Ida stomped towards him. "Don't you dare wake that baby."

Billy peered in the room. The infant was swaddled, asleep in his crib. "He's sleeping, ma'am."

"Fine. Keep a watch on him. I've got to go back out to the garden and have a talk with Father Preti." Ida rotated on her black boot heels, teetering from side to side. She swung her arms from side to side to propel herself forward faster.

Billy heard her clomp through the kitchen. *Screech. Slam.* He ran into the kitchen, stood on his tip-toes and peered out the window towards the garden in the backyard. Ida's hands and arms flailed in the air as she summoned Father Preti to her side. Billy ran to the phone. He picked up the earphone and mouthpiece. "Hello? Is anybody out there?"

The telephone operator replied, "Hello. Where would you like to place your call, sir?"

Billy swallowed and lowered his voice, mimicking a stuffy grown-up. "Patch me through to Sacred Heart Hospital. Stat!" He had overheard Dr. Springer using that term often on the pediatric ward. He watched the nurse scurry whenever they heard that word. Oblivious to the meaning, he thought it would apply here. His heart raced; he was embarking on a secret mission like ones he read about in his favorite book.

"Yes, sir. Whom shall I say is calling?"

"Uh, Dr. Swanson." Billy listened for approaching footsteps or voices.

"Sacred Heart Hospital. This is Moira. How may I help you?"

"This is the operator. I'm connecting this physician's call to you. Go ahead, Doctor Swanson."

Click. Silence.

"Is anybody on the other line?" Moira probed. "Hello?"

Billy's legs trembled. "This is Dr. Swanson. I need to speak to Nurse Engle about a patient...stat."

"Give me just a moment while I connect you to the pediatric ward, sir."

"Pediatrics. This is Nurse Engle. How may I help you?"

"I've got a Dr. Swanson calling for you, Nurse Engel. He's on the line."

"Is this Nurse Engle?" Billy paced.

"Yes, sir. I've connected you to pediatrics where Nurse Engle is assigned to work today."

"Moira, thank you for connecting the call. You can hang up now."

Silence. *Click.*

"Please proceed, uh, who is calling? I'm sorry I didn't catch your name, Doctor."

Click.

Billy resumed talking in his normal voice. "Nurse Engel, it's me, Billy."

"Are you okay, Billy? Is everything all right?"

Frantic, Billy remained vigilant. "I'm not sure. I can't talk long. I overheard Ms. Preti talking on the phone to someone named, Mr. Chang. He's sending men to come here tonight to pick up a boy."

"Oh, my goodness!"

"Will you call the detective to let him know?"

"Of, course."

Billy heard Ida's voice through the house walls. "I gotta go."

Click. Moira disconnected from the call.

Screech. Slam.

Billy quietly set the phone down and bolted around the corner towards the back bedrooms.

Ida appeared in the main hall. The hall darkened. Her wide frame blocked the light flowing from the front of the house. "Is that baby still sleeping?"

Winded, Billy tried to remain composed. Without looking at her, he replied, "Yes, ma'am." He bent over and scooped up his pile.

Ida walked back toward the kitchen, stopping to adjust the position of the phone. She looked back over her shoulder and heard Billy sweeping. "I must have not put it back properly in my haste," she muttered.

THURSDAY AFTERNOON, SIXTH WARD

Addie walked with purpose towards Randall. "Dr. Springer, I need to speak with you privately, if you please." Her cheeks flushed, hives erupted on her neck.

He bent over a little girl whose appendix had been removed a few weeks ago. "Give me just a moment. I've got two more stitches to remove." He held a pair of silver hemostats in his left hand and a pair of suture scissors in the other.

"Yes, of course. I'll be over here." Addie pointed at the nurse's desk.

"Are you alright, Nurse Engel?" Opal pointed at Addie's cheeks and neck.

"I'm fine." Addie returned to her desk and resumed charting on her patients.

"Please place a sterile dressing over this, Nurse Alexander." Dr. Springer handed Opal his instruments.

"Yes, Doctor Springer." Opal watched Randall walk over to Addie.

"What is it, Nurse Engel?"

"I just got a call from Billy Swanson at the orphanage. He overheard Ms. Preti talking to someone named Mr. Chang. Billy said men are coming to the orphanage tonight to pick up a boy."

"That's very odd." Randall crossed his arms.

"I know. He sounded scared. We've got to do something to save those poor boys."

"I'll call Detective McGee to let him know."

"Tell him we'd be happy to help him in any way we can."

"I will." Randall uncrossed his arms. "I'll call him from the doctor's lounge. I'll be back in a minute. Can you hold down the fort until I get back?"

"Yes, sir." Addie saluted.

"Attagirl!"

Randall left the ward.

Opal returned her dressing supplies to the tray and rolled it over to Addie. "What's going on? You're all broken out."

Addie debriefed her.

"Father told me in private about the investigation. Gosh, count me in to help in any way I can. I know he wouldn't have it any other way." Opal returned her supplies to the medical cabinet and washed her hands.

Randall returned.

"What happened? How did your conversation go with Detective McGee?" Addie looked over at Opal. She motioned her to come join them. "Don't worry. She knows everything."

Opal approached. "It's okay. Father told me all about it."

"Well, Detective McGee was very appreciative of the information. He's in a bit of a quandary. However, without going into too many details, he said he will need our help tonight. Finish up your charting." He looked at his wristwatch. "You've got another fifteen minutes before your shift ends. Be quick and concise with your report to the next shift." He tapped his toe on the floor. "Head back to the dorms, change your clothes, and meet me in the garage in one hour."

Addie fanned herself using a manila-colored file folder. "What about Nurse Hartman? We can't simply leave the property without her permission. She'll give us demerits."

He folded and unfolded his arms again.

"Don't worry about her. I'll also have a quick chat with Dr. Williams, too."

"What about Mr. Posey?" Opal asked with furrowed brow. "You know he's covering for Father during his absence."

"I'll let Dr. Williams handle him. Mr. Posey is his boss, not mine." Randall removed his white medical jacket and hung it on the brass hook on the wall. He picked up his black leather doctor's bag and opened the ward door. "I'm off to do my shift report and transition my patients' care to the oncoming doctor. Don't dawdle, ladies. I'll see you in an hour." He shut the door behind him.

THURSDAY EVENING, FIRST WARD

Knock. Knock. Ida shuffled to the front door and opened it. "Good evening to you both. Father Preti and I have been expecting you."

Jo folded *The Atlanta Dispatch*, got up from the sofa in the living room, and walked over to greet the two Chinese gentlemen. Familiar with the men, she smiled and extended her hand.

"Where are the boys?" Gang asked as he reached behind his suit jacket with his right hand.

"Locked in their bedroom, like always. I've picked out the perfect boy for you tonight." Ida reached into her navy skirt pocket.

"Not so fast." Gang pulled out his .38 revolver.

Chongan did the same, revealing he held rope in his other hand. "Sit down."

"What's the meaning of this?" Ida stumbled back into Jo.

"Shhh. Keep your voices down. Don't want to cause a fuss."

They pointed their guns at the women's heads. "Sit down."

Ida and Jo took a seat on the couch.

Ida started crying. "Sister, what have we done?"

"We haven't done anything wrong," Jo snapped. "Why is Mr. Chang doing this to us?"

Chongan handed his gun to his older brother. He tied Jo's wrists behind her back. He did the same to Ida while Gang held both guns on them. He pulled out two handkerchiefs. He stuffed them into their mouths, securing them with red bandanas.

"Get up and walk." Gang handed his brother's gun back to him.

Chongan directed them out of the house. Ida struggled, knocking off her cross-stitch masterpiece from the front hall wall, which read *Sow seeds of hope so you can reap your future potential.* She stepped on it. *Crack!* The hand-made oak frame broke. Mr. Chang's henchmen shoved Jo and Ida out the front door and down the front porch steps, towards the back of their black truck.

Gang pulled out a dark green bottle. He uncorked it, poured the liquid onto a rag, and forced it over Jo's face. Jo kicked and fought, but the powerful drug overtook her. She fell limp. The men lifted her large frame into the back of the truck. Ida took off running. Chongan pursued her. He wrapped his arms around her, tackling her to the ground. He jumped up, grabbed her upper arm, and forced her up at gunpoint to walk back to the truck. She wiggled and tried to yell. Her eyes darted wildly. Saliva dribbled from her chin.

Gang subdued her with his medicated towel. He grabbed her under her shoulders as she slipped into unconsciousness. "God, she's heavy." He stumbled. "Get her legs before I fall."

Chongan hoisted her feet up. Together, they rolled her next to her sister. "I think she need more medicine. Don't want her waking up during our drive. She like wrestling a pig in mud." He laughed, wiping sweat from his brow. He pulled out two more bandanas, blindfolding them.

Gang handed him the bottle and the towel. "Don't use too much." He disappeared around the side of the truck, got into the driver's side, and turned the engine over.

A mile down the road, Gang heard sirens off in the distance.

"Faster, brother, faster!"

"No, slower. Faster raises suspicions. Faster means we did something wrong. We go slow. We blend in."

The Sacred Heart ambulance flew by them. Sirens whined.

"Hurry, Dr. Springer. Time is of the essence."

Randall glared. "Look, if you feel more qualified to drive, then I'll be happy to pull over and let you."

Addie blanched.

Opal howled. "Now that's funny. Addie has no idea how to drive."

"Well, I bet I can hitch up a horse to a wagon faster than you can."

"Well …"

Randall barked, "Ladies, really? Can you manage to quiet yourselves while I'm driving at top speed? Goodness gracious! You remind me of two cackling hens."

"Hey!" they snapped in unison.

Addie turned around and peered through the back windshield. "Mr. McDaniel isn't far behind us." *My heavens, what are we getting ourselves into?*

Randall pulled the ambulance into the dirt driveway, passing the *Holy Cross Orphans' Asylum* sign, and guided the vehicle towards the back of the house, grinding the gears into park. He turned off the engine. "There's no sign of Detective McGee yet. I was told we need to wait for him before we do anything."

We can't wait. We must safeguard the children. Addie scrambled out of the ambulance and darted towards the front of the orphanage. She flew around the corner, her navy-blue nurse's cape flapping behind her.

"Addie! No! Wait!" Randall objected.

Brice spun his ambulance into the side yard and hopped out. "Jesus, Mary, and Joseph! Doc, you sure you don't want a job working for the McDaniel Brothers? I think you topped 'er out, don't you?"

"Hey! Over here!" Addie shouted out before she ran inside through the open front door.

Suddenly, the black truck pulled up.

Chongan leapt out and brandished his gun. *Bang! Bang!*

Randall, Opal, and Brice dove to the ground and scrambled for cover behind Brice's ambulance.

Bang!

"Oh, dear God! ADDIE!" Opal screamed.

Chongan lit the long fuse to the TNT and tossed it through the open front door. The truck began to pull away. *Bang! Bang! Bang!* He grabbed on to the passenger door and flung himself inside the cab. The door shut.

As the truck sped off, Randall, Opal, and Brice raced around the vehicle only to witness Addie throwing the sparkling red stick out the front door. It landed on the front lawn.

"Get out of the way! It's gonna blow!" Addie yelled as she ran inside the house again. *Dear God, protect us all from harm.*

"Holy f-beaver balls! Get down!" Brice pulled on Opal's cape and hurled his massive frame over Randall and Opal.

Detective McGee punched the accelerator in his patrol car. From Chapel Road, he saw a red and orange fireball erupt through the wooded tree line. He turned his steering wheel sharply to the right. The patrol car tires squealed and a cloud of dust trailed behind him as he drove up the orphanage driveway. He slammed on the brakes and quieted the siren. "Oh, God! Am I too late?" Black smoke billowed, disappearing in the night sky. Spotting Randall behind the ambulance, he got out of his car and sprinted over to him. He found Opal curled up in Brice's arms, weeping. "Are y'all alright? Is anybody hurt?"

Randall looked panicked. "We don't know yet."

"Oh, no! Did we lose the children?"

"I don't know." Randall ran around to the front of the house. "I don't know," he cried out. "ADDIE! ADDIE!" The front porch was gone, the front windows blown out, and pieces of lumber hung from the outside walls that were still intact. He raked his fingers over the sides of his head and pulled on his hair. "NO!" He dropped to his knees. "Oh, dear Lord! What have I done?"

Detective McGee ran to the back of the house. He emerged a few minutes later. In tow were the orphan boys, two helping Billy walk, and Addie, who carried a fussy baby boy. All sustained a few scratches and were a bit sooty and dirty.

Randall, Opal, and Brice ran to them. Opal hurled herself at Addie, hugging them both. Addie trembled. The baby continued to cry. Opal carefully lifted the baby out of Addie's shaking hands.

A silly grin spread on Billy's face. He reached out to Randall. "Ya shoulda seen it, doctor, miss-ter, sirrr. We were s-s-saved by an angel, I tell ya. She swoo-ooped in, broke down our bed-room-room door, and got us-s-s out before KA-BOOM!"

"I think he's been given some kind of sedative." Addie wrung her hands.

"Sh-sh-she even managed to grab my book off my night stand." One of the orphans held up Billy's copy of *The Iliad & the Odyssey.* "This is quite the adventure, I'd s-s-say! Did they teach you how to do all th-th-that in nurs-shing s-s-school?"

Addie's eyes fixed on Randall. "Prioritize, act, analyze, evaluate, and reprioritize."

"Addie, I think you're in shock. Have a seat. I'll be right back to check on you." Addie sat cross-legged on the cold ground. Caressing the fescue with her fingers, she watched Randall assess Billy and the rest of the orphans.

"Mr. McDaniel, load them up, and you and Opal take them to the ED. Dr. Williams will be expecting you." Randall whispered, "Beaver balls?"

Brice whispered back. "I started to blurt out the f-word and realized I couldn't use that word in front of Miss Opal. Me mutha raised me and me brothahs to be a good ol' Irish gentlemen." Brice slapped Randall on his back with such force, he almost toppled over. "We need to put some lead in your shoes, Doc!"

"You're a funny guy! We're really lucky to have you." Randall called back to Brice as he made his way to Addie. "God speed to you."

Randall knelt down and cradled Addie's face in his hands. "That was the bravest thing I have ever seen." He wiped soot from her nose. He felt her whole body quake. "Are you hurt?

Addie shook her head.

"Are you okay?"

Addie nodded.

"I thought I lost you." He pressed his lips against hers.

Addie responded, wrapping her arms around him, and pulling him in tight.

Brice revved the engine and sounded the siren. The ambulance sped away.

Detective McGee approached them and cleared his throat. "I hate to interrupt you two lovebirds, but we have more pressing matters to attend to." Randall and Addie separated immediately. "I'll need for you to follow me to Mr. Chang's emporium. It's not far from here. I'm afraid we're going to find more young children there. They're going to need medical attention." He paused. "I need to get to a phone. I've got to call this in and make sure I've got back up at the emporium."

"I saw one inside. It's in the main hallway just outside the kitchen."

Detective McGee darted past them.

"Addie. I'm so sorry. I don't know what just happened. I was so overcome with emotion."

"I think a sweet kiss is the perfect medicine to cure shock, don't you, Doctor Springer?"

"Now, there's my Addie." Randall combed back Addie's short auburn locks off her forehead as he examined a few of her superficial scratches.

"Don't worry. This will be our little secret. No one needs to know. Besides, if Nurse Hartman ever found out, I'd get kicked out of nursing school for sure."

"I won't let that happen, ever."

Detective McGee returned and motioned for them to follow him. "No sirens!" he shouted. Turning his palm to the sky, raindrops pooled in his hand and cascaded down his forearm. McGee got into his patrol car.

"Come on." Randall grabbed Addie's hand. They returned to the ambulance and tailed the detective's car through the First Ward.

Once at the emporium, patrol cars had already blocked the streets around the bordello. With a flash of his badge, Detective McGee pulled through the barricade. Randall and Addie were instructed to park on an adjacent side street.

Detective McGee ran up to Randall's driver side window. Rain rolled off the brim of his hat. "Stay put." He pointed at Addie. "And that goes for you, too, young lady. No shenanigans." He opened his raincoat that covered his navy-blue jacket, pulled out his gun from the holster, and checked it for ammunition. "We'll bring the children out to you. It will take a while to clear the place, so be patient." He disappeared into the dark shadows of the street. Lightening streaked across the sky. A few seconds later, thunder rolled. He joined the policemen gathered outside the front door. Detective McGee ordered, "On three, men. One... two..." *Boom!* The front door swung open. "Be careful and clear every room in this place!" He grabbed two officers by the shoulders. "Go find the children and take them to the Sacred Heart ambulance the next street over to the west, just outside the barricade. I have a pediatrician and a nurse ready to care for them and transport them back to the hospital for medical care."

"Will do!" The men ran past the screaming women and protesting clientele being rounded up in the lounge and cautiously slipped behind a gold velvet curtain partition.

Detective McGee spotted the dragon banister leading to the second floor. He ran up the stairs, taking two at a time. He called out, "Does anybody have Chang yet?" He watched the officers shake their heads as he walked by the various colorfully decorated bedrooms containing nude or partially clad male clientele and naked male and female prostitutes. He walked to the end of the hall and kicked the black door open. He found Mrs. Lee naked, sitting cross-legged in a tall, jade green, winged-back chair. Her long ebony hair flowed over her shoulders, covering her breasts. She dipped her long gold nails, one by one, in her teacup on the end table. Her index finger was covered with a gold, razor-sharp talon.

McGee scanned the small room for additional threats. There were none. White orchids, a wood-burning fireplace, a fully stocked book shelf, a jade-green sofa and another end table occupied the low-lit room. "Where's Chang?"

"Don't you mean *Mr.* Chang?"

"Don't get smart with me. Where is he?"

"He's not here." Mrs. Lee refused to divulge that Mr. Chang escaped through a secret passage located behind the bookcase moments earlier. She chose not to accompany him, but rather decided to serve as a distraction. She grabbed the armrests of the chair and slowly rose to her bare feet. She parted her hair, exposing her dark brown nipples and tiny breasts, and raised her hands in the air. "As you can see, I'm not armed."

McGee took one step closer, keeping his eyes on her dark irises. The years had taught him that the eyes were the first thing to betray one's true intent. Her eyes frosted. She lashed out at him with her right hand. The talon lacerated his left cheek. She tilted her head to the right, reached across her body, and sliced the side of her neck before he could gain control of both her wrists. Blood spurted with every beat of her heart; she had hit the carotid artery. He kneed her in the gut. Mrs. Lee doubled over. He lost his grasp on her and stumbled backwards. Images in the room blurred and whirled.

He fell to the floor. "Sandra…."

Mrs. Lee lay motionless on the oriental carpet, her mouth agape. Searing pain surged through McGee's entire body. Paralyzed, he felt his heart beat erratically. He desperately wanted to breathe, alert and aware that he was suffocating. McGee's heartbeat slowed, rendering him unconscious. *Ba-dum…ba…dum… ba….*

THURSDAY NIGHT, STONE MOUNTAIN, GEORGIA

Gang and Chongan hoisted Ida's lifeless body out of the back of the truck and threw her into the rectangular wooden crate that sat on the make-shift barge on the shoreline.

Gang chided his younger brother. He whispered angrily, "You use too much. You use too much."

Chongan fired back, "Sorry, my brother. She so big. Thought she needed more sleep medicine."

Ida's heart had stopped beating fifteen minutes earlier. The towel saturated with chloroform had taken its toll. The men returned to the truck to retrieve Jo. Her shallow chest movements brought relief to Gang. He had received strict instructions from Mr. Chang to not kill the Preti sisters before they were placed into their final resting place. 'Return those vile lotus flowers back to the mud,' he'd said.

Drifting in and out of consciousness, Jo felt as if she were floating. Blindfolded, she tried to cut through her foggy thoughts. Overhearing the men speaking in Chinese, she instinctively began to struggle to free herself from their grip. One arm broke free; she flailed. They dropped her upper body onto the damp grass and continued to drag her by her feet to the water's edge. Jo felt sharp stabbing pains in her scalp, neck, shoulders, and upper back as rocks and pebbles cut through her priest's jacket and tore her flesh. She felt her upper body rise again. The floating sensation returned. Jo heard the familiar sound of water lapping along a shoreline before she was thrown. She landed on a hard surface. *Thud.* She smelled fresh cut wood and then heard the pounding of a hammer on nails. *Bam. Bam. Bam. Bam.* Silence. The box began to rock gently. Jo inhaled, noting her sister's familiar perfume—roses. Frantic, she ripped off the blindfold and gag and groped around the container. She felt cotton fabric and panicked. She ran her hands up Ida's lifeless body and held her hand in front of her sister's nose and mouth; her breath was absent.

"Oh, God! Sister, what have they done to you?" Jo cried out, banging on the sides of the box. "Let me out! Help! Someone help me please! Dear God, help us!"

Gang's reply in Chinese told her that her pleas for help were futile. Jo patted her pockets to find anything she could use to aid in her escape. She found her rosary beads in her left pants pocket. She rapidly rolled the beads between her fingers, locating the metal cross attached at the end of the strand. She used it to claw and scrape at the wooden siding. Splinters lodged underneath her fingernails. Despite the agonizing pain, she persisted.

The crate tilted left. *Splash.* Jo felt the box bobble before water began seeping in the sides, flooding the compartment.

Jo screamed. "HELP ME! For the love of God, help me! I didn't mess with the dragon! Please, we didn't do anything wrong. We never snitched to anyone!" She kicked and banged her fists against the sides and top of the container. The water level rose. She sobbed and pleaded, "Please get me out. HELP! HELP!" The water reached her chin. Jo tilted her head back, struggling to breathe. Hyperventilating, she continued to blindly feel around the box in the darkness for any signs of vulnerability in its structure. Nothing. Water entered her nose. Jo inhaled one last time as water cascaded over her head. Shivering, she tried to fight the urge to exhale. However, reflexes took over. Jo exhaled, then inhaled water.

27

"Is it sunny out?" Charlie leaned on his elbows. He watched Scout, who stood in front of his executive desk, fiddle with his tweed cap. He motioned for him to take a seat. He mouthed, "I'm waiting for a reply from Moira." His lit cigar rested in the blue glass ashtray. Swirls of smoke rolled under his nose and disappeared.

Scout picked up the stack of bound newspapers that were occupying the chair by the strings and placed them on the floor.

"Cloudy? You don't say." Beams of sunlight streamed through his office windows. "Do you think it will be cloudy for a while? Uh, huh. Who's Alan? Uh, huh. Well, the information you provided me with yesterday about the orphans was very helpful. In fact, everything checked out. I plan on publishing a big story next week, provided it gets cleared by Sam and the editorial department. Uh, of course I kept your name out of the article." Charlie rolled his eyes. "Whatever. Gotta scoot. Call me later." Charlie hung up the phone. "What a broad. She's a real piece of work and really knows how to work it." He picked up his cigar. "What do you have for me?"

"According to the coroner, it appears that the detective in charge of the murdered kids' case was poisoned by the mamasan at Mr. Chang's emporium. I believe he said her last name was Lee. She committed suicide."

"How?"

"She slit her throat. Evidently, she put some kind of poison on her fingernails. When she scratched the detective, she introduced the stuff into his system."

"That sounds like a nasty way to die."

"Oh, it is. Do you want to know how the poison works?"

"No, kid. Spare me the details. I don't want the little ol' ladies writing me to tell me that I was too graphic in my article. It's bad enough that I have to pen a story about a vile children's sex ring operation in Atlanta. But, it is a reality and it's my job to tell the story." He puffed on the cigar and made o-rings in the air. "Is there anything else that might be of interest to *The Atlanta Dispatch* readers?"

"When the coroner flipped the Chinese lady over on her stomach, she had an enormous colorful dragon tattoo on her back. Its hind legs extended across her butt cheeks and the tail wound down the back of her left leg. He said the mark symbolizes power, strength, and longevity, and it can also mean 'good luck.'"

"Well, I would say that it didn't serve her very well, did it?"

Scout laughed. "I guess it depends on your perspective." He twirled his cap on his finger. "She won't be rotting in a jail cell and hung for her crimes."

"You got me there." Charlie leaned back in his burgundy leather chair and propped his well-worn black cowboy boots on the edge of his desk. "So, you have greedy caretakers at the Holy Cross Orphans' Asylum who are looking to make an extra buck by selling young boys to some Chinaman." He scratched his head.

"Mr. Chang."

"Mr. Chang. So, the million dollar question is, where's Father Preti, his sister, Ida, and Mr. Chang? Why aren't they in custody yet?"

Scout shrugged his shoulders. "Dunno. The APD is baffled. They're freaked out about the loss of one of their own, not to mention the fact that they can't find these people. It's like they vanished into thin air."

Charlie threw his hands up. "What am I missing?"

"According to one of the officers, there appears to be a link between Chang and the murdered boys they've been finding all over Atlanta. They think that Chang procured some of those kids from Holy Cross Orphanage."

Charlie brooded. "My stomach turns at the thought that there are perverted bastards that get off on little kids, and that there are soulless, evil bastards who can murder them. Regardless, there's a special place in hell for both kinds."

"There is a silver lining to all of this. The kids they rescued from Mr. Chang's basement, where they were kept heavily drugged and imprisoned, were all okay. There were eight boys and five girls, all under the age of twelve. They are being medically cared for at Sacred Heart."

"That's what Moira told me yesterday, too. She said the hospital has converted the medical library on the A-wing of the second floor into a make-shift dorm for the orphan boys. The five girls are being supervised on the pediatric ward. They plan on keeping the children until proper arrangements can be made to safeguard them." He tapped the cigar ashes in ashtray. "While the physical wounds might heal, the psychological scars are going to linger." Charlie peered out his office window. "If I'm going to write this story, I want to have a call to action for the public. Perhaps those rescued children can end up in decent homes and not be placed into another orphanage. I'll reach out to the hospital and give them a heads-up about my plan. If their phones are going to start ringing from calls from attorneys with interested adoptive parents, I want them to be prepared."

"Don't forget about those orphan boys from Holy Cross."

"Oh, I won't."

"Am I seeing a softer side to you, Mr. Finch?"

Charlie took his feet off his desk. He slammed his fist onto his desk. "Don't get used to it. Now get out of here. I've got work to do."

Scout got up to leave. "It looks good on you."

"Oh, shut up. Get the hell out of here. And, shut that damn door on your way out!" he ordered.

"Yes, sir." Scout put his cap on his sandy blonde hair, closing the door behind him.

SATURDAY AFTERNOON, SIXTH WARD

"There's a letter for you, Addie." Opal handed her a white envelope. Addie recognized the handwriting and the return address from the Fourth Ward. It was marked *Special Delivery*. Opal sat down next to her on her bed.

"Hey, what about giving me a little bit of privacy?" Addie scooted down a few inches.

Opal turned her back to Addie. "Fine." Opal glanced at the mirror on the far wall. Spotting her reflection, she saw a piece of hair sticking out from under her cap. She tucked it behind her ear. She looked up at the clock hanging above it and noted the time. "We've got about ten minutes before we have meet with Nurse Hartman in her office." She stood up. "You're going to have to read it while we walk over there."

Addie had flipped to the second page of the letter by the time they descended the back stairs and exited through the back door. Opal and Addie walked in silence through the garden.

Opal looked up at the sky. "Isn't it just a beautiful afternoon? I love the fall and a cloudless, blue sky."

Addie stuffed the letter back in the envelope and tucked it away in her nursing uniform pocket. "Me, too."

They walked up the hospital's back stairs.

"Aren't you going to at least give me a little bit of a hint who it's from?" Opal opened the back door to the hospital.

"Nope."

Once inside, Addie and Opal took a right at the concierge desk, and walked toward Lena's office.

"You know, you aren't supposed to keep secrets from your best friend."

Addie knocked on Nurse Hartman's door. "You'll find out soon enough."

"You're impossible, Addie."

"Come in," a male voice commanded.

Addie and Opal looked at each other and shrugged their shoulders. They entered the room, shutting the door behind them. Nurse Hartman sat behind her desk. Clyde stood to her left.

Carefully eyeing them, he pointed at the empty chairs. "Make yourself comfortable, ladies."

Nurse Hartman folded her arms across her chest.

"I hear you were quite the brave souls on Thursday evening. Sacred Heart Hospital thanks you for assisting Dr. Springer and that poor detective."

Addie and Opal looked confused. "What do you mean by 'poor detective?'" Addie unfastened her cape, removed it, and laid it across her lap. She smoothed out the wrinkles.

"He died," Clyde blurted out.

Opal gasped. "What?"

"How?"

Nurse Hartman bit her lip and remained silent.

"He succumbed to injuries sustained at the …."

"Oh, for the love of Pete." Nurse Hartman wasn't going to tolerate Clyde's pompous nonsense. "Ladies, Detective McGee was poisoned; he died."

"How do you know?" Addie continued to smooth out her wrinkle-free cape.

"I can take it from here, Nurse Hartman. Thank you." He placed his hand on her shoulder. Lena shrunk away. He removed it. "In our debriefings with the chief at the APD, he disclosed the tragic incident." Clyde stuck his hands in his pockets as he walked behind Addie and Opal.

Lena reached in her pocket and pulled out a white lace handkerchief. She dabbed her eyes.

"Did either of you observe or hear anything out of the ordinary while you were at the orphanage?"

Like what? Ducking gunshots? Hurling TNT out the front door? Rescuing orphans from an orphanage? Receiving a kiss from Randall? Saving kids from a life of hell? I know we all swore not to talk about the details of that night with anyone. If the Sacred Heart administrators found out what really happened, it could mean the end of medical and nursing careers for all involved. Oh, dear Maw! How do you tell the truth, yet not reveal the whole truth, so you can avoid telling lies?

Addie and Opal shook their heads.

"What about at the emporium?" Clyde paced back and forth.

Opal turned to Addie.

Be short, brief, and factual, just like I do in my oral shift reports. "Opal wasn't there. Dr. Springer and I were the ones dispatched to that location. Detective McGee kept us outside of the barricade. We never stepped foot inside the place. Two officers brought the children to us."

Addie stared ahead at Nurse Hartman, studying her face and body language. *Arms crossed, wrinkled brow, glaring eyes, downward turned mouth, and lips pressed tight—that speaks volumes. I hope she isn't mad at us.*

Opal squirmed. "Why are you so curious about the details?"

No! Opal, please don't ask him any more questions. More questions leads to more questions.

Clyde stopped. "Well, I'm just trying to make sure I give your father a full report."

Lena grabbed the sides of her desk and stood. She extended

her hand to Clyde. "Thank you, Mr. Posey. Thank you for being so thorough. If you don't need anything else, I need to have a brief meeting with these ladies."

Oh goodness! She is mad at us! Addie felt her insides warm and prickling heat surged up her neck.

Clyde shook her hand. "I can manage to stay a few more minutes longer."

"Well, we'd be delighted to have you with us to discuss the latest stomach virus outbreak in the TB ward. It appears that every time our patients are coughing or vomiting, they are experiencing explosive diarrhea. I would like to challenge their professional thoughts on how best to 1) contain the outbreak; 2) prevent the spread of this virus; and 3) dispose of soiled linens. Since you are now in charge while Mr. Alexander is out, what are your thoughts on the matter, sir?"

Clyde plucked his silver pocket watch out of his green and blue plaid vest pocket. "Oh, silly me. Look at the time! I've had a lapse in memory. I've got to be downtown for a meeting." He turned and strutted out of Lena's office.

Lena sat back down.

"Goodness gracious! We have a stomach bug on 2-B?" Addie reached out and grabbed Opal's wrist.

"Heavens no. I didn't know how else to get that weasel of a man out of my office. He's always meddling."

Addie leaned forward. "So, you're not mad at us?"

"Heavens no, ladies! After all that you have done, whatever would make me cross with either of you?"

"Thank the good Lord above." Opal clapped her hands together.

"So, I'm not the only one who thinks that man is creepy?"

"Addie, that's my mistake. It's probably best that I keep my personal thoughts to myself." Lena tried to hide her laughter behind her hand. "Opal, I'll be so glad when your father returns. This place just isn't the same without him." Lena folded her hands and placed them on her desk. "Ladies, I had no idea what this simple investigation would lead to. Had I known, I wouldn't have given my blessing for you to accompany Dr. Springer. However, with that said, I couldn't have sent two better ambassadors of this nursing program into the field to assist in rescuing the orphans. While the physicians and I may provide you with invaluable clinical class instruction, it is how you choose to apply those lessons in your daily care of patients and in life that really matters."

"You taught us to listen for the clock chimes at night and ask ourselves, 'What did I do today to help another human being.' I believe that stuck with us, Nurse Hartman."

"Addie's right. Your lessons do stick with us, Nurse Hartman."

Lena reached for her handkerchief, again. "You both are so full of hope and promise. I couldn't be more proud of you."

Addie retrieved the white envelope from her pocket. *Muster the courage to ask for what you want, Addie. Don't be afraid. You never gave up hope about earning better marks this month. You really applied yourself and you did it. Maw, I know you would be so proud of me. Cleanliness, Work—B; Cleanliness, Person—B; Reliability, Patients—B; Reliability, Records—B; Economy—B; Adaptability—B; Observation—B; Industry—B; Disposition—A; Executive Ability—B. Now that I'm off probation, what's the worst thing Nurse Hartman can say?*

"Nurse Hartman? I have a personal request. I have been invited to travel back to Hope to visit the Darling family for Thanksgiving. Since I'm no longer on probation, would it be at all possible to have a few days off?"

"Of course." Lena blew her nose. "In fact, the both of you may take leave to celebrate the holiday with your families. Opal, you need to be with your mother and father. I'll work with Nurse Scott to make sure your shifts are covered from Thursday through Saturday. Be back in the dorms by Sunday night for supper. If you are one minute late, you know what you'll get?"

"Demerits." Opal made a check-mark in the air with her finger. "Check. Got it."

Addie was lost in thought, recalling her Sacred Heart Nursing School contract for the term 1914–1917.

This is an agreement between Miss ____________ and the Sacred Heart Hospital Board, whereby Miss ____________ agrees to participate in the Sacred Heart Nursing School's three-year program beginning April 1, 1914, concluding on March 31, 1917. Sacred Heart Hospital agrees to pay Miss ____________ the sum of $5 per month.

Miss ____________ agrees:

1. Not to get married. This contract becomes null and void immediately if the nurse marries.

2. Not to keep company with men.

3. To be at compliant with dorm rules and regulations, remaining on the hospital grounds between the hours of 8:00pm and 6:00am unless approved by Nurse Hartman.

4. Not to smoke or possess cigarettes.

5. Not to drink or possess beer, wine, or whiskey.

6. Not to be incompliant with uniform dress code to include dying of hair, wearing make-up or jewelry of any kind, keeping nails trimmed, and securing hair from face and off nape of the neck, and maintaining personal cleanliness.

7. Not to wear perfumes or scented lotions of any kind.

8. Not to wear dresses more than two inches above the ankle when out of uniform and to wear at least two petticoats.

9. Not to ride in a carriage or automobile with any man except her brother or father during time off.

10. Not to loiter in downtown ice-cream stores, bars, or establishments of ill repute during time off.

This contract becomes null and void immediately if the student is found in violation of rules #1-10.

I think I might be violating the second and ninth rules if I travel to Hope…with Garrett. Addie's cheeks flushed. "Nurse Hartman, according to our contract, I'm not to keep company with men or travel in a car or buggy unless it is with my father or brother. Since I don't have either, Garrett is asking to be my escort from Atlanta to Hope. Will that be alright?"

Opal kicked Addie's foot.

"Addie, don't you consider Garrett like a brother?"

"Yes, ma'am."

Opal kicked Addie's foot again.

"And, since your family is gone, God rest their dear souls, haven't the Darlings embraced you into their family?"

"Yes, ma'am."

Opal took another swing, but Addie had moved her foot.

"I don't see a problem with Garrett being your escort to Hope." Lena sniffed. "It is so noted. I want you both to have a very happy Thanksgiving with your respective families."

"Thank you, Nurse Hartman. That is a very generous gesture." Opal felt something tickle her right ear. Feeling a stray strand, she tucked her short blonde lock behind her ear.

Addie stood and wrapped her nurse's cape around her shoulders.

"Come back clear-headed and ready to work. Duty calls." She winked.

28

Clyde pulled out the heavy wooden chair and took his seat at the head of the board room table. He observed various members of the Sacred Heart leadership team huddled in three different groups across the room, all in private conversation. He cleared his throat. "Excuse me, it's time to begin our leadership meeting. Take your seats, if you please."

The groups ignored his request and continued to converse.

Clyde jumped up and commanded, "I am not to be ignored! I am in charge of this place and you must do what I say." He stomped his foot and huffed. "I said…."

The door to the board room opened. Edward entered the room. "Good morning, everyone. Boy, how I've missed this place and being with y'all." He sniffed at the air. "And, boy, how I've missed Miss Maybelle's buttermilk biscuits." He patted his belly.

"Edward!" The group broke apart and congregated around him.

Edward shook their hands. He gave Lena a big hug.

"It is simply wonderful to have you back here. It just wasn't the same without you." Lena followed the others as they took their seats in their respective places.

Clyde picked up his stack of papers and scooted his coffee cup back over to his usual seat as Edward slipped in his seat at the head of the table.

Alan couldn't resist. He folded his hands four times before saying, "It matters where one sits at the table if one is to run an effective meeting. Don't you agree, Clyde?"

Clyde huffed and stiffened his bottom lip.

Edward opened his notebook. "Alan, I'm sorry. I wasn't listening. What was that you said?"

Clyde sneered at Alan. "You can disregard Alan's comment. It wasn't meant for you, Edward."

"How was the Carolina shore, Edward?" Dr. Williams picked up his glass of orange juice. "You look full of vim and vigor, tan and rested."

"It was time well spent with Trudy and the family." Edward, relieved that Trudy forgave him for his misconduct, was ready to tackle today's meeting. "Clyde has informed me that quite a lot has happened since I've been away." He checked off an item at the top of his agenda list. "First, I want to express my sincere appreciation to Clyde and to all of you for keeping Sacred Heart running smoothly in my absence. However, I did get a chapped ass after I read the article written by Charlie Finch in *The Atlanta Dispatch* last week about the Holy Cross Orphanage and its ties to child prostitution." He looked down the table at Lena. "Sorry about my colorful use of language this morning, Nurse Hartman."

Lena waved him off. "I'm not offended. Please carry on."

"The fact that Sacred Heart and other area hospitals in Atlanta were unknowingly involved in any way or could have contributed to this horrendous crime makes my gut churn."

Clyde squirmed, sticking his index finger between his white Arrow shirt collar and his neck.

"I can't believe my daughter, Nurse Engel, and Dr. Springer were providing medical care in the field during the whole ordeal."

"They did an amazing job," Dr. Williams clarified. "Dr. Springer kept Nurse Hartman and I apprised of the situation. I, in turn, made sure Clyde was aware that we were providing any and all of our professional resources to help the orphans and those children rescued from the bordello." He added, "And, what a tragic end for Detective McGee."

"Simply tragic." Clyde drew a series of circles on his paper.

Edward noticed. His gut rumbled and rolled for the first time in a month. "Dr. Williams, you did the right thing. It's exactly what I'd expect from this hospital. I think what chapped me were the facts about the kids once they were patients of Sacred Heart. While the story didn't reveal who its source was, the paper had to have had someone on the inside sharing details with them that only we would know. I spoke with the chief at the APD and he said he didn't supply those details about the kids and where they were staying. So, who did?"

Clyde continued doodling, making squares and triangles.

"I have no idea, Edward." Lena shrugged her shoulders.

The rest of the group remained silent.

Edward looked over at Clyde. "Clyde..."

Busy making cubes out of the squares, he failed to respond.

Edward grabbed Clyde's pencil from his hand. "Clyde, what the hell is wrong with you." He snapped the pencil in two. "While your sketching skills are as impressive as those of my son, Tripp, will you please track down whoever is leaking information to *The Atlanta Dispatch*?"

Clyde pulled out his tiny notepad from his breast pocket and retrieved a new pencil. "Yes, Edward."

Alan took a bite from his buttermilk biscuit and then patted his napkin four times. While he'd been keeping a keen eye on someone, he preferred to keep it to himself until he could be sure of his suspicions. He didn't want to accuse anyone, especially if he was wrong. He had plenty of time to gather facts and evidence.

"Clyde, keep me posted on your progress." Edward ticked off another item on his list. "The next thing I'd like to talk about is the disposition of the orphans and all of the calls the hospital has been receiving from interested families and their attorneys regarding adopting the children. Dr. Williams, what updates do you have for us?"

"I have some wonderful news to share, finally. It beats giving weekly updates on the death totals from the pellagra epidemic and other disease and surgical complications." Dr. Williams chuckled. "We've had more callers than we've got children. I've got the hospital attorney working to sort out the details, vet the families, and fast-track these cases through court. Rest assure that all of the boys and girls from Mr. Chang's place will have a home by Christmas."

The group clapped and cheered.

"What about the boys from the orphanage?" Oliver reached for another biscuit from the silver bowl in the center of the table.

"I'm glad you asked. Y'all are familiar with Officer Evans, who is part of our security detail at night?" John watched heads around the table nod. "He and his wife lost a baby boy during child birth. They've been trying to have another child, but have been unsuccessful. He came to me after he heard about Billy and how he played a key part in the investigation with Detective McGee. They want to honor Detective McGee by adopting Billy Swanson and the baby boy who was under our care after it was born."

Lena gasped. "Praise the Lord!" Her eyes moistened.

"They're going to have their hands full." Flippant, Clyde twirled the pencil between his fingers.

"God works in mysterious ways and He is good all the time." Oliver held his right hand up in the air.

"What mighty generous hearts God has given the Evans family." Edward made a note on his agenda. "Clyde, will you reach out to *The Atlanta Dispatch* to let them know this bit of good news? Make sure they get plenty of photographs, preferably under the Sacred Hospital sign over the front door."

"Yes, sir." Clyde stopped twirling his pencil and made a note in the small notepad.

"As I said earlier, we have more callers than kids, so I predict the remaining children will be in good homes by the holidays."

Edward looked over at Lena, who was wiping tears from her cheeks with her white cloth napkin. "Nurse Hartman, what updates do you have for us about the status of the nursing students?"

"I, too, am the bearer of good news this morning. I'm happy to report that all of the nurses on probation, to include Addie Engel, Alice Fein, and Isabelle Esposito, have turned a corner. As of the beginning of this month, they are no longer on probationary status."

"A true mark of a leader is to be able to turn a situation around and make it better. It's always easier to simply rid yourself of poor performers. However, if they truly show potential, it is our job to cultivate that skill set inside them and provide them with the opportunities to grow and develop. I appreciate you and Nurse Scott for investing your time and energy into these ladies."

The leadership team clapped.

"Thank you, Edward." Lena soaked in the applause. "I also must thank you for the evening gowns and accessories from Rich and Brothers. They are due to arrive in plenty of time for the ladies to be properly fitted. We are all looking forward to your exquisite Christmas party."

"I, for one, am ready for the holiday season." Alan cracked a smile.

"Me too, Alan." Edward pointed at Oliver. "Oliver, I understand the construction project for Alexander Hall is still on schedule?"

"Yes, Edward. It is. As we approach winter, I hope we have a mild one that doesn't linger until March or April of next year. That could possibly mess us up a bit."

"Georgia weather can be very fickle. She can tease us with her warm temperatures and then whip up a snow and ice storm in a matter of days." Edward sipped his coffee. "It reminds me of a time when my father and his friend, President Teddy...."

Clyde looked at his watch. "Edward, pardon the interruption, but I know Dr. Williams needs to get to the surgical suite in time for his case."

"Actually, I'm good on time this morning. We had to cancel my first case. I found out from the nurses that my patient snuck food off another patient's dinner tray and ate it. I can't perform surgery on someone with a full stomach. We've rescheduled him for tomorrow. Edward, please continue. I can't wait to hear this story."

"Great!" Clyde grimaced. "Me, too!"

MONDAY AFTERNOON, SIXTH WARD

Dr. Leventhal and Dr. Paine stood in the corner of the medical-surgical suite closest to the nurse's desk. Addie charted, but couldn't help but overhear their conversation.

"Mr. Danielson's stomach cancer is in the area of the fundus. He is experiencing quite a lot of pain, vomiting, loss of weight, and is anemic. The tumor is evident on x-ray as well as on manual physical examination." David fiddled with the reflex hammer in his hands.

"While surgery is an option, depending upon the size of the tumor, you're going to have to do a partial or a complete gastrectomy."

Addie translated. *That means Dr. Leventhal will have to remove part or all of the stomach from the patient.*

"My dilemma is that the operation could throw him into a state of shock, and you and I both know the mortality rate is extremely high."

"Either way, he's going to end up on my table downstairs. It's just a matter of when."

David hung his head, resigning himself.

"You don't have to make that decision alone. Be honest with Mr. Danielson and give him the option to either do nothing or have the surgery. By the way, how old is he?"

"He's thirty-two years old. Two years older than I am."

Mr. Danielson yelled out from his bed, "Nurse! Give me more pain medicine right now!"

Deborah walked over and removed his chart that was hanging on the foot of his bed. "Mr. Danielson, I just gave you a morphine injection an hour ago." She returned the chart to the hook.

"It's not time yet. You have to wait another three hours."

Mr. Danielson reached for his water glass on the bedside table and hurled it at her. Deborah ducked. It struck the floor and shattered. "Where's my doctor? I want to see my doctor, NOW!"

David shook Dr. Paine's hand. "Thank you for your solid advice, as always." He rushed over to Mr. Danielson's beside. "What's the meaning of this?"

He pointed at Deborah. "That nurse won't give me my pain medicine."

Deborah bent over to pick up the large shards of glass. "Dr. Leventhal, I just gave him an injection an hour ago."

Addie retrieved a dust pan and broom from the utility closet and returned to help Deborah.

"I simply can't have you acting out while you are on my unit, sir. I understand you are in pain." David reached for Mr. Danielson's left wrist. He palpated his pulse. It was rapid and irregular. "Listen, I need to have a frank discussion with you." He looked over at Addie and Deborah, then back at Mr. Danielson. "Your stomach cancer is very advanced. The tumor is growing larger daily and I'm sorry to say that your condition is going to get much worse, not better. This means your pain level is going to increase, too."

Mr. Danielson groaned and wrapped his arms around his abdomen. He curled his legs up and turned over on his left side. "Go on, doc, tell it to me straight."

"You have two choices. The first, I can take you to the operating room and I can remove your tumor. However, by doing that, it means I would have to remove a portion or all of your stomach. I won't know until I explore the affected area. There are numerous risks with that type of surgery, and there is a high death rate associated with it, too."

"What's the second?" Mr. Danielson scrunched himself into a tight ball.

"We do nothing. The bottom line is you are dying from stomach cancer. However, I can mitigate the pain with medicine. Instead of injections, I can have the nurse start an IV and administer pain medicine to you on a larger, more consistent and frequent basis. You have the right to have a pain-free death. While the cancer may claim your life in a matter of weeks or months, the large amount of opiates I would order will cause you to go into an unconscious state, eventually depress your respirations, and hasten your death."

"How much longer will I have to live?"

"It would be a matter of days."

Mr. Danielson writhed in excruciating pain. "I'll take the second option. Let's just keep the details between you and me. When my wife and kids come to visit, please break the news to her gently. I want her to be prepared and I want to get the chance to tell my loved one's good-bye. Will you keep me awake enough to do that?"

"You have my word." David patted him on the shoulder. "Would you like a visit from the hospital chaplain?"

"Yes, that would be nice. Thank you." Tears streamed down his face and dampened his pillow.

David walked over to Deborah and Addie. "I believe you heard his wishes?"

Deborah stood up. "Yes, Doctor. I will see that he is taken care of."

Picking up the chart, David updated the medication orders and then handed it to Deborah. Addie finished sweeping up the debris and discarded the shards in the metal trashcan. She walked over to the sink and washed her hands. She returned to her desk to complete her report on her patient's status after gall bladder removal surgery and the current state of the incision site. Occasionally, she glanced up to watch Deborah compile her medical supplies and medications. Deborah kept a keen eye on the medical staff in the room as she reached in her nursing uniform pocket and pulled out one of the wax pouches that read *Strychnine Sulfate*. She poured out the white pills and immediately pocketed it again. She crushed the pills using a mortar and pestle and diluted the drug with the liquid morphine before injecting the contents carefully into the glass IV bottle. She watched the cloudy contents swirl, dissipate, and become clear again.

The ward door swung open. Mr. Danielson's family entered. His wife, a slight, fair-haired, weathered woman, held the hands of their two adolescent children, a plump, albino boy, and a pudgy girl with dark brown eyes and hair. All were dressed in their Sunday best. Spotting her husband's frail form from across the room, she wept.

Addie stood, stepping out from behind her desk. "You must be here to see Mr. Danielson." She escorted them to his bedside.

Dr. Leventhal picked up a tri-fold white cotton screen, unfolded it, and set it up around the bed.

Addie clasped her hands in prayer. *Dear God, please let this man find comfort in his final days.* She walked back to pick up a chart and returned it to the foot of the post-surgical patient's bed. She looked at her watch. *Two forty-five. The evening shift nurses should be reporting for duty any time now.* As soon as Addie looked up at the door, two nurses entered the room.

Deborah rolled a silver tray stocked with silver metal needles, gauze pads, tape, rubber tubing, tourniquet, and the glass IV bottle over to the nurse's desk. "Who's going to be taking care of Mr. Danielson tonight?"

A nurse with dark blonde hair and almond-shaped green eyes raised her hand. Her name badge read *Nurse Blackwell.* "That would be me. I took care of him last night, too."

Deborah rolled the cart toward her. "Dr. Leventhal spoke with Mr. Danielson about his treatment options for his terminal stomach cancer. The patient has opted for the morphine infusion to help quell his severe pain."

"Did the doctor explain the risks involved?"

"He did. Mr. Danielson is saying good-bye to his family as we speak." She pointed at the white partition. "When they leave, you can start his IV. I've labeled the bottle with the drug, dose, time, and date."

"Thank you." Nurse Blackwell took the tray from Deborah.

Addie and Deborah gave their shift reports about their respective patients to the nurses. When it was time to leave the unit, Addie and Deborah grabbed their capes off the brass coat hooks on the wall, stepped out into the main corridor, and turned left towards the concierge desk.

"What a stressful day." Addie fastened the button at the neck and stuck her hands in her cape pockets. They made a right turn at Mira's desk and exited out the back door of the hospital. The wind blew up their capes. They held on to their caps as they walked.

"How do you mean?"

"That poor Mr. Danielson. He's so young and will be leaving behind his family. I can't even imagine having to face your mortality and make that kind of life and death decision."

"But it's our job to help our patients and be supportive of the decisions that transition them between life and death. It's our duty to make it as humane and dignified as possible. I think it's empowering to know we can be there to help ease their suffering."

Deborah and Addie walked past the gurgling fountain and through the flower garden. Yellow mums swayed in the breeze.

"Yeah, but I struggle with the moral and ethical issues of snowing them with massive doses of opioids."

"Don't you think euthanasia is justified? We don't give it a second thought when it comes to animals, like shooting a horse after it has suffered a broken leg. How is it any different when it comes to humans? Isn't it our job as medical professionals to be angels of mercy, too?"

"Angels of mercy?" Addie stopped dead in her tracks. "Whatever do you mean by that? I'm studying to be a nurse, a darn good one at that. I'm not sure that I'm angelic. Isn't that status meant for the Catholic nuns or people like that?"

Deborah laughed and kept walking. "Oh, Addie, you are a funny girl."

Addie ran to catch up with her. "Funny? I wasn't trying to be funny. I'm just trying to understand your turn of phrase."

Deborah waved her off. "Never mind, poor girl. I'm just messing with you. Come on. Let's get out of this blustery wind before we catch our death."

You are one strange girl, Deborah Owens. I still don't get you at all.

After supper, a hearty meal consisting of meatloaf; green beans cooked in butter, bacon, and onions; fresh rolls; and blueberry cobbler, Addie curled up in the brown leather wingback chair in the library. The wood fire popped and crackled. She pulled out her pencil and stationary from its box. Placing the beige paper on top of the box lid, Addie wrote a thank you note to Garrett's father.

Dear Mr. Darling,

Thank you so much for your hospitality at Thanksgiving. I truly enjoyed my time in Hope. I can hardly believe all of the work that has been done to transform the farm into Hope's Guardian Angel Cemetery. Seeing the white wooden crosses replaced with granite, engraved headstones for my parents, Sissie, and Ben took my breath away. Your generosity astounds, and I am forever grateful for the kindness you have bestowed upon me. I rest peacefully at night knowing I, too, have an eternal resting place with my family when the good Lord chooses to call me home. I wish you only the best. I promise to continue to study hard and be a good servant of God.

Sincerely,

Addie

P.S. I know it's a bit early, but I want to wish you a very Merry Christmas and a Happy New Year!

Addie folded the letter, addressed it, and sealed the envelope.

Opal walked into the room. "Are you writing your lover boy?" she chided.

Which one? "Cut it out, Opal. No, I'm writing Garrett's father a thank you note."

"Tell me about your trip. I'm dying to hear all about it." Opal tugged at her gray shawl and hoisted up her nightgown and bathrobe. She stepped out of her slippers and took a seat in the chair opposite Addie. She tucked her feet under her, settling in and waiting to hear the long version of the tale.

"What do you want to know?"

"You're impossible, Addie! For starters, how's Garrett?"

Knowing I could be violating rule #2 of my nursing contract, I best not reveal the details of my late-night rendezvous with Garrett in the Darling's barn on Thanksgiving night. I simply couldn't resist him as I helped him brush my family's old chestnut mare, Ol' Girl. All of our old familiar feelings came alive. I adored his warm passionate kisses to the back of my neck, followed by the chills that ran down my spine. My, oh my, how he cradled me in his arms and caressed my skin. I felt so alive, so loved, and so protected. Thank goodness Garrett spotted the straw tangled in the back of my hair as we walked hand in hand back to the house. I would have died of embarrassment if Mr. Darling saw it first! "Garrett is just fine. We had a lovely ride up to Hope in a Model T that he borrowed from one of the boys at the firehouse. Opal, you should have seen him teaching me how to drive that contraption!"

"What? Garrett taught you how to drive?"

"He did! Can you believe it! You should have seen me swerving down the dirt road. Once I quit grinding the gears and nearly hit a Jersey cow, he taught me to listen to the engine and the noises it makes when it's ready for a gear change. It took me almost an entire day, but I finally got the hang of it."

"What a remarkable year for you. You've managed to learn how to ride a bicycle and drive a car!"

"How crazy is that? We've birthed babies, shaved our heads, dealt with the grossest of gross, witnessed miracles, and we're just beginning. Can you imagine what's in store for us next year?"

"Gosh, what could be in store for us in 1915? Think about it, Opal, we'll only have one more year left of nursing school after that. Where will we go? What will we do?"

"Only the good Lord knows." Opal watched the burning embers.

"Tell me about Thanksgiving with your family? How did it go?"

"It went well. Father has hired Ms. Mattie's replacement, a lovely woman by the name of Ranzell Romans."

"Ranzell? That is quite an unusual first name."

"She said her first name means 'caretaker.' She was employed by the Robinson family in Augusta. They had to move to New York. She told me she couldn't bear living up north in the cold and be that far away from her immediate kin. Mr. Robinson and father are childhood friends, and he reached out to him to see if he'd be interested in hiring her. The rest, as they say, is history. Now, she's a new member of our family."

"Do you like her?"

"Yes, I do. While she's not like Ms. Mattie, who was very willing to put my sister, Pearl, in her place, I think it will only be a matter of time before she finds her place in our home. Mother and Tripp have taken to her, so that's always a good sign. Pearl, on the other hand, is so needy and contrary. No one could possibly please her."

"I look forward to meeting Ranzell at your Christmas party next month. By the way, it is quite generous of your father to purchase evening gowns for us to wear to the party. Nurse Hartman said that she was allowed to order costume accessories and wiglets for us, too!" Addie clapped her hands together. "I'll never forget getting all gussied up for the affair last year. Mrs. Gray and her sister, Mary, loved dressing me. They even made sure my hair was teased and adorned with ostrich feathers in order to achieve the appropriate height for the evening event."

Opal ran her fingers through her short blonde hair; it stuck straight up in the air. "Will this hair-do, do?"

Addie doubled over in hysterics. She did the same. "Will this do do, too?"

"Oh my! You said, 'do-do!'" Opal laughed so hard she snorted.

Addie couldn't compose herself. "I think we're delirious!"

"My sides hurt." Opal clutched her waist with her hands.

"Make it stop." Addie wiped the tears running down her cheeks. "I can't remember the last time I laughed this hard."

"Laughter is the best medicine. That's what Father always says."

"I think we've overdosed tonight!"

"Addie, you are truly my best and dearest friend. I'm so glad to know you."

"Friends till the end. Pinky promise?" Addie held up her right pinky finger and leaned over toward Opal.

Opal leaned out of her chair, interlocking her pinky with Addie's.

"Promise."

MONDAY NIGHT, SIXTH WARD

"Doctor Southerland, Mr. Danielson's pulse is faint and erratic." Nurse Blackwell handed the stethoscope to the physician, a middle-aged, short fellow with warm, caring eyes and greying sideburns.

"Mr. Danielson? Can you hear me?" Dr. Southerland pulled the sheets back. He extracted a needle from his pocket and stuck it into the bottom of the patient's feet. There was no reaction.

He balled his right hand in a fist and forcefully rubbed his knuckles up and down the sternum. Again, there was no reaction. "Please note that he is unresponsive to painful stimuli. This is not a good sign. I'm sorry to say, he's taken a turn for the worse."

"And so quickly, too," Nurse Blackwell whispered.

"I think Dr. Leventhal and I thought it would be a matter of a few days. However, his condition must be further along than we once thought. He will be dead within the hour."

Mr. Danielson was experiencing agonal breathing, gasping for air at times.

"Please make his final preparations and set up the privacy screen."

"Yes, Doctor. Should I summon the chaplain, too?"

"Yes, please do."

Fifty-three minutes later, Dr. Southerland noted the time on his wristwatch. "Time of death, twenty-two twenty-eight."

29

Lexie put the finishing touches on Deborah's wiglet, which was attached to her natural hair. "There, that should do it. Look in the mirror and see what you think of it."

Deborah got up from the chair in the dorm bathroom and walked over to fuss over her reflection in the mirror. "Not, bad, Carmichael. Not bad at all." She patted her hair.

"Don't touch it! The more you mess with it, the greater the chances it will come undone." Lexie called out, "Who's next?"

Addie entered the bathroom. "I'm next and I think Opal is after me."

"Great. Take a seat." Lexie pulled out a few falls. "Which one would you prefer? This one?" She held up a very curly jet black wig. "Or, this one?" The auburn-colored hairpiece matched Addie's strands perfectly.

"Ha! Ha! Very funny, Lexie. Can you imagine seeing the look on Nurse Hartman's face if we all chose to put mismatched wigs on our heads?"

"She would give us demerits for sure. I don't know where that failing grade would appear on our monthly report card, but I'm sure she'd find a place."

"Don't make it too fussy. I prefer a more natural look. We're so lucky that you know how to do hair." Addie spotted a sparkling rhinestone headband. She reached over to pick it up from the stack of Rich and Brothers boxes surrounding her feet on the black and white tile floor. "Here, see if you can work this into your coiffed masterpiece. I'm wearing the sapphire blue gown."

"That will look stunning on you, Addie."

"Which one are you wearing, Lexie?"

"I chose the emerald dress. I thought that one looked the best on me."

"Who took the ruby red one?"

"I did." Opal held the beaded dress up to herself, admiring the image in the mirror as she twirled around.

"Wow! You're going to look like a princess in that number."

"Poor Shelby Maddox won't know what hit him when he sets his eyes on you tonight."

"Addie Engel, whatever do you mean by that?"

"Oh, please...."

"Addie, quite fidgeting." Lexie bopped her on the shoulder with her teasing comb.

"I'm not very good at being still, am I?"

"No, you're wound up tighter than a tick."

"I think you're going to get even more wound up tonight." Opal swayed as she spoke.

"Whatever are you talking about? I don't plan on having any episodes like I did last year, I'll have you know."

"Never mind. I'm going to skedaddle. I'm off to get my make-up done by Susan. You two better hurry up. The cabs are picking us up in two hours." She called out to Lexie, "Holler at me when you're ready for me, Lexie."

"I will."

Two hours had almost passed when the grandfather clock in the main hall struck five bells. Lena walked through the front door of the nursing dorm. She stopped to admire the fragrant, five-foot pine tree in the hallway adorned with ornaments and cranberry and popcorn garland made by the remaining orphans still waiting to be discharged to their new families. She proceeded to the back stairwell. Hearing frantic footsteps running back and forth upstairs, she called up to the second floor, "Ladies, Nurse Scott and I are here. The cabs are ready to take us to the Second Ward. I expect to see y'all down here in the next two minutes."

A voice replied; the Irish brogue did not go unnoticed. "We're finishing up, and we'll be down in a jiffy, Nurse Hartman."

"Thank you, Mary Margaret."

A few seconds later, the stampede began. Belle and Alice were the first to descend. Belle wore a copper and tan gown with three-quarter length beaded sleeves while Alice was dressed in a beige lace formal. Bertie followed, wearing the jet black curly wiglet and a shiny black dress that had a pale matte pink skirt underneath. Four rows of black, teal, clear, and pink sequins beads were strung across her décolleté. Susan walked hand in hand with a tentative Mary Margaret down the stairs. Susan wore a yellow gown with embroidered red, blue, and green flowers down the front of it. Tiny crystals were hand-sewn on the intricate pattern.

Lena tried to suppress her giggles.

"I'm trying to get used to walking in me new shoes." Mary Margaret held up her velvet amber princess-waist gown, which had long, flowing, sheer sleeves. She took each step, one by one, with care. "I hope I don't break me neck!"

Lexie, Opal, and Addie peered over the top railing down at Nurse Hartman. "Oh, you look like precious jewels!" Lena exclaimed as they came down the staircase, clapping her black silk gloved hands together. "Look at you ladies in emerald green, ruby red, and sapphire blue."

"Holy moly! Look at you, Nurse Hartman. You look just radiant!" Addie gawked at Lena's appearance.

Lena removed her black, full length, mink coat and spun around in her garnet and black gown. Sequins caught the light and sparkled.

"I can clean up pretty good when I have to, girls." Lena glanced up the stairs. "Deborah, we're all waiting for you."

"I'm coming." Deborah balled up her butterscotch-colored dress, which had an open neckline and illusion sleeves, and clomped down the stairs.

"My, you look lovely, Deborah." Lena watched the white ostrich feathers flail and fly with each step.

"Thank you." Deborah unrolled and smoothed out her dress when she reached the bottom step.

Lena followed behind Deborah as they weaved their way through the kitchen and down the hall to the front door.

Nurse Hartman summoned the girls.

The nurses shushed each other as they gathered around.

"Y'all look breathtakingly beautiful tonight. Shine like the angels you are and please remember to behave yourselves. Do not imbibe too much; some of you have shift duty in the morning. Remember, you represent Sacred Heart's Nursing Program while you are in public. Mind your manners and make a point to thank Mr. Alexander individually for his generosity." Pausing, Lena added, "More importantly, have a wonderful night. We will all arrive together, and we will leave together by… midnight." As the girls cheered, she opened the front door. "Ladies, please make your way to the cabs. They are lined up out back by the garage."

The procession of black cabs departed from Sacred Heart Hospital and wound their way out of the Sixth Ward, crossed over the railroad tracks, and traveled to the Second Ward. One by one, the cars pulled up to the front of the Alexander's mansion, let out their passengers, and drove off. The girls gathered at the bottom of the stairs, waiting for Nurse Hartman and Nurse Scott, who rode in the last vehicle.

Once out of their car, Lena and Claire, who was barely recognizable and dressed in a silk fuchsia formal, walked up the grand front entrance. They passed butlers at the front doors wearing black tuxedos with black top hats. Each wore a white rose boutonnière and asked to take the coats of the guests, exchanging it for a ticket to be claimed at the end of the evening.

Once inside, red and white poinsettias were used to create a fourteen-foot tall Christmas tree in the foyer. A cluster of pheasant feathers adorned the top.

Bertie stopped and pointed. "Oh, look at this tree! I have never seen anything like it!" She walked in a circle around the entire structure. She raised her nose in the air. "Something smells simply divine. I'm starving." She grabbed Susan's free hand since she was still holding Mary Margaret's with the other. The three disappeared into the massive dining room.

A quartet of carolers strolled by singing, "Here We Come A-Caroling" in four-part harmony. Cinnamon, pumpkin spice, a variety of colognes and perfumes, and the scent of fresh cut evergreens and roses permeated the mansion. Garland, sprigs of Baby's Breath, and massive bouquets of red and white roses adorned table tops, fireplace mantles, and banisters.

Belle and Alice spotted the exotic trophies collected over the years by Edward and his father on their hunting expeditions with Teddie, a family friend and former United States president. A mounted cougar, buffalo, and red fox were just a few of the animals in the room on the left, dubbed the "Zoo."

"I want to pet the bear." Alice pulled Belle by the hand toward the thousand-pound Grizzly bear, who stood on its hind legs with raised claws, baring its ivory teeth, in the far corner of the Zoo.

"Come on, Addie. I have a surprise for you." Opal grabbed Addie by the hand and pulled her through the crowd of guests, crossed the main hallway, and entered into the Great Hall, a room that extended across the entire back of the house.

Addie spotted Tripp standing on one of the celadon-colored couches, trying to stick a purple grape into the open mouth of a silver fox fur stole wrapped around the shoulders of an oblivious woman with white, fluffy hair who was hard of hearing. He squished the fruit into place and then began swatting the feet dangling down her back. "Opal, I think your brother is trying to feed someone's fox stole." Addie tried to point him out, but Opal tugged her through the throng. "Where are we going?"

"Over here." Opal stopped. She swung Addie around her.

"My, you look simply beautiful tonight." Garrett, dressed in a black tux and a white bow tie, stood up and greeted her with an embrace. He gave her a light peck on the left cheek.

"I must say, you are a sight for sore eyes, Nurse Engel." Randall, who sat next to Garrett, also rose to his feet.

Addie reached out and shook his hand. *Oh, my heavens!* "To what do we owe this honor?" *Remain calm. Don't get anxious.*

"Mr. Alexander asked me to bring a guest. I thought it best to bring my best friend and roommate."

Opal nudged Addie. "Isn't this just perfect! Dr. Springer told me about his plans when I worked on the pediatric ward yesterday. He begged me not to tell you." She spotted Shelby talking with her father. "Please, excuse me. I see someone I need to talk to."

Opal, I could wring your neck. So, that's what you meant earlier today in the bathroom.

Garett extended his hand. "Would you like to dance, Addie?"

"I'd love to." Addie took his hand. "If you'll excuse us, Dr. Springer."

"Certainly, you two run along and enjoy yourselves. I plan on doing some mingling of my own tonight."

Addie and Garrett walked over to an open area near the ebony Steinway grand piano and joined a small group of guests slow dancing to a medley of holiday classics. Garrett took Addie by the waist and glided her across the floor. Addie spotted the elderly lady with the fox wrap walk by. The grape was still protruding from the fox's mouth. Addie buried her head in his shoulder, laughing.

"What's so funny?"

"I watched Opal's little brother stick a grape in the open mouth of a fox stole worn by a woman who just passed by."

Garrett threw back his head, laughing. "That sounds like something I would do if I were that age again."

"Your mother would have tanned your hide if she had caught you doing something so naughty."

"Yes, she would have." Garrett, lost in Addie's eyes, leaned over, smelled her lilac-scented hair, and whispered in her ear, "I had a wonderful Thanksgiving. Can you imagine what it will be like when we have a family of our own?" He reached in his jacket pocket and pulled out a small black velvet box. "I know it's a bit early. But I have to work next week over the Christmas holidays. I wanted to give you your present early. Happy birthday, Addie."

Addie stopped dancing, walked off the dance floor with Garrett, and took the box from his hand. She opened it, slowly. Inside was a gold heart-shaped pendant. It took her breath away.

"You will always have my heart, Addie. I see such hope and promise with you. I will wait for you to give me your heart someday. Life without you is like living in the dark. I can't see where I'm going and my path is unclear. You light the way for me. I see such possibilities with you." He took the box from her hands, removed the necklace, and fastened it around her neck while she secured the box in her beaded evening bag.

She caressed it. "This is the nicest birthday present I have ever received in my whole life. Thank you so much!" She threw her hands around his neck and then hastily removed them. "Oh, goodness! I'm so sorry, Garrett. I must remember where I am and that my behavior is being monitored."

"I understand. We've got to be very careful."

"You didn't say anything to Dr. Springer about us? Did you?"

"Heavens no. Gentlemen don't talk about such things with each other. I'm aware of the risks we are taking and in no way want to jeopardize your education and career."

"You are too good to me."

"Just keep that in a safe place."

"I will. I'll keep it with the pebble you gave me last year." She popped him in the upper arm.

"Hey! Remember, your actions are being monitored. I don't want you to get in trouble with the APD for assault and battery."

"Very funny!"

"Speaking of APD, Randall told me about your rescue operation with the orphans. He didn't go into great detail. However, he did mention that you were very brave and kept your composure. You were a real asset in the field."

"Did he mention anything else?" *Like kissing me, for example?*

"No. Why do you ask?" He studied her face.

"No reason." Addie spotted Opal talking with Shelby and Randall. "Come, let's step out of this room and find something to eat."

"Great. I've not had a chance to partake in anything delectable yet."

"Lead the way."

Addie turned to follow him. *Turn around.* She obeyed the voice in her head. She turned and spotted Randall staring longingly at her. *Oh, my stars! How can I possibly yearn for two men? Maw, I wish you were here to give me guidance. I hope and pray I never have to choose between them.*

30

Opal entered the kitchen in the nurse's dorm carrying a red velvet birthday cake with cream cheese icing on a crystal cake plate. Nineteen candles burned bright. Deborah and Lexie removed the plate of turkey from the middle of the table as she placed the cake down in its place.

The nurses sang, "Happy birthday to you. Happy birthday to you. Happy birthday, dear Addie. Happy birthday to you!"

"Make a wish!" Mary Margaret clapped.

"Hurry and blow out your candles!" Bertie retrieved a knife from the drawer and gathered dessert plates from the cupboard.

Opal pulled out two stacks of construction paper cards in a variety of colors from one of the kitchen cabinets. "Here, I had these stowed away for safe keeping." She handed Addie one stack. "These birthday wishes are for you. They're hand-made cards from the orphans. When Billy found out your birthday was on Christmas Day, he wanted to do something special just for you to thank you before they left. He made me promise not to tell you." She handed Addie the other. "And these are from us."

"You tend to keep a lot of secrets, Opal." Addie stood up, took both stacks, set them on the table, and hugged her.

Opal stood by her side and took a hold of her hand. "Make your wish a good one, Addie."

Addie took a deep breath. *What should I wish for, Maw? Mark Twain's quote came to mind: "The two most important days in your life are the day you are born and the day you find out why." Maw, this year has been so trying. I know I'm supposed to find my purpose and I'm being tested with every day and with every year that passes. As Nurse Hartman once said, 'I believe, in this great big world of ours, that we all have a purpose. We are all meant to help guide each other along our journey through life. It is through compassion that we find connection.' I hope and pray that I continue to find the inner strength to pass those tests. And, if I fail, I hope my failures become my testimony. Hope is all I have and it just never seems to rest, does it, Maw? Addie picked up her heart pendant and rubbed it between her fingers. Well, I wish....* Addie blew out the candles, hoping her wish would come true... one day. *One can hope. One can always hope.*

FRIDAY EVENING, SECOND WARD

"Here is your one-way ticket to San Francisco, ma'am." A man wearing a monocle with sparse grey hair passed the yellow ticket under black iron the bars as he sat behind the ticket counter at the train depot. "Merry Christmas. Have a safe trip."

"Thank you, sir." The Asian woman tipped her hat as she walked away, carrying a large tapestry bag.

"Would you like for me to carry your bag to the platform, ma'am?" a male voice said over her right shoulder.

"Why, Mr. Washington, how kind of you." Mr. Chang handed his bag to him. "It's heavy. Be sure not to hurt yourself." Mr. Chang looked to his left. "How nice of you and Mr. Lincoln to personally escort me out of town."

The three walked through the train station toward the outdoor platform.

"We've been keeping you under surveillance these past few weeks."

"Of course you have."

"Nice get-up." Mr. Lincoln snickered. "You make a pretty good-looking gal, I must admit. This blue velvet coat looks mighty fetching on you."

"Why you not arrest me?" Mr. Chang pouted, pushing out his rouged bottom lip.

"We think that it is best that you disappear quietly." Mr. Washington held the door open.

Mr. Chang paraded through, stuffing both of his hands in the white rabbit fur muff. "What? Like Father Preti and her sister?"

"What do you mean by *her* sister? Don't you mean *his*?" Mr. Lincoln tossed a look at Mr. Washington, who shrugged his shoulders as he put on his brown bowler.

Mr. Chang kept walking down the wooden platform, keeping an eye on the approaching locomotive. "You didn't know?"

"Know what?" Mr. Lincoln flanked him.

"He was a she?"

"Really?" Mr. Washington walked on Mr. Chang's left side.

"Good to know." He took a few more strides. "Will we ever find them?"

"Like lotus flower, they have returned to the deep, dark water and mud."

"Is that a 'no' or is that some kind of ancient Chinese saying?"

Mr. Chang laughed in a delicately feminine way. "My house: my rules."

The locomotive was less than fifty-feet away. Brakes squealed and white clouds of steam billowed out from under the train. The noise from the engine was making it difficult to carry on a conversation.

Mr. Washington raised his voice. "Well, this is my city: my rules."

In a swift series of choreographed moves, Mr. Lincoln extended his right foot out, causing Mr. Chang to trip. Mr. Washington bumped him with the bag, causing Mr. Chang to fall on the tracks, directly into the path of the oncoming train. The train whistle drowned out Mr. Chang's screams.

Mr. Washington and Mr. Lincoln casually walked back to their unmarked car.

Mr. Washington opened the back door, tossed Mr. Chang's luggage in the back seat, and closed the door. As he got behind the wheel, he removed his hat and tossed it in the back seat too. "It appears that we got all our loose ends tied up. Merry Christmas to us."

"Not all of them, dammit." Mr. Lincoln removed his hat and held it in his lap.

"What did we miss?"

"We forgot to ask him why he chose the names Lincoln and

Washington." He paused, looking out the window, observing relatives greeting each other with hugs and handshakes in the parking lot. He looked back at Mr. Washington. "I still think I should have been Washington."

"Really?" Mr. Washington started the engine.

WESTERN FRONT, SOMEWHERE IN EUROPE

The Great War had begun five months earlier. Invasions, gun fire, and explosions destroyed towns and country sides from Luxembourg, Belgium, to France. While the Battle of the Marne proved to be a pivotal turning point in the war, a line of fortified trenches were dug, stretching from the North Sea to France, as the armies raced to the sea.

The night before and tonight, British, French, and German soldiers participated in an unofficial cease fire in some areas along the line. Some chose to climb out of their trenches and some came together in the area between them called no man's land. Reportedly, soldiers swapped stories, cigarettes, food, and souvenirs, and shared black and white photographs of loved ones. The dead were retrieved and buried; prisoners were exchanged. Some soldiers opted to play soccer, while others sang Christmas carols in their respective languages, like "Silent Night." The Christmas truce of 1914 would forever be remembered as a remarkable event, symbolizing peace, unity, and hope.

Hope in humanity never rests.

About the Author

Katie Hart Smith, a published author for over 20 years, has a wide array of work, ranging from medical to academic essays, to historical fiction, non-fiction, and children's stories. She served on the editorial board and was a manuscript reviewer for the *Orthopaedic Nursing Journal* and was a former member of the advisory board for *Atlanta Sports & Fitness Magazine*. Currently, she is a staff correspondent and a writes a monthly column called "From the Heart" for the *Gwinnett Citizen* newspaper.

She published her first memoir, *Couch Time with Carolyn* in 2014 and was a nominee for the Georgia Author of the Year award. In July 2016, Smith released *Aspirations of the Heart* through Deeds Publishing. It is the first book in the Sacred Heart historical fiction series, which is set in 1900s Atlanta and profiles the emerging medical community. *Aspirations of the Heart* has been placed in the Governor's Mansion Library by Georgia's

First Lady, Sandra Deal. The second novel, *Hope Never Rests*, will also become a part of Georgia's literary collection.

Born in San Diego, California, Smith moved to Dunwoody in 1976. Metro Atlanta has remained her home ever since. She is a graduate of Dunwoody High School, obtained a BS in Nursing from Georgia State University, and earned her MBA from Troy State University. Smith is an active member in the Gwinnett community to include her service on the City of Lawrenceville City Council from 2009—2011. She was even the first recipient of the Gwinnett Chamber of Commerce's Healthcare Professional of the Year award in 2011.